# A Beautiful

# Death

## Sins of the Mother

### Danielle Siler

DANIELLE SILER

# A BEAUTIFUL DEATH

Published in the United States of America ISBN 13: 979-8-218-74584-4

Fiction / African American / Urban

1. Fiction/Drama/Romance

DANIELLE SILER

# A Beautiful Death

## Sins of the Mother

# Danielle Siler

DANIELLE SILER

# *Book Dedication*

This book is dedicated to my two beautiful daughters Jasmine and Jaylen, my greatest gift. I am so proud that God chose me to be your mommy. To my husband Chad, I love you more than words can say. To my wonderful Graves family for always standing behind me, supporting me and catching me when I fall; without you, I would not have made it this far. And to my guardian angels in heaven, my grandparents Jazz and Yvonne Siler, my parents Suzette Siler and Lamont Jenkins and my twin Richard Steele. I love you all!

# *Acknowledgment*

I would like to give all praises to God for giving me this talent; and never letting me fall, no matter how many times I may have stumbled! Thank You!

# A BEAUTIFUL DEATH

DANIELLE SILER

# Prologue

## Jesse

Thirteen years had passed since Jesse Braxton's incarceration. Initially sentenced to 10 years for a drug charge, his time in prison took an unexpected turn upon his arrival. His boyish good looks caused him to become the target of two unwitting prisoners. They were looking to have some fun with the "new fish in the pond". The coup ended with the two prisoners in the infirmary: one with a broken jaw, black eye and three missing teeth and the other in a temporary coma.

Although it was clear that Jesse had not instigated the altercation, the severity of the fight earned him a week in solitary confinement and an additional three years added to his sentence. Despite the setback, the incident proved to have an unintended benefit.

When Jesse emerged from solitary confinement, he was no longer perceived as "the new guppy in the pond". Instead, he was recognized as a force to be reckoned with—a shark in the prison's ocean. His newfound reputation as the "King Fish" quickly spread through the prison grapevine, solidifying his status and ensuring that no one dared challenge him again.

# Carolyn

After another disastrous relationship, Carolyn was back to her usual antics, leaving everyone astounded yet again. When Jesse was imprisoned, Carolyn reverted to her familiar habits of exploiting others to serve her own needs. She vanished to Florida with a married man—one who happened to be on the run from the Cuban mafia. Her escapades ended with a frantic call to her parents, asking them to rescue her after her car broke down during her attempt to return home.

Carolyn then briefly embraced the idea of an instant family by marrying a man with two sons. Once the initial surprise settled and her daughters and parents welcomed the new family members, Carolyn's restless nature resurfaced. Leaving behind her picture-perfect family setup, she set her sights on new adventures, eventually following her daughter Jordan to Atlanta, where Jordan had started college.

Atlanta brought Carolyn back to a role she knew all too well—being the girlfriend of a kingpin. She found herself living in a luxurious penthouse, armed with credit cards, cash to burn, and the thrill of danger that always seemed irresistibly enticing to her. However, her time in Atlanta and her interference in Jordan's life led to profound consequences. Once the dust settled, Carolyn was back on the prowl for her next adventure.

Regardless of the fallout, Carolyn continued to make poor decisions regarding both her relationships and her daughters. Throughout their lives, she frequently left her daughters in the care of their grandparents while she pursued love and wealth in all the wrong places. Ironically, entrusting her daughters to their grandparents during her reckless escapades may have been the most responsible act of motherhood she ever demonstrated.

## Jordan and Jessica

Jordan and Jessica were learning to navigate the challenges of adulthood, shaped by the absence of their parents—one through voluntary absence like Carolyn's selfish pursuits, and the other through Jesse's incarceration. Despite the presence of supportive family and friends, these efforts could only soften the blow but never fully mend the emotional void left behind. The pain of abandonment, whether intentional or circumstantial, continued to cast a long shadow over their lives, influencing their decisions and relationships in profound ways.

Jordan worked through her grief over the abortion, allowing her and Miles to rekindle their relationship. While Miles gave his all and dreamed of marrying Jordan as soon as they graduated, her focus remained on pursuing graduate school and building her career. She loved him but struggled to commit, held back by her deep-seated fear of abandonment. This fear made her keep emotional barriers, especially with men, believing that maintaining distance would shield her from hurt when things inevitably ended.

Jordan's unresolved issues stemmed from a fraught relationship with her mother and the absence of her father, Jesse, who was incarcerated for much of her life. Despite this, Jordan maintained a connection with her father, regularly writing and visiting him. However, she chose to withhold certain details about her life, not wanting to burden him further or make his remaining time in prison even harder than it already was.

After graduating from Clark Atlanta University, Jordan and Miles settled in a small apartment in LeDroit Park neighborhood of Northwest Washington, DC. Jordan pursued her Master of Fine Arts in Fashion Design at Howard University, while Miles enrolled in the Master of Fine Arts program in Film.

Though their love for each other remained strong, they approached their relationship with contrasting perspectives. Miles envisioned a future together, dreaming of making their commitment official through marriage. Meanwhile, Jordan wrestled with lingering doubts, anticipating the day Miles might let her down and quietly preparing for an eventual exit.

Throughout their relationship, Miles had been nothing but kind and devoted to Jordan. However, her past wounds, largely shaped by her mother Carolyn's tumultuous and reckless relationships, left Jordan continuously braced for disappointment. She couldn't help but anticipate that Miles would eventually show their love was an illusion. Consumed by this fear, Jordan spent so much time searching for flaws in Miles that she failed to recognize and appreciate the genuinely good man he already was.

Jordan's unpredictable and mistrustful actions were her way of building a shield against potential heartbreak from Miles. However, these very actions ended up causing her more harm than good. She constantly sought reassurance that Miles was genuine and committed to their relationship, but her erratic tendencies and overt suspicion began driving a wedge between them. Consumed by her fear of abandonment, Jordan inadvertently jeopardized their bond, turning her anxieties into a self-fulfilling prophecy.

After graduating high school, Jessica decided to follow her sister Jordan's example by enrolling at Clark Atlanta University in Atlanta, Georgia. Awarded a full academic scholarship, she chose to major in criminal justice, driven by a deep passion for reforming a justice system she perceived as flawed.

Jessica believed her father Jesse's prolonged incarceration stemmed from inadequate legal defense, a conviction that shaped her aspiration to become a defense attorney. While her determination to challenge systemic injustices was unwavering, the emotional void left by her father's absence also left Jessica grappling with unresolved "daddy issues."

Jessica, while undeniably intelligent and strikingly beautiful, often displayed a certain innocence that bordered on naivety. Unlike her father's street smarts, her mother's cunning, or her sister Jordan's guarded approach, Jessica was open-hearted, trusting others far too easily. This openness, coupled with her yearning for love, made her vulnerable to individuals who might exploit her good nature.

As she embarked on her college journey, she was thrilled by the idea of being independent and enjoying the freedom it offered. Yet, her first hard-learned lesson was that freedom comes with its own costs—overseeing her life could be liberating, but neglecting caution could lead to dire consequences.

# Chapter One

(Jordan)
Chocolate City

Jordan and Miles rented a cozy studio apartment in the LeDroit Park neighborhood of Northwest Washington, DC, conveniently located near Howard University for an easy commute. Jordan had chosen Howard for its renowned Fine Arts program, which had produced many prominent African American alumni. She was drawn to the vibrant creative energy of the institution, as it perfectly aligned with her passion for the arts and her desire to express that passion through fashion design.

Meanwhile, Miles pursued a master's degree in film, eager to bring compelling stories to life on the screen. He was thrilled not only about attending school but also about living with Jordan, as he cherished every moment they spent together. For him, the arrangement was ideal, blending their personal and academic lives seamlessly.

Jordan, however, had reservations. She feared that living and studying together might feel stifling. Thankfully, once their classes began, they became deeply immersed in their respective programs, which left them with little overlap at school—a balance Jordan found comforting.

The shrill ring of the alarm echoed through the room, marking 8:00 a.m. and signaling it was time for Jordan and Miles to begin their day.

"Good morning," Miles murmured softly, placing a gentle kiss on Jordan's forehead.

"Good morning. Why are you awake so early? Your first class doesn't start until 10:30," Jordan remarked, her eyes still shut.

"I know, but I just love waking up to your beautiful face before you head out," Miles said, sitting up in bed. "How about I make you some breakfast before you go?"

"Nah, I'll just pick up a muffin at the coffee shop on my way to class," Jordan said, her voice groggy as she sleepily made her way to the bathroom to get ready.

"Well, if you'd rather trade my legendary bacon and eggs for a simple muffin, that's entirely up to you," Miles quipped with a grin, leaning back into the bed.

"Aww, that's so sweet of you, baby, but I really can't be late today," Jordan said with a warm smile. "It's the first day of class, and we're being paired with our models, so I need to be on time." She blew Miles a quick kiss before heading into the shower.

Twenty minutes later, Jordan stepped out of her room dressed in a pair of jean shorts, hoop earrings, a cropped white DKNY t-shirt, and white sneakers. Her hair was styled with one side tucked behind her left ear, while the other flowed gracefully over her right shoulder in a style reminiscent of Aaliyah. She kissed Miles goodbye briefly, grabbed her bag, and left the apartment.

As soon as Jordan opened the front door of their building, the intense summer heat hit her like a wave. August in D.C. was suffocatingly hot—like stepping straight into a sauna. Determined not to let the weather slow her down, she made her way to the coffee shop. As she entered, searching through her bag for money, she accidentally bumped into the person in front of her in line, causing their muffin to fall to the floor. Flustered and apologetic, Jordan quickly bent down to clean up the mess she had caused.

"Oh my God, I'm so sorry!" Jordan exclaimed, quickly bending down to retrieve the muffin from the floor.

"Don't worry about it, accidents happen," a deep voice said reassuringly, helping Jordan back to her feet.

Jordan opened her mouth to speak, but the words eluded her as her gaze fell upon the striking figure before her. Standing tall at 6'3", he had light honey-brown skin that accentuated his toned, athletic frame, and mesmerizing light green eyes that seemed to hold her in place.

"Are you alright?" the stranger asked, noticing Jordan standing there momentarily lost in thought. Steadying herself and adjusting her hair and outfit, Jordan gave a nervous smile and said, "Yes, I'm fine. Sorry again about your muffin."

"No worries, I wasn't that hungry anyway. I'm Aaron," Aaron said with a warm smile, extending his hand toward Jordan.

"Jordan," she said, offering a polite smile as she shook Aaron's hand with a hint of hesitation. "I really feel bad about this—please, let me replace your muffin."

"It's alright, really, you don't need to do that," Aaron responded.

"I insist," Jordan said firmly, approaching the counter. "Could I get two blueberry muffins and two orange juices, please?"

The woman at the counter placed the muffins and orange juice into two bags and handed them to Jordan.

"Thanks," Jordan said, taking the order and handing Aaron his bag.

"Thanks," Aaron said, his fingers lightly brushing against Jordan's hand as he took the bag. A jolt of energy coursed through her as their hands touched, prompting her to pull away abruptly.

"Are you alright?" Aaron asked, his voice filled with concern as he noticed Jordan's startled reaction to his touch.

"Yes, I need to get to class," Jordan said, her voice tinged with nervousness as she tucked her hair behind her ear, deliberately avoiding his gaze.

"Really? Which school do you attend?" Aaron asked, his grin widening as he noticed Jordan's flustered reaction.

"Howard," Jordan replied as she hurried toward the door. "It was nice meeting you—have a great day," she called over her shoulder, her pace quickening as she made her exit.

"Nice to meet you as well," Aaron said, chuckling to himself at the visible effect he seemed to have on Jordan.

His light green eyes sparkled with amusement, but there was a softness in them too, as though he didn't want to push her too far.

*What is wrong with you? That man has you acting like a schoolgirl who just spotted her first crush in the hallway! Pull yourself together, you have a boyfriend waiting at home. Jordan scolded herself internally as she hurried to class. Still, she couldn't deny it, he was undeniably attractive, and if just a fleeting touch of his hand could send shivers down her spine, heaven help her if he ever truly touched her. But there was no need to dwell on it; after all, she'd never see him again. Problem solved.*

Resolving to shake off the encounter, Jordan continued her inner dialogue, steeling herself as she entered the classroom and settled into her seat. Ms. Stanton, the instructor, was already addressing the class as Jordan tried to focus her mind.

"Settle down, everyone, and take your seats," Ms. Stanton said, her voice commanding yet warm. "I'm Gloria Stanton, and I'll be your instructor for today." She gestured for the class to get seated.

Ms. Stanton was a tall, slender, middle-aged Black woman with cinnamon brown skin, and striking silver and dark gray hair styled into a neatly coiled bun at the back of her head. She wore a sleek black jumpsuit, complemented by a white, diamond-studded belt and layered with an oversized white cashmere cardigan. Her outfit was completed with high-heeled black boots. Her demeanor was effortlessly composed, radiating elegance and sophistication.

"Ladies and gentlemen," Ms. Stanton began, her voice commanding yet approachable, "this class offers a unique experience where you and a partner will collaborate throughout the semester. You'll alternate between the roles of model and designer. Now, please select your partner so we can begin today's exercise."

Jordan glanced around the room, realizing that everyone had already paired up, leaving her the only one without a partner. She hesitated for a moment before raising her hand to alert Ms. Stanton of the situation. Just as she opened her mouth to speak, she sensed someone approaching from behind. That familiar jolt shot through her, the same one she'd felt earlier, as a deep and unmistakable voice said, "I'll be your partner."

Jordan closed her eyes, trying to steady herself as she absorbed the masculine energy that was pulsating behind her. She inhaled deeply, gathering her composure, and turned to meet those familiar light green eyes, the same ones that had left her breathless in the coffee shop earlier that day.

*Could it really be Aaron? Was he following her? What were the odds that he'd end up in this class too?* Jordan's thoughts raced as she struggled to find her voice. Just as she was about to respond, Ms. Stanton quickly made her way toward them.

"Ah, Mr. Garrison, glad you could join us. It seems everyone now has a partner," Ms. Stanton said with a welcoming tone. "Please take a seat beside Miss Alexander so we can begin."

Jordan hesitated for a moment before sliding over to make space for Aaron at her workstation. The warmth of his presence beside her and the subtle scent of his cologne seemed to envelop her, stirring a flurry of butterflies in her stomach. She couldn't help but think to herself, *this is going to be a long semester.*

"Ah, we meet again, Miss Alexander," Aaron murmured, his voice low and smooth as he added her last name to the familiarity of her first.

"So, it appears, Mr. Garrison," Jordan responded, mirroring his use of her last name with a subtle smile.

Jordan managed a tight smile in response, her hands fumbling with the edge of her notebook. Her mind raced, searching for something clever or neutral to say, but her thoughts were a tangle of butterflies and apprehension. Why did he have to smell so good? And why did he have to look at her like that—as if he could see right through her feigned composure?

"So, any idea how this whole modeling and designing thing is going to work?" Aaron asked, breaking the silence as he leaned slightly closer, his elbow resting casually on the desk they now shared. His tone was easy, confident, as though he were oblivious to the storm raging in Jordan's chest.

Jordan cleared her throat and forced herself to meet his gaze, which only seemed to intensify the quiver in her stomach. "I… uh… I guess we'll figure it out as we go," she said, her voice steadier than she expected, though it still betrayed a hint of nervousness.

"Good. Because I'm terrible at figuring things out alone," Aaron said with a grin that could have melted steel, "but I have a feeling you're going to be a great partner."

Jordan opened her mouth to reply, but before she could, Ms. Stanton's voice drew their attention back to the front of the room.

Jordan couldn't quite understand why everything about this man seemed to make her feel so vulnerable. She understood continuing to have him as her partner might be risky, yet she couldn't help but feel exhilarated by the spark he ignited within her. She reassured herself that she could keep those feelings under control, but deep down, she knew that playing with fire often leads to someone getting burned.

After class, Jordan and Aaron exchanged numbers and shared what started as a friendly hug goodbye. However, the warmth of his embrace, the intoxicating scent of his cologne, and the way being in his arms made her feel as though she might melt turned that hug into something that lingered far longer than what "friendly" typically allowed.

When their embrace ended, Jordan hurried to the ladies' room, splashing cold water on her face to steady her racing thoughts. Yet even that proved insufficient; after that hug, what she truly needed was a cold shower.

For the rest of the day, Jordan couldn't concentrate. Her mind was a whirlwind of thoughts about Aaron and the undeniable chemistry that seemed to spark between them. No matter how much she tried, she couldn't push him out of her head or regain her focus. Her curiosity about him only grew stronger.

That evening, she returned home later than usual, telling Miles she had been at the library working on a class project. In truth, she was avoiding going home. Instead, she took a train to Pentagon City Mall in Virginia and wandered through the shops. She eventually found herself in Victoria's Secret, picking out alluring lingerie sets along with new yoga outfits and athletic wear for a campus fitness class.

*Maybe I can work off some of this sexual tension.* Jordan mused as she browsed through the selection of athletic wear.

Jordan tried to tell herself that the new underwear was for Miles, but in her heart, she knew that was a lie. Although at the time, she never intended for Aaron to ever see the lingerie, it was the beginning of decisions that were made with Aaron in mind. She wrapped up her shopping and decided to grab some food from the food court. After she placed her order and sat down, her phone buzzed with a text message. It was Aaron. Jordan opened the message and read it.

"It was nice to meet you today; I am glad we were partnered up. Let's meet up at the coffee shop at 6:00pm tomorrow to start working on our first project. I can't wait to see you again. – Aaron".

Jordan read the message over and over with an uncontrollable smile spreading across her face and butterflies in her stomach. *Bzz bzz*, the phone buzzed again, but this time it was a message from Miles.

"Hey babe, I just wanted to say I love you and I can't wait to see you when you get home. Dinner will be waiting for you, and so will I. – Miles."

Soon a wave of guilt replaced those warm fuzzy feelings, and Jordan sat back in her chair for a moment and let out a heavy sigh.

*What are you doing Jordan? You love Miles, and he loves you. He is a good man, and he does not deserve this. You have got to stop this before it goes too far.* Jordan thought to herself.

Then just like that, her insecurities and past trauma took over and rationalized her behavior. *It's just harmless flirting; you haven't done anything wrong. Besides, Miles is a man, and sooner or later they all cheat, and break your heart. You must keep your options open; you are not married. Who says Miles is your soulmate?*

Jordan decided it was time to go home. She threw her trash away, grabbed her bags and hopped on the train. Her apartment was a short walk from the Shaw Metro station and in turn was also a short walk to school. When Jordan arrived at her apartment, she paused momentarily and stared up to her second-floor apartment.

Miles had the window open, so she could see him moving around in the kitchen. He looked like he was preparing dinner. Jordan slowly walked in the building and walked up the stairs to their apartment. As soon as she opened the door, she eased the shopping bags in the closet, before Miles turned around.

"Hey baby, I missed you today. I made your favorite, stuffed salmon, with broccoli and mashed potatoes. Why don't you put your bag down and come eat." Miles said with a smile, when he realized she came in.

"Thanks babe, but I am not feeling well. Can you put my plate up for me? I had a long day." Jordan replied, feeling bad, about the mental affair she had been having with Aaron since they first locked eyes in the coffee shop this morning.

"Oh no, I'm sorry you are not feeling well babe. I tell you what, I will put this food away and bring you something to help settle your stomach. Maybe rub your tummy for you. How does that sound?" Miles asked with genuine concern.

"You don't have to do that; I think I just need to get some sleep" Jordan responded.

"Ok, you sure? You know I don't mind taking care of my baby." Miles offered.

"I'm sure. I am just going to lay down, I will see you in the morning baby. Good night." Jordan said.

"Ok…good night." Miles responded, feeling like something was off.

Jordan jumped in the shower and tried to wash off the stench of her growing duplicitous behavior, and thoughts of Aaron. She dressed in a comfy pajama short set, tied her hair up, brushed her teeth, and laid down. Miles slid into bed beside her, wrapping his arms around her. This was the second time today, she had been in a man's arms, but this time, it wasn't the flutter of butterflies that she felt, it was the pangs of guilt.

# Chapter Two
## (Jessica)
## Daddy's Little Girl

Jessica was up before her alarm had the chance to go off. A freshman at Clark Atlanta University, she was eager to start strong. With a full academic scholarship riding on her performance, there was no room for mistakes—Jessica was focused and disciplined. She dressed quickly and was out the door before her roommate, Amina, even stirred. Jessica and Amina did not reside in the regular dorms, they were roommates at Carter Hall, a renovated hotel now being utilized as off campus housing for college students.

Their routines almost never aligned. Jessica favored early classes so her afternoons could be free for studying and personal projects, while Amina, a Senior, who had started her college career at 26, scheduled everything in the latter half of the day, often sleeping late into the morning.

Amina was stunning. With her tall, elegant frame, radiant ebony skin, and long flowing hair, she naturally turned heads wherever she went. As an Atlanta native, she moved through the city with confidence and ease. She had an air of mystery about her—cool, composed, and extremely private.

Jessica often wondered what filled Amina's nights. On weekdays, she returned just before curfew, and on weekends, she wouldn't reappear until late Sunday. But since their relationship remained distant and polite, Jessica kept her curiosity to herself.

Jessica made it through her classes without issue and spent a quiet hour in the library, getting a head start on her assignments. When she returned to her dorm, she was surprised to find Amina still there—lingering in the shared space for once, rather than breezing in and out like a passing shadow.

Amina stood in front of the mirror, applying a final swipe of lipstick. She wore a pair of sleek, fitted jeans, a white strapless top that hugged her curves, and heels that added an extra inch or two to her already statuesque frame. She moved with effortless grace, like someone who knew the effect she had when she entered a room.

Jessica hadn't realized she was staring until Amina turned slightly and spoke, her voice calm but edged with awareness.

"You good?" Amina asked, catching Jessica's gaze in the mirror.

Jessica blinked, caught off guard by Amina's question. "Yeah—sorry," she said, flustered. "I didn't expect to see you here this early. You usually head out later."

Amina gave a half-smile, adjusting a silver hoop earring. "Got somewhere to be."
Jessica hesitated. "You always do," she said lightly, trying to sound casual, but her curiosity had slipped through the cracks.

Amina raised an eyebrow, catching the edge in Jessica's tone. "You thinking I'm up to something?" Jessica shook her head, embarrassed. "No, no. It's not like that. I just—never mind."

For a moment, Amina studied her, then turned back to the mirror with a shrug. "You're not wrong to wonder," she said, voice calm but cryptic. "Some things just aren't meant to be explained in daylight."

With that, she slipped on a denim jacket, grabbed her small clutch, and made for the door. "Don't wait up."

The door clicked shut behind her, leaving Jessica standing in the quiet, a dozen questions suddenly loud in her mind. Jessica stood by the door long after Amina was gone, the air still faintly holding the scent of her perfume—floral with a hint of something darker. Curiosity burned in her chest. She'd always respected Amina's privacy but tonight felt different. The way she'd spoken, that cryptic almost-challenge—"some things just aren't meant to be explained in daylight"—stuck with her like a thread begging to be tugged.

On impulse, Jessica slipped out of her sweats and into jeans and a hoodie, tying her curls into a loose bun. She didn't have a plan—just a quiet resolve as she headed into the hallway and down the stairs. She didn't have to go far. Amina wasn't even out of sight yet—just across the quad, her silhouette lit by the soft orange glow of streetlamps. She walked like she knew exactly where she was going, her heels clicking lightly against the pavement, not once looking back.

Jessica followed at a distance, staying just far enough to avoid attention. It felt ridiculous, juvenile even—but something told her this night would be different. Amina crossed the street, stepped into the back of a sleek black car waiting at the curb, and it pulled away with quiet urgency. Jessica stared as the taillights vanished into the city. This wasn't over.

The city at night thrummed with a different kind of heartbeat—lower, silkier, full of secrets. Jessica stepped out onto the sidewalk, the air still warm from the afternoon sun but tinged with a restless breeze. Streetlights cast golden pools along the pavement, broken only by the hum of passing cars and the occasional laughter spilling from a restaurant patio.

Jessica didn't know where the car had gone, but something told her it wouldn't be back on campus. So, she walked. Not aimlessly but guided by a quiet intuition that pulled her toward the pulse of downtown Atlanta. The sound of jazz floated from an open doorway as she passed a tucked-away lounge. A couple leaned close together outside, cloaked in shadows and cigarette smoke.

Jessica's hoodie didn't match the after-hours crowd—heels clicked, dresses shimmered, cologne and confidence perfumed the air. She hugged her arms a little closer. As she waited at a crosswalk, a sleek black car pulled up beside the curb. Not the same one Amina took—but close. Its tinted window rolled halfway down. A man inside, dressed sharply in dark slacks and a crisp shirt, glanced at her and smiled—too long, too knowing—before the light changed and the car slipped away. Goosebumps flared across Jessica's arms. She pressed forward.

Blocks later, something caught her eye: a quiet, upscale lounge tucked beneath a boutique hotel. No sign, just a velvet rope and a pair of bouncers in black. Through the frosted glass, Jessica glimpsed silhouettes—women in heels, men in suits, the slow swirl of conversation and secrets. And there, just for a second, moving through the crowd with unmistakable grace—Amina.

Jessica's breath caught. She backed away into a nearby alley, her heart hammering. She'd seen enough to know this wasn't just a night out. It was a world entirely separate from campus life. And Amina wasn't just navigating it—she belonged to it. Jessica lingered in the shadows a moment longer, pulse thudding beneath her hoodie. The faint bass from inside the hidden lounge pulsed like a second heartbeat—low, seductive, charged. She couldn't tear her eyes away.

Then, slowly, she stepped out from the alley and crossed the street, keeping close to the edge of the sidewalk. She didn't try to get in. Instead, she perched on a nearby bench, pretending to scroll through her phone. From her spot, she watched the door like it might open and reveal some crucial clue.

People came and went in sleek black cars and whispered laughter. Most looked older, polished. They moved with the kind of ease that came from money—or power. She spotted two women in designer dresses greet the bouncer with a subtle nod before being waved in, no ID check, no questions.

Behind them, a man in a tailored trench coat lit a cigar, glanced at Jessica, then looked away as if dismissing her entirely.

Jessica tucked her chin lower into her hoodie. Just as she started to question what she was even doing there, a familiar voice drifted from behind. "You know, it's not really safe sitting out here like that."

Jessica turned. A young man—maybe a few years older than her—stood nearby, leaning against the lamppost. He wore a charcoal-gray suit without a tie, collar open, cufflinks gleaming faintly in the streetlight. His smile was easy, but his eyes were sharp.

"I'm fine," Jessica said, instantly guarded.

He tilted his head slightly. "Let me guess... college student, journalism major, maybe? You don't exactly blend in out here. That's not a judgment," he added quickly, raising his hands. "More like... an observation."

Jessica stood slowly, slipping her phone into her pocket. "I was just heading out."

He took a step closer but didn't block her path. "Sure. But if you're looking for someone... Amina, maybe?" He said her name like it held weight. Like a test.

Jessica's heart skipped. "She's... a friend," she lied, too quickly.

He smiled again, this time with a little more edge. "Right. Well, if you're going to follow people, maybe be a little more subtle next time."

Then, he turned and walked toward the lounge entrance. The bouncers stepped aside without a word. Jessica watched him disappear inside. Her feet felt frozen to the sidewalk. The door swung shut behind him with a soft finality. Whatever world Amina belonged to—it was layered, exclusive, and very much awake. And Jessica had just cracked the edge of it.

# Chapter Three

## (Carolyn)
## Same Man, Different Money

Carolyn could smell money the way a shark smells blood in the water. So, when her unstable ex-husband Evan rolled into town behind the wheel of a brand-new Mercedes, throwing cash like it grew on trees, her instincts lit up. Something had changed. Evan wasn't just back—he was back with power.

After asking around, Carolyn got the full story: Evan had landed a quiet fortune. While working construction on a high-profile development site, he'd been electrocuted due to faulty wiring. The company, mid-negotiation on a multi-billion-dollar deal, couldn't afford the press nightmare of a court case. Instead, they paid Evan off—$1.3 million in hush money, sealed tight with a nondisclosure agreement.

Now he was rolling in money, and Carolyn could almost hear the numbers clicking behind her eyes. She knew Evan's weak spots. She knew how to make a man like that feel needed. And more importantly—how to make him feel generous. The question wasn't whether she'd make a move. It was how soon. It happened, as these things often do, in the least glamorous of places—a strip mall parking lot near a liquor store, just before sundown.

Carolyn spotted him before he saw her. Evan was leaning against that glossy new Mercedes, sunglasses on despite the fading light, tossing a wad of twenties to a kid selling mixtapes from a backpack. The watch on his wrist probably cost more than her rent. He looked clean, confident— like someone who'd finally figured out how to polish the madness into something charming.

Carolyn smirked, then called out to him - "Evan."

He turned at the sound of his name, froze mid-sip of his drink, then broke into a wide grin. "Well, I'll be damned…"

Carolyn sauntered closer, hips swaying with familiarity and calculated sweetness. "You gonna offer me a ride, or just stand there acting like I didn't used to sleep on the left side of your mattress?"

He chuckled, lowering his shades. "You still remember that?"

"I remember everything." She let the words linger in the humid air. "Heard you hit it big."
He shrugged, but not modestly. "Let's just say karma finally paid out for all the hell I've been through."

Carolyn glanced at the car, then back at him. "Looks like she paid in full."

"You here to congratulate me… or collect?" he asked, half-joking.

She leaned in close enough for him to smell her perfume—something warm and nostalgic. "Maybe a little of both."

Evan didn't move. But his smile slipped just the tiniest bit. He remembered who she was. He also remembered what she could do with one whispered secret, one well-placed smile, one carefully told lie.

"Get in," he said finally, unlocking the car. "Let's catch up."

Carolyn slid into the passenger seat with a slow grin. Hook set.

The inside of Evan's Mercedes smelled like leather, new money, and overcompensation. Carolyn crossed her legs slowly, making a show of adjusting the hem of her skirt. She knew how to make a man lean in without realizing he was doing it. Evan turned down the music—some overproduced rap song that had no business playing in a car this expensive—and glanced over with that old, manic glint in his eye.

"You look good, Carol," he said. "Better than I remember."

"Memory's a funny thing," she replied, cool as ice. "Selective. Foggy when it wants to be."

He laughed, tapped the steering wheel. "So, what's the real reason you waved me down like a groupie outside a concert? You lonely, or just casing the ride?"

She let that sit between them like smoke. Then, soft and just a little bitter: "I heard you got paid." Evan's knuckles whitened slightly against the leather. "People talk too damn much in this town."

"You think I came to beg?" she said, voice tightening just enough to feel real. "Evan, I'm not here for your money. I'm here because maybe—just maybe—I remember when you were something besides angry and broke."

He looked at her then, for real. For the first time since the parking lot.

"And maybe," she continued, eyes still forward, "you remember what it felt like to have someone see you as more than the guy everyone called crazy behind his back."

Silence stretched long, interrupted only by the turn signal clicking as he pulled out onto the road. Then, softly, he said, "You hungry?"

Carolyn smiled without looking at him. "Starved."

The car glided through the twilight like a lie whispered in velvet. Carolyn kept her gaze on the road, but her mind was a storm.

*He still wants to believe I need him. Good. That's leverage. That's warmth in the water. Evan smelled different—clean, but chemical. Like something trying too hard to scrub itself into a new identity. His nervous laugh earlier, that slight delay when she mentioned the money... He hadn't changed. Not really. Money just gave his delusions a shinier coat of paint.*

Carolyn she wasn't here for nostalgia. She was here because a man like Evan didn't deserve to be lucky twice. Not without paying someone for it. All those nights of chaos, the hospital visits, the lies I used to tell just to keep him from coming undone in public—he owes me. Even if he doesn't know it yet.

Carolyn glanced at him from the corner of her eye. He was humming now, relaxed. Comfortable. That was dangerous. She'd have to fix that. I don't want forever. I just want enough. A few months. A few quiet withdrawals from that accident settlement he's pretending doesn't exist. And when he starts slipping—which he always does—I'll be gone before the ink smudges on the next meltdown. She smiled. He didn't see it. It wasn't for him. It was the kind of smile you wear when you've already counted the money.

Carolyn let Evan take her to one of those rooftop lounges with overpriced cocktails and waitstaff trained to pretend they didn't recognize trouble when it walked in wearing designer sunglasses. She sipped a drink she didn't like and laughed just loud enough to keep him feeling interesting. But even across the table, over the low thrum of jazz and clinking glass, she could tell the cracks were already spidering behind his new veneer. The manic energy was still there—it just wore cologne now. And Carolyn knew how to wait out a storm like that. Smile. Nod. Let him talk long enough to give himself away.

"I've got people now," Evan bragged, swirling his glass. "Connections. Lawyers. You wouldn't believe the kind of doors open to a man with money and no conscience."

Carolyn tilted her head. "No conscience? That sounds familiar."

*He didn't catch the jab. Too busy feeding his own myth. Good, she thought. Let him puff up. Men like Evan never notice when the tide's already rising around their ankles.*

Back at her motel that night, she kicked off her heels and pulled out the small notebook she used to keep her chaos straight—dates, details, pressure points. Carolyn jotted a note:

*Evan = flashy. paranoid. high probability of relapse. Not watching his accounts.* Then beneath it, in smoother script: *Potential exit strategy: let him think it was his idea to bring me in. Let him write the check. Let him get messy.*

Carolyn underlined that last part. Let him get messy. She didn't need to destroy Evan. She just needed to make sure that when he self-destructed… she was the one holding the match and the alibi. Carolyn's long game wasn't about revenge. Not exactly. It was about correction. She sat alone that night in the motel's chipped vinyl chair, a Styrofoam cup of cheap wine sweating on the nightstand and reviewed her mental ledger. Evan's money wasn't the goal—it was a means. She had spent too many years watching men stumble into luck and call it *justice.*

So, Carolyn would play the loyal ex-wife, the one who *just wanted to reconnect.* She'd ride shotgun in that Mercedes, laugh at the right moments, and ask no questions about the money— yet. Evan was arrogant, but fragile. That combination made him predictable. He wanted validation as badly as he wanted power, and

Carolyn could serve him both—just long enough to loosen his grip.

The plan? Get close. Rebuild trust. Then leverage the truth: that settlement money was off-the-books, bound in NDAs and quietly wired. The kind of funds that wouldn't stand up well to scrutiny. The kind of funds someone might want to keep quiet—*especially* if she hinted at a little blackmail. But Carolyn was careful. She wouldn't press too fast. She'd let him feel safe. Then she'd turn the screws. And when he spiraled—as he always did—she'd already be gone. With just enough cash to disappear. Or start over. Whichever came first.

# Chapter Four
## (Jesse)
## New Fish/King Fish

Thirteen years had swum by, and the tide that carried Jesse Braxton into lockup was nothing like the one that held him there. When the judge banged the gavel—ten years for possession with intent—it felt like drowning. But prison? Prison didn't drown Jesse. It woke something in him.

The moment Jesse Braxton stepped off the transport bus, he felt it—the eyes. Sizing him up. Hunger, boredom, and malice all simmering beneath the surface like oil waiting for a spark. He kept his head down, hands behind his back. This wasn't his first time. But it had been a long while. He was twenty-nine. Still smooth-faced. Lean. With eyes that hadn't yet lost hope. That hope was dangerous behind bars—like blood in shark water. It only took three days for trouble to find him.

At rec, two inmates—older, mean, bored— caught sight of Jesse coming through the intake yard. One leaned against the wall, grinning like he already owned Jesse's future. The other circled like he'd done this before.

"Fresh meat," one of them said with a grin. "That's a pretty one. Bet he sings sweet when he gets scared."

The other laughed. "Let's find out."

Jesse clocked the threat instantly. He'd learned back home that charm didn't protect you. His good looks didn't help either. Not in this place.

Later, in the showers, they cornered him. No guards. No mercy. But they underestimated him.

"Well, look what we got here," said the taller one, stepping into Jesse's space. "Didn't think introductions were necessary but call me Trigger. My boy here? He don't talk much, but he gets real expressive when folks get mouthy."

Jesse didn't flinch. "You picked the wrong nigga, Trigger."

"Oh, is that right? You don't look like much." Jesse gave them a small smile. "Looks'll fool you." Trigger grabbed Jesse's arm. The other moved behind him. What happened next became legend.

It happened fast. Jesse twisted, slamming Trigger's head into the tile wall. The second man lunged, but Jesse ducked low and launched a punch into his gut that made him crumple. He turned back to Trigger—now bleeding from the nose—and cracked him across the jaw so hard, teeth clattered against the drain. A mop handle. A broken faucet. A slam against tile that left one man with a shattered jaw, fractured orbital, and three missing teeth. The other had his head bounced off a cinder block so hard he spent two days in ICU under neurological watch.

Blood. Silence. Then alarm. Jesse stood over both of them, breathing hard. He didn't speak. He didn't apologize. There was no noise. Except for the guards shouting and dragging Jesse off the pile. The altercation resulted in Jesse receiving One week in the hole and three years tacked on.

Solitary confinement was cold, concrete, and deafeningly quiet. The lights stayed on just enough to keep your thoughts loud. Jesse didn't mourn the fight. He didn't regret defending himself. But the extra three years they tacked onto his sentence— those weighed differently.

Still, that week alone did something unexpected. It hardened what was already starting to reshape. The inmate who walked out of that cell wasn't fresh-faced anymore. He was a message. When Jesse emerged, everything had changed. Inmates who used to size him up now stepped aside. The whispers started. *"King Fish."* A title he hadn't asked for—but learned to wield.

Later, Jesse became the talk of the yard. It started in whispers, then spread like wildfire.

"Y'all hear what happened to Big Marcus and Trigger? That dude Braxton was behind it, he did that."

"The Little dude with the curls?"

"Don't let the curls fool you. He's a shark."

The grapevine rebranded Jesse overnight. No longer "guppy." No longer "new fish." Now he was the King Fish—calm, calculating, untouchable. And prison respected stories more than stats. Jesse's story was blood-inked and passed from cellblock to cellblock.

Nobody challenged him again. In fact, they started coming to him. For protection. For advice. Even for mediation. A young inmate once asked Jesse why he didn't start a crew. Jesse just lit a cigarette and said, "Because a king doesn't need soldiers to remind people he's a king."

Fast forward to ten years inside, Jesse Braxton had survived by learning how not to flinch. The first three were hard and full of anger. The next three were the ones where the anger quieted and clarity crept in. And the next three was when he made the decision to make use of the time he had inside.

By the time Jesse hit year ten, he'd become a ghost of what most men called "a problem." Not because he had faded—but because he'd learned to live in the silence, to move beneath it, like a current. He trained. Read. Wrote more letters than he ever sent.

The rest of his sentence wasn't easy—but it was controlled. He studied law in the library. He wrote letters to his daughters he never sent. He broke up fights with words instead of fists. Started programs to help other inmates give back to the community. Jesse didn't waste his prison time. He built something in it. And when he finally walked out thirteen years later—it would not just be with time served, but a reputation earned—he wasn't looking to reclaim what he'd lost. He was ready to build something better.

But sharks never stop swimming. And peace still felt like open water. When Arturo Delgado's son Juan landed in lockup years later, it was Jesse who stepped in before things turned bloody. That act of quiet leadership became his real currency.

Barely twenty, rail-thin, sharp-tongued with a chip on his shoulder the size of his sentence, Juan Delgado had gotten three years for moving weight across state lines. He walked in talking tough, trying to puff up in the yard. Jesse clocked him within two minutes: a rich kid playing gangster, headed for a long fall unless someone intervened.

At lunch, Jesse spotted him eyeing an empty seat.

"Don't sit there," Jesse said without looking up from his tray. "That's Monroe's spot."

Juan hesitated. "So?"

"So, Monroe's got six inches on you and a craving for theatrics. He'll stab you and cry about it later."

Juan shifted to the next seat over. "Appreciate it, old man."

Jesse smirked. "Keep talkin' slick, I'll let him have you next time."

A few weeks later, Juan found out the hard way, why he should have listened to Jesse's advice. Juan was cornered—three guys, twice his size, laughing low and mean.

"You got soft hands, pretty boy," one of them said, pinning him against the fence.

"I said I don't got nothing else, man!" Juan barked, panic overtaking bravado.

One of the guys raised his fist. And then Jesse's voice cut through the noise. "Back away."

The men turned. Jesse stood still. Calm. Not posturing—just *present.* "I said," he repeated, "back away."

The guy in front grinned. "This ain't your business."

Jesse cracked his neck slowly. "It is now."

The one closest to Juan took a step forward—then paused, recognizing the name stitched into the back of Jesse's reputation.

"Yo, that's Braxton," one of them whispered. *"King Fish."*

The men scattered. Juan sat down hard on the bench, shaking. "Why'd you do that?" he asked.

Jesse handed him a water. "Cause I've seen what happens to kids like you in here."

"You don't even know me." Juan stated.

"I don't need to," Jesse said. "Just saw someone who didn't belong in hell yet."

Later that night in Cellblock C. Juan appeared with a fresh bruise on his cheek but eyes shining. "You ever heard of Gabriel Orozco?"

Jesse squinted. "The artist?"

Juan walked over to Jesse who was laying on the bottom bunk and continued, "My old man has a sculpture of his in our backyard. Don't know why— I used to hate it. Thought it was ugly. But he told me art like that's meant to change depending on where you're standing."

Jesse looked up. "That's how I'm starting to feel about you."

Over the next year, they fell into rhythm.

Jesse taught Juan how to move quietly, speak less, watch more. Juan—smart, hungry for more than status—started reading the books Jesse passed down. They traded stories. Laughed more than anyone expected. And one night, over a game of chess played on a board carved into the table, Juan told him the truth.

"My father's connected," he said. "Real connected."

Jesse raised an eyebrow.

"I didn't want to pull that card. Didn't think I should. But I told him about you."

Jesse folded his arms. "What'd you tell him?"

"That you saved me. Twice. Once from them... and once from becoming one of *them*." Juan paused.

"My old man says anything you need, anytime—you got it." Jesse didn't answer. But he remembered.

# Chapter Five

## (Jordan)
## Pinned at the Seams

The hum of machines and the sharp scent of muslin hung in the air as Ms. Stanton tapped a manicured nail against her clipboard. Jordan sat up straighter, clutching her sketchbook like it was armor. Beside her, Aaron lounged with that effortless ease that always made the room lean just slightly in his direction.

Ms. Stanton smiled—tight, sly. "This year's showcase will be unlike any before," she said, scanning the class. "In four weeks, you'll debut one signature piece before a panel of industry guests. Editors. Buyers. Designers. The winner will receive a summer internship in New York with Maison de Luxe."

Gasps echoed. Pens dropped. Jordan's heart thudded.

*Maison de Luxe.*

"That internship could change your whole life," someone whispered behind her.

Ms. Stanton continued. "Partnerships remain the same. You'll alternate roles as before—one model, one designer. Switch for the next round.

53

Concept and execution must be original. Cohesive. Elevated."

Jordan caught Aaron's eye. He winked.

*God help me.* She thought.

That night in the studio, fabric was scattered on the floor like fallen petals. Jordan crouched beside a half-finished dress, pinning folds along the hip of the muslin form. Aaron sat on the stool behind her, sketching in silence.

"Crimson chiffon," he said finally.

Jordan looked up. "That's what you want for yours?"

Aaron shrugged. "No. For yours. Draped low in the back. Clean lines, but suggestive. That color would kill on you."

Jordan tried to laugh. "Not every garment has to seduce someone, you know."

Aaron smirked. "Sometimes it helps."

Jordan stood, brushing lint from her jeans. "You're ridiculous."

"And you," he said, crossing the room toward her, "are working yourself into a stress coma."

His voice dropped. "You're gonna win this, J."

"I don't need you to say that." She said.

"No. But I need to." Aaron replied softly.

Later that week on the cafeteria balcony, Jordan toyed with the edge of a croissant. Beside her, Aaron flicked through design photos on his phone.

"Camille's using ostrich feathers. Feather *everything,*" he muttered. "It looks like a high-fashion chicken coop exploded."

Jordan tried to laugh, but her smile didn't land.

"Hey," Aaron said softly, nudging her. "You good?"

Jordan stared out at the campus green. "Everyone in that class wants the same thing," she murmured. "They'll smile at you while they're stealing your lining. And every time I think I'm climbing—"

"You look back and see you left pieces of yourself behind," he finished.

Silence.

"I just... I've always had to be the responsible one. The one who didn't screw up. I can't afford to want anything that could burn it all down."

When she finally turned to him, Aaron's expression shifted.

"Jordan," he said, voice low. "If wanting me is what you're afraid will ruin you... don't."

"I didn't say—"

"You didn't have to."

Two days later in the design lab, steam curled from the iron as Jordan pressed the pleats in Aaron's trousers. He was shirtless, arms stretched above his head as he examined a sleeve on the mannequin.

Jordan hated how good he looked under harsh fluorescent lights. "Don't do that," she said.

"Do what?" Aaron asked slyly.

"Make this harder than it has to be." Jordan uttered softly.

Aaron walked behind her, voice at her ear. "I think it's supposed to be hard. That's how you know it matters."

When Jordan turned to face him, her breath caught. They were too close. Always too close. She couldn't remember how the distance vanished—but when Aaron's hand brushed her waist, Jordan didn't step away.

The air between them sparked, fragile and loaded. Jordan was balancing on a ledge made of ambition, fear, and fire. And she had no idea which way she'd fall.

# Chapter Six
### (Jessica)
### Love Lessons

Jessica returned to her dorm that night, but sleep didn't come easily. Visions of the exclusive club, the flicker of Amina through frosted glass, and the mystery of the man in the suit replayed in her mind. When she heard Amina slip in later, Jessica stayed still, feigning sleep—but her mind was wide awake. Eventually, exhaustion won. It felt like only minutes later when her alarm blared, slicing through the stillness. As usual, Amina slept undisturbed, untouched by Jessica's groggy scramble. The detective work from the night before had dulled her usual morning spark, but she still managed to pull herself together and head out.

Just as she reached the sidewalk, a voice drifted out.

"You really shouldn't stay up past your bedtime following people... if you can't hang."
Jessica froze.

There he was—Bryce. But gone was the sharp suit from last night. Now he wore jeans, Timberlands, and a gray hoodie, blending in effortlessly with the campus crowd. Her surprise was evident.

He chuckled. "Looks like the cat's got your tongue. I'll go first. I'm Bryce. And you are…?"

"Jessica," she said, hesitating for a split second before giving her real name. "My name is Jessica."

"Well, nice to meet you in the daylight, Jessica. Headed somewhere?"

She was suddenly aware of how good he looked, something she'd overlooked the night before. "Class," she replied simply.

"Same. Which one?" Bryce quizzed.

"Freshman Orientation." Jessica shot back.

Bryce smirked. "I remember that. Hated it. Glad that year's behind me—I'm a junior now. Mind if I walk with you? Chemistry's in the same building. Thought maybe we could get to know each other a little better."

Jessica paused, then cut through the flirtation. "How do you know Amina?"

He let out a short laugh. "Dang—straight to it, huh? We work at the same place."

"The club?" she asked.

"Yeah. I'm a bouncer there." he answered.

"What about Amina? What does she do?" she continued.

His tone shifted, even, cool. "That's a question for her."

"What kind of club is it?" Jessica continued like an interrogation.

Bryce studied her. "Let's just say it's an upscale spot. Private. Offers... adult experiences for exclusive clientele."

Jessica raised an eyebrow. "Maybe I'll check it out."

He chuckled, but his grin held a warning. "Not your crowd, princess."

"Maybe I'll be the judge of that." she countered.

His smile faded. "No, seriously. It's not a place for girls like you. Things happen there that don't belong in your world. Promise me you won't go."

She caught the edge in his voice. Something beneath the charm had sharpened. "Okay," she said finally. "I promise."

The tension eased. They walked the rest of the way to class in easy conversation. Before they parted, they exchanged numbers. From that moment forward, Jessica and Bryce were inseparable—but the questions about Amina still whispered at the edges of her mind.

Before Jessica realized, weeks had passed, and she and Bryce had been talking every day and spending every available moment together. She sat on the edge of her bed, phone in hand, rereading Bryce's last text for the third time.

"You're full of questions, but I don't mind. Keep 'em coming, princess."

There was something about the way he said things—light enough to make her laugh, but with an undertone that made her want to read between the lines. She knew better than to let herself get distracted, especially by someone who guarded his world behind velvet ropes and half-truths. But it was already happening. She was thinking about him too much.

She glanced across the room. Amina's side was still neat, untouched. She hadn't come back since last night.

Jessica's stomach tightened. What did Bryce mean when he said that place wasn't for girls like her? And why had it felt like more than concern—like warning? Like guilt?

Across town, Bryce leaned against the brick wall outside the club, gone was the hoodie and casual dress. He was back on the clock and back in his suit, the weight of his earlier conversation with Jessica still pressing against his ribs.

She was asking questions. Smart ones. The kind that didn't just want answers—they wanted truths. And that was dangerous.

He liked her. More than he should. There was something different about her curiosity, it was tinged with innocence and intelligence. It came from boldness. From a quiet need to know things deeply. That kind of pull was hard to push back against, but her naiveté in this world could get them both killed.

But if she stepped even one foot too far into the world Amina inhabited, the world he helped guard... there was no coming back clean.

He took out his phone and typed a message, paused, then erased it. Instead, he shoved his hands in his pockets and stared down the block, already knowing she'd ask again.

And next time, he might not have it in him to lie.

A few days later, Bryce and Jessica were sitting at a quiet corner table at the campus café. The afternoon sunlight spilled through the wide windows, striping the table in gold. Jessica stirred her iced coffee with deliberate slowness, watching the swirl of cream dissolve like clouds in her cup. Across from her, Bryce leaned back in his chair, one arm draped lazily over the seat beside him.

"You've been quiet," he said, eyeing her over his drink. "Did I scare you off the other day?"

Jessica looked up. "No. Just… thinking."

"Still trying to decide whether or not I'm a danger to your GPA or your peace of mind?"

A corner of her mouth lifted. "Both, probably."

Bryce chuckled, tapping his fingers against his cup. "Look—I wasn't trying to be cryptic about Amina or the club. I just don't want you wandering into something without knowing how deep it goes."

"Then tell me," Jessica said softly. "Explain it. You keep saying I don't belong in that world, but you never say why."

Bryce exhaled, his expression shifting—less guarded, more raw. He leaned forward, forearms resting on the table. "Because once you see everything, you don't unsee it. The people, the choices, what they expect from you. It changes how you look at the world. And maybe at yourself."

Jessica studied him, her voice barely a whisper. "And Amina? She's in deep?"

"She's not who you think she is," Bryce said carefully. "But that doesn't make her bad. Just... good at compartmentalizing."

Jessica nodded slowly, her throat tightening. "And you?"

There was a pause. Then he smiled—wry, unflinching. "Me? I'm already on the inside. I just try not to forget where the door is."

The silence between them was heavy, but not uncomfortable. It pulsed with something unspoken—fascination, maybe even fear, edged with the faintest trace of longing.

When Jessica stood to leave, she hesitated, then glanced over her shoulder. "For what it's worth... I don't scare easily."

Bryce's eyes lingered on her as she walked away. And for the first time in a long time, he wondered if he was the one who should be afraid.

Later that night, Jessica continued with her possum routine, she had developed whenever her roommate came back from one of her mysterious late nights at the club. Amina shut the dorm door quietly behind her, the soft click echoing louder than expected in the still room. Jessica was still curled under the covers in that familiar sleep posture—but Amina didn't miss the faint shift in her breathing. Eyes closed, body stiff.

So... she's pretending. She thought watching Jessica try not to move.

Amina didn't blame her. The curiosity had been building for weeks, threading through every glance and polite exchange. Jessica watched everything—even the things she thought she didn't. That, more than anything, was dangerous.

Amina stepped out of her heels and padded to the mirror, peeling off the layers of the evening's persona: lipstick, lashes, silk. Beneath the performance, her face stared back—still beautiful, still composed—but tired in a way that makeup couldn't mask.

The club had been routine tonight. The same patrons with their predictable appetites. The same music, low and pulsing. But Bryce had been tense when she left, and now she knew why.
Jessica.

He liked her. That was the problem. There was an innocence in Jessica that wasn't annoying, just naive—it was sincere. Genuine. The kind of innocence you wanted to shelter… or corrupt.

Slipping into her sleep shirt, Amina sat at the edge of her bed and opened her phone. A text from Bryce blinked at the top of her screen.
"She followed you. We talked. Told her to stay away. Don't think she will."

Amina stared at the message, then slowly typed.

"I know. I could feel her watching."

She didn't press send. Not yet.

Instead, she looked over at Jessica's sleeping form and whispered—so softly it could've been her own heartbeat—

"You really don't want to know what I've seen."

# Chapter Seven

(Carolyn)
Second Time Around

After a whirlwind of exotic vacations, champagne dinners, and soft-spoken apologies, Evan had convinced her he was a changed man. She even let herself think that maybe the electrocution had done more than just shock his body—maybe it had rewired his soul. He was attentive, generous, and—by all appearances—healed. When they remarried during one of their sun-drenched island getaways, Carolyn felt like she'd finally secured the life she'd always chased.

The island breeze had smelled like mango and saltwater the day they remarried. Carolyn wore a white silk slip dress that caught the wind just enough to make her feel cinematic. Evan's vows were soft, reverent, almost trembling. He cried when he slipped the ring on her finger. She let herself believe it.

For a while, it seemed true. Evan was attentive. He booked surprise trips to Morocco, Paris, Santorini. He ordered her favorite wine before she asked. He listened—really listened—when she talked about the girls, about her regrets, about the years she'd spent trying to outrun her own shadow. He even apologized for the past.

"I was sick," he said one night, their feet tangled beneath Egyptian cotton sheets. "But I see it now. I see *you*. And I'm not going to lose you again."

Carolyn had turned toward him, heart aching with the kind of hope that felt like a dare.

"I want to believe you," she whispered.

"Then do," he said, brushing her hair back. "Let's start over."

And she did. Until the night she came home fifteen minutes late.

Carolyn stepped through the door, laughing softly to herself, still glowing from dinner with old friends. The house was quiet. Too quiet.

"Evan?" she called.

He appeared from the hallway, barefoot, holding a glass of scotch. "You're late."

Carolyn blinked. "Fifteen minutes. I texted."

He didn't respond. Just stared at her, eyes flat.

"I said I'd be home by ten," she added, trying to keep her voice light. "It's 10:15."

Evan set the glass down. "You think I don't know what this is?" he said, stepping closer. "You think I don't see the game?"

"What game?" Carolyn asked feeling uneasy.

"You testing me. Seeing how far you can push before I snap."

She took a step back. "Evan, I'm not—"

The slap came fast. Open palm. Sharp. Her head turned with the force of it. Silence.

Then his voice, low and trembling. "Look what you made me do."

Carolyn didn't cry. She didn't scream. She just stood there, one hand on her cheek, and stared at the man she had once loved enough to marry twice.

The next morning, she stood in front of the mirror, tracing the faint bruise beneath her cheekbone. It wasn't fear that stirred in her chest. It was memory. She'd lived this before. The tension. The apologies. The way the violence always came wrapped in silk and scented candles. But this time, she wasn't the same woman. She had daughters now. Secrets. A spine made of scar tissue. So, she recalibrated.

"Where's your travel bag?" Evan asked one morning, sipping espresso.

"In the closet," Carolyn replied, folding laundry. "Why?"

"Just making sure you didn't run off on me," he said with a smile that didn't reach his eyes.

Carolyn laughed. Kissed his cheek. "You'd miss me too much."

Inside the lining of that bag was a burner phone. On it: photos of bruises. Audio clips of threats. A spreadsheet of dates, times, and receipts. Carolyn emailed copies to a lawyer in Charlotte. She wasn't just surviving this time. She was building a case.

One night, after a tense dinner, Evan cornered her in the kitchen. "You think I don't know what you're doing?" he hissed. "You think I don't see the way you look at me when you think I'm not watching?"

Carolyn kept her voice even. "I'm just tired."

"You're always tired. Always somewhere else." Evan grabbed her wrist.

Carolyn didn't flinch. Instead, she leaned in, kissed his cheek, and whispered, "I'm right here, baby. I'm not going anywhere." He let go. And she smiled. Because she knew exactly where she was going. And how to get there.

Evan still had money. And if he was going to spiral, Carolyn intended to land on her feet—preferably with enough leverage to walk away with half of everything and a clean escape route. But the game was dangerous, because she knew something else too: Evan's rage ran deeper now. It wasn't the drunken recklessness of their past—it was colder, more focused. And if he ever caught on to what she was doing, there wouldn't be a second chance. So, she smiled when he touched her cheek too hard. Kissed him when he said he needed her. Let him think she was still convinced of the fairytale. All while plotting the ending.

# Chapter Eight

## (Jesse)
## The Weight of the Crown

In prison, respect came in two currencies: fear and purpose. Jesse Braxton had earned both. They still called him "King Fish" in hushed tones—part reverence, part warning. But Jesse hadn't thrown a punch in years. He didn't need to. His presence alone kept the chaos at bay. But what made him dangerous now wasn't his fists. It was his vision.

The workshop room was an old storage room that had been converted into a makeshift workshop. Shelves were lined with fabric scraps, yarn, and donated sewing machines. Inmates hunched over tables, stitching quietly.

Juan stood at the door, skeptical. "Dolls?" he said, raising an eyebrow. "You got grown men in here making dolls?"

Jesse looked up from his station, needle in hand. "Handmade comfort dolls. For kids in foster care."

Juan stepped inside, eyeing the half-finished plush animals and soft-stitched bears. "You serious?"

Jesse nodded. "Dead serious. You ever seen a kid come into the system with nothing? No bag, no blanket, no one? These dolls—they're not just toys. They're something that says, 'You matter.'"

Juan picked up a half-sewn rabbit, its button eyes still loose, one ear flopping sideways. "You really think this makes a difference?" he asked, skeptical but curious.

Jesse met his eyes. "I know it does." He set down his own doll and leaned back, voice quieter now. "Before I was adopted by the Braxton family, I was in foster care. Given up at birth. Shuffled from home to home until I was thirteen."

Juan blinked. "Damn. I didn't know that." Jesse nodded. "Most people don't. But I remember one home—when I was about five. I had this social worker, Miss Evelyn. She gave me a stuffed bear. Nothing fancy. Just soft, brown, with one eye stitched crooked." He smiled faintly at the memory. "She told me, 'Anytime you feel scared, you hug that bear and remember—somebody loves you.' I didn't understand it then. But I held onto that bear like it was the only thing in the world that wouldn't leave."

Juan looked down at the rabbit in his hands, suddenly more reverent. "So, what happened after thirteen?"

"That's when the Braxtons adopted me. Good people. Church folks. They already had a son— Jody. He was older. Strong. Smart. He became my protector. My hero."

Juan grinned. "So, you had a big brother?"

"Yeah," Jesse said, his voice softening. "Jody was everything I wanted to be. He taught me how to fight, how to fix a bike, how to talk to girls without sounding like a fool."

Juan's smile faded. "Where's he now?"

Jesse looked away for a moment, jaw tightening. "Vietnam," he said. "He got drafted. Went over there a boy, came back... different. Quiet. Jumpy. And hooked on heroin."

Juan's eyes widened. "Damn."

"Yeah," Jesse said. "He convinced me to get into the game. Said we could make real money, take care of the family. I was just boosting cars before that. Petty stuff. But with Jody? We started moving weight. People started calling us the Braxton Brothers."

Juan nodded slowly. "So, what happened?"

"Jody started using more than he sold. Got sloppy. Started lying. Stealing from his own stash. One night, he OD'd at home – I found him. Left behind a wife—Lynette—and a baby girl he had just met. She was born while he was deployed and three when he got home."

Juan swallowed. "That's rough."

Jesse's voice dropped. "That baby girl... reminded me of my daughter, Jordan. She was just a few months old when Jody died. And I remember holding her one night, thinking—*I can't do to her what Jody did to his.* I can't disappear. I can't leave her with nothing but a name and a folded flag."

Juan was quiet for a long moment.

"So that's why you're doing all this," he said finally. "The dolls. The classes. The letters."

Jesse nodded. "I couldn't save Jody. But maybe I can help someone else's brother. Someone else's kid. Maybe I can still be the man I should've been back then."

Juan looked down at the rabbit again, then picked up a needle and thread.

"Well," he said, "guess I better learn how to sew."

Jesse chuckled. "That's step one. Step two? Learn how to stay."

Jesse continued to show Juan how to make use of his time in prison. The parenting circle met every Thursday, Jesse ran a class in the chapel. Folding chairs in a circle. No guards inside, just the chaplain, and the men—some broken, some bitter, all trying.

Juan sat in the back at first, arms crossed.

Jesse stood at the front, holding a worn photo of Jordan and Jessica.

"This is who I lost," he said. "Not because I didn't love them. But because I didn't know how to show up. I thought providing was enough. I thought being feared meant being respected. I was wrong." Jesse looked around the room. "You want to be a father? Start by learning how to listen. How to apologize. How to stay."

One man raised his hand. "What if they won't talk to us?"

"Then you write," Jesse said. "Every week. Even if they don't write back. You show them you're still trying."

Juan shifted in his seat.

Later that week on the yard, Juan jogged beside Jesse, sweat glistening on his brow.

"You really think we can change?" he asked.

Jesse didn't answer right away.

Then he spoke: "Change isn't a lightning bolt. It's a choice. Every day. Every minute. You mess up, you start again."

Juan slowed. "You think your girls will forgive you?"

Jesse looked up at the sky. "I don't know. But I'm gonna be the kind of man worth forgiving."

The next day, Jesse sat with a few inmates in the library, helping them fill out GED prep forms and job readiness packets. Juan leaned against the doorframe, watching.

"You ever sleep?" He asked.

Jesse chuckled. "Not much."

Juan stepped in. "I've been thinking. When I get out... I want to do something like this. Real. Not just hustle."

Jesse nodded. "Then start now. Help me run the next class."

Juan blinked. "You serious?"

"Dead serious." Jesse answered with steady eyes.

And with that, Juan led the next parenting class. He stood at the front, nervous. "My dad... he's a powerful man. But Jesse? He taught me what kind of man I want to be."

Juan looked at Jesse, then back at the group. "I used to think being hard was the only way to survive. But maybe being soft—being real—that's the only way to live."

The room was quiet. Then one man clapped. Then another. Jesse smiled.

That night, Jesse wrote in his journal – slowly, deliberately, reflecting on what led him to this point in his life, including his time in prison and how he chose the path that he was now walking.

*"They still call me King Fish. But I'm not ruling anything. I'm building. One stitch. One letter. One man at a time. If I leave here with nothing else, let it be this: I didn't waste the pain. I turned it into something that mattered."*

He closed the notebook. And for the first time in years, he slept without dreaming of bars.

# Chapter Nine

(Jordan)
Lust by Design

The design studio pulsed with the low thrum of late-night jazz someone had left playing through an old speaker. The floor was a soft chaos of muslin, sketches, and frayed thread. Jordan stood in front of the mirror, running her fingers along a seam she couldn't quite get right. Behind her, Aaron adjusted the hem on the pants he'd spent the last two days fitting to her specs. Clean lines, sharp tailoring—he moved like he was born into the silhouette.

"What do you think?" Aaron asked, glancing up.

Jordan turned, ready with a critique, but the words caught. His eyes—light green, framed by thick lashes—met hers with the kind of focus that made everything else in the room dim. Jordan had always found them distracting. But tonight? They were devastating.

"You're staring," he said, voice low and amused.

"I'm... evaluating," she lied.

Aaron smiled—just enough to tease. His close haircut gave nothing for the chaos to cling to. Always sharp. Always clean. But that smile? That was the part of him that unraveled her. He stepped closer, running his palm down the finished seam of the waistband.

"You know," he said, fingers lingering, "when we win this thing…"

"*If* we win—" Jordan quipped

Aaron grinned. "When. The internship goes to *both* of us."

Jordan looked away. "Aaron—"

"Just picture it," he cut in, voice suddenly velvet. "New York. Maison de Luxe's artist's workroom. You and me. Morning coffees in SoHo, evenings at the studio, fittings that run too late."

"Dangerously late?" Jordan asked, unable to help herself.

Aaron shrugged, playful. "Creative tension's a good thing."

Jordan folded her arms. "Is that what this is?"

Aaron stepped even closer. "What do *you* think it is?"

Jordan's breath hitched. Everything in her wanted to lean in. To let him make her forget the weight she always carried—expectations, perfection, Miles. Especially Miles.

"I can't—" Jordan whispered.

"You *can*," Aaron murmured. "You just won't. And that's fine. But you need to be honest… with yourself. With *him*."

Jordan wanted to argue, but the way he said *him*—so casual and cutting—it twisted something inside her. Because Aaron wasn't wrong. She wasn't being honest – With anyone.

Jordan hadn't meant to stay late that night. The studio was near-empty, lit only by the blue glow of desk lamps and the hiss of steam from the iron. Her final piece was due in six days. She hadn't eaten. Had barely slept. But that wasn't what kept her wired.

Aaron was now pacing behind her, shirt rumpled, eyes hungry—not just for her, but for the prize. They'd both been pushing, breaking themselves open to make something that mattered.

"Zip me," Aaron said, holding the half-stitched jacket against his bare torso.

Jordan swallowed. Her hands moved on instinct, fingers tracing the line of his spine. The zipper stuttered halfway. "This needs to be tighter in the shoulders," she mumbled, stepping back.

But Aaron didn't move. "I know what this is for you," he said softly. "The internship. Your way out. Your way *through*."

Jordan froze.

"I see how you break yourself for everyone else," Aaron continued. "How you never ask for anything because you're afraid no one'll show up. But I would. Jordan—I'm already standing here." He stepped closer – Too close.

"Don't," Jordan whispered. "I can't afford to want this."

"Why?" Aaron asked. "Because of Miles?"
Jordan didn't answer. Because *yes*. Because *no*. Because wanting Aaron felt like setting fire to the life she'd spent years trying to build—and still, part of her already smelled smoke.

Aaron touched her face. "Tell me to stop."

Jordan didn't. Their mouths crashed together like the last gasp before a storm breaks. Fabric scattered. Pins clattered to the floor. And for one reckless, breathless moment, Jordan let herself burn.

# Chapter Ten

## (Jessica)
## Private Dancer

Jessica waited until they were alone—both seated on their respective beds, the quiet hum of the mini fridge the only sound in the room. Amina was scrolling her phone, legs crossed, dressed casually for once in sweats and a loose tee. Her hair was wrapped, her face bare.

"I need to ask you something," Jessica said, her voice steady but soft.

Amina didn't look up. "Okay."

Jessica hesitated, then said it: "The club. I want in."

That made Amina glance up. Her expression didn't change, but the air shifted. "Why?"

Jessica pulled her knees to her chest. "Because I want to take care of my grandparents for once instead of them always taking care of me. Because I saw that car, and your clothes, and I know tuition doesn't cover that. And because... I don't want to keep wondering who you are when you leave here at night."

For a long moment, Amina said nothing. Then she set her phone down gently and looked Jessica in the eye.

"You think this life comes without a cost? The money's real. The lifestyle is real. But so is the weight. Once you step through that door, you don't get to pretend anymore. You don't get to unsee things."

"I'm not afraid," Jessica said.

Amina studied her. "Maybe you should be." She stood, walked to her desk drawer, and pulled out a black envelope—sleek, unmarked. She handed it to Jessica without ceremony.

"Be ready Saturday night. Wear black. Nothing flashy—just clean, simple, like you know how to blend. And when we get there… don't speak unless someone speaks to you."

Jessica took the envelope, pulse thudding in her ears.

"Once you're inside," Amina added, "you're not a student anymore. You're part of the show." Jessica spent the rest of that night turning the envelope over and over in her hands, its weight heavier than paper should feel. Inside was a single card—black, sleek, embossed with the club's emblem in silver. No address, no name. Just a time: 11:00 PM.

All week, Jessica moved through her classes in a fog. Professors spoke, students laughed, but she couldn't shake the sense that her world was about to tilt on its axis. Every time she looked at Amina— cool, unbothered, as if nothing had changed— Jessica felt like she was keeping a secret that hadn't fully formed yet.

Jessica didn't tell Bryce. Something in her told her not to. Not yet.

At night, she lay in bed rehearsing how she'd carry herself. How she'd walk. How she'd speak— if she were even allowed to. Was she being reckless? Or finally bold?

Jessica dug through her closet and tried on every black outfit she owned. Nothing seemed right. Everything either screamed trying too hard or freshman budget. On Thursday, she used the last of her saved-up tutoring money to buy a simple black dress—elegant, quiet, form-fitting in a way that made her feel... new.

On Saturday, Jessica lit a candle on her desk while she got ready. A nervous ritual. The vanilla scent reminded her of home, of her grandmother humming while folding laundry. Of a version of herself she wasn't sure she'd be able to return to after tonight.

As Jessica tied her curls up and slid on a coat, her heart beat not just with anxiety—but with purpose. She wasn't walking into this for vanity. She wanted a better life. She wanted control. And tonight, might be the first step toward claiming it. Behind her, Amina stood in the mirror adjusting her earrings. Their eyes met in the reflection. She didn't smile, but she nodded.

"Ready?" Amina asked.

Jessica took a breath, then nodded back. "Yeah. I am."

The car eased to a stop in front of an inconspicuous building nestled between a designer showroom and a closed-for-renovation jazz club. There was no sign above the door, just a single red light glowing over the awning, casting the sidewalk in a muted pulse.

Amina didn't speak. She simply stepped out, her heels clicking with familiar certainty, and waited for Jessica to follow. Jessica hesitated, her hand tightening around the black envelope in her coat pocket before she climbed out of the car into the warm hush of the Atlanta night.

A tall man in all black opened the door for them without a word. He didn't ask for ID. He didn't ask who they were. He just looked at Amina, nodded once, and stepped aside.

Inside, the air was velvet. Low lighting bathed the club in shadows and gold. The music was slow and seductive, not loud enough to overwhelm conversation but deep enough to settle in the bones. Laughter, soft and polished, flitted between crystal glasses and candlelit corners.

Jessica blinked. The crowd was unlike anything she'd ever seen—men and women dressed like secrets, like wealth and stories wrapped in silk. No one looked surprised to be there. They belonged. And suddenly, she wasn't sure if she did.

Amina leaned toward her. "Keep your eyes open. Mouth closed."

Jessica nodded, heart racing. Amina led her past plush booths, a sleek onyx bar, and a private back hallway guarded by another bouncer. She stopped before reaching it, turning to Jessica.

"This is the front of the house," she said. "The part people are allowed to remember. Don't wander. Don't ask questions."

Jessica swallowed hard. "And the back?"

Amina's lips curved into a faint smile, but her eyes didn't. "You're not ready for that part yet."

Then she disappeared into the haze of the room, leaving Jessica surrounded by velvet and shadows and the sharp, thrilling edge of something dangerous—something she'd asked for. And she wasn't sure whether to run from it... or deeper in.

Jessica hovered near the edge of the bar, unsure where to stand or what to do. Amina had vanished into the room like smoke, leaving her to navigate the velvet hush alone. She tried to steady her breath. It helped to focus on details—the chilled glass of water placed in front of her by the bartender without a word, the low thrum of music vibrating through the soles of her heels, the flicker of candlelight across marble tabletops.

A man in a tailored suit brushed past her, his cologne sharp and expensive. He didn't look at her, but others did—subtle, assessing glances that made her simultaneously shrink inward and square her shoulders.

Jessica caught her reflection in a bronze mirror behind the bar. Her dress fit her well. Her makeup was clean, precise. But her eyes betrayed her— wide, alert, quietly trembling with the weight of not knowing what came next.

"First time?" Jessica turned. A woman— elegant, probably late twenties, with deep brown skin and box braids piled into a crown—slid onto the stool beside her.

Jessica hesitated. "That obvious?"

The woman smiled knowingly. "Only to people who've been through their own first night. You're not staff… but you're not here to watch, either. Not really."

"I'm here with someone." Jessica responded, not wanting the woman to think she was alone.

"Someone smart enough not to hover," the woman said, sipping from a champagne glass. "You look like someone who's about to make a decision they can't undo."

Jessica's stomach fluttered. "What kind of decision?"

The woman leaned in just slightly. Her voice lowered. "Whether you're going to keep pretending this world doesn't tempt you… or admit that you want to understand it."

Before Jessica could respond, movement near the hallway caught her eye—Amina, emerging from behind the guarded door, her expression unreadable. But when she spotted Jessica, her gaze lingered a heartbeat longer than usual.

Jessica straightened. She didn't feel ready. But she was here now. And something told her the night was far from over.

Behind the guarded hallway, the club shed its velvet polish and transformed into something quieter, more charged. The lighting dimmed further, casting everything in amber and shadow. Plush walls absorbed conversation. Every movement was deliberate. Controlled.

Amina walked those halls like someone with authority—not flashy, but undeniable. Staff greeted her with slight nods, a few with subtle deference. She slipped through a curtained doorway and entered a room far more private than the lounge Jessica had seen.

Inside, a woman in a deep burgundy suit waited, reviewing something on a tablet. She glanced up as Amina entered. "Right on time." Amina removed her coat and hung it on the rack by the door. "Any changes to the list?"

"Two substitutions. One VIP request. Room three." The woman replied.

Amina nodded, her gaze flicking across the screen briefly. "I'll handle it."

Amina wasn't a hostess. Not really. She was what the club called a liaison—a term that barely scratched the surface. She managed introductions between high-paying clients and the curated atmosphere the club promised: experiences tailored to indulgence, secrecy, and emotional precision. Amina didn't dance, didn't perform. She orchestrated. She observed. She protected the line between fantasy and danger.

But tonight, Amina wasn't just thinking about her rotation. She was thinking about Jessica, upstairs, sipping water and soaking in gold and velvet like a sponge. She admired her. Maybe even envied the part of her that still flinched with wonder. But she also knew—if Jessica stayed curious long enough, something would change in her. Things always did.

Amina checked her phone quickly. No new messages. No updates from Bryce. She slipped her earpiece in and straightened the lapels of her suit. "Let's begin."

Amina adjusted the earpiece in her ear as she moved with quiet precision through the backstage corridors of the club, the kind of space that operated like an ecosystem—smooth, sleek, meticulously maintained. Here, she wasn't just a liaison; she was a handler of atmospheres, a gatekeeper of masks. Her presence meant things ran without mess, without questions, without incident.

Tonight's assignment was Room Three—an exclusive suite lined with velvet and soundproofed walls, reserved for the club's elite. One of the club's top-tier clients had made a personal request. That alone meant Amina would oversee the exchange herself.

Amina entered the suite moments before the guest was scheduled to arrive. Everything was in place—crystal glasses, chilled champagne, the low flicker of candlelight, and a performer already poised by a bed with red satin sheets with a serene expression and eyes trained on Amina for the signal.

There was a knock. Amina opened the door to find a man dressed in quiet wealth: tailored charcoal suit, pressed collar, skin the color of roasted pecans, and the kind of eyes that missed nothing. He stepped inside without hesitation.

"Ms. Amina," he said, voice smooth but clipped. "I trust everything is as I asked."
Amina gave a small nod. "Precisely. You'll have complete discretion. No interruptions."

The man moved toward the bed and dropped his phone into the locked tray provided for high-tier clients—no electronics, no distractions, no trace.

As Amina closed the door behind her, she paused just long enough to watch the man relax into the room, as if shedding the armor, he wore outside. These were the moments she understood better than most—not the performance, but the surrender beneath it. The hunger for control, intimacy, anonymity… safety, even, in its strange way.

Walking back down the corridor, she checked her messages. Nothing from Jessica. Good. Amina didn't need her anywhere near this version of her life—not yet. The club had rules. The shadows were curated, not kind. And if Jessica kept stepping toward them with wide eyes and a bright heart, someone would have to choose whether to shield her or let her learn the hard way.

And Amina… wasn't sure which side of that line she'd fall on.

# Chapter Eleven

## (Jesse)
## Cuban Connection

The visitation room buzzed with low voices and the occasional scrape of plastic chairs. Jesse sat at the far end, arms folded, eyes scanning the room like he always did—out of habit, not fear. He'd learned long ago that the most dangerous men didn't raise their voices. They watched. They waited.

Juan had told him his father was coming. Jesse didn't know what to expect. He'd heard the name— Arturo Delgado. A man with money, reach, and a reputation that stretched from Miami to New York. Not flashy, but formidable. The kind of man who didn't need to raise his voice either.

Juan appeared first, grinning like a kid who knew he was about to change the game, he was being released later that month, but he couldn't leave without introducing Jesse to his father.

"Pop's here," he said, sliding into the seat across from Jesse. "Told him he had to meet you." Jesse raised an eyebrow. "You sure that's a good idea?"

Juan shrugged. "He doesn't do anything he doesn't want to."

A moment later, the door opened, and Arturo Delgado stepped in.

He was tall, silver at the temples, dressed in a tailored navy suit that somehow didn't look out of place in a prison. His eyes swept the room once, then landed on Jesse.

Arturo walked over slowly, extended his hand. "Mr. Braxton," he said. "I've heard a lot about you."

Jesse stood, shook his hand. Firm grip. No posturing. "Likewise," Jesse said. "Juan talks about you like you're a ghost story."

Arturo chuckled. "That's because I taught him to respect silence."

He sat beside his son, folding his hands on the table. "I wanted to thank you," he said. "For looking out for my boy."

Jesse shrugged. "Didn't do it for thanks. Just didn't like the way they were circling him."

"Still," Arturo said, "you stepped in when you didn't have to. That means something to me."
Juan leaned back, arms crossed, watching the two men like he was witnessing a chess match.

Arturo continued. "I've kept my distance from this place. Let Juan learn what he needed to. But I also believe in paying debts."

Jesse's eyes narrowed slightly. "I'm not looking for favors."

"I'm not offering one," Arturo replied. "I'm offering a door. When you get out—and I hear that's soon—you'll need options. Clean ones. Quiet ones. I can help with that."

Jesse studied him. "Why?"

Arturo moved closer. "Because you protected my son. And because I know what it's like to be underestimated by people who think they've already written your ending."

After a long pause. Then Jesse nodded once. "I'll think about it."

Arturo stood. "That's all I ask." He turned to Juan. "I'll see you next week."

Then he was gone. Juan looked at Jesse, eyes wide. "Told you he was serious."

Jesse didn't smile. But something in his posture eased. "Yeah," he said. "You did."

After Arturo's visit Jesse began to think about his release date. The days moved differently once you had a date. Jesse had spent thirteen years watching the clock without ever really caring what time it was. But now, with release just weeks away, every tick felt louder. Every sunrise sharper. The air even smelled different—like something was waiting.

Jesse kept his routine tight. Morning laps in the yard. Weights. Reading. Writing. He'd started journaling again—something he hadn't done since the early years, when the guilt still kept him up at night. Now, the words came slower, but they came. Mostly about the girls.

Jordan, who had grown up too fast. Jessica, who he barely knew anymore. And Carolyn—who had once promised to wait, then disappeared into a life he couldn't touch. And now there was Arturo Delgado. A man who didn't offer favors. Just doors. Jesse didn't trust anyone easily. But he trusted what he saw in Arturo's eyes: calculation, yes—but also code. The kind of man who didn't forget who protected his blood. Still, Jesse had questions.

*What would freedom even look like?*

*Would his daughters want to see him?*

*Would they forgive him?*

*Would he forgive himself?*

Jesse guessed those questions and more would be answered in a few short weeks.

The next day on the yard, Juan jogged up beside Jesse, breathless. "You ready?"

Jesse didn't break stride. "For what?"

"For the world, man. For sunlight without fences. For real food. For women who don't wear a uniform and carry military grade pepper spray."

Jesse smirked. "You're not out yet."

Juan grinned. "Soon. And when I am, I'm calling you. You better answer."

Jesse nodded. "I will."

Juan slowed, then added, "My dad meant what he said. You call him, he'll set you up. No strings."

"There's always strings," Jesse said.

"Maybe. But some of them pull you forward." Juan replied.

That Night, Jesse sat on the edge of his bunk, flipping through a stack of letters he'd never sent. One for Jordan. One for Jessica. One for Carolyn, though he wasn't sure why anymore. He picked up the one for Jordan. The envelope was worn, the ink faded. He opened it.

*I don't expect you to understand why I left. I don't even expect you to forgive me. But I need you to know I never stopped thinking about you. About your sister. I wanted to be better. I just didn't know how to be free without breaking something. I'm trying now. I hope that still matters.*

Jesse folded it again. Slipped it into his pocket. Tomorrow, he'd ask the chaplain to mail it.

The weeks before his release, Jesse couldn't sleep. He lay on his bunk, staring at the ceiling, listening to the hum of the lights and the distant echo of someone laughing too loud in the next block. He thought of the girls. Of Juan. Of Arturo's card, tucked into the back of his Bible. And he thought of the gate. The one that would open in a few short weeks. Not just the one made of steel and wire—but the one inside him. The one he'd kept locked for years, afraid of what might come through. Now, he wasn't afraid. He was ready.

# Chapter Twelve

(Jordan)
Late Nights & Early Mornings

The apartment felt different when Jordan wasn't in it. Not just empty—*uncertain*. Like the air had changed density somehow, and nothing stayed where he left it.

Miles sat on the edge of their bed, her side still untouched from the night before. The sheets were cold, but what unsettled him more was the silence. Jordan had always let him in, even when she was buried in deadlines or tangled in her family's mess. But this... this distance felt different – This felt chosen.

Miles stared at the sketchpad Jessica left on the chair by the dresser. It was open to a half-finished design—a gown, dramatic and powerful. It wasn't her class assignment. It looked like it had been drawn from memory – Or for someone.

Miles rubbed his eyes, exhausted. He wasn't jealous by nature. But he wasn't naive, either. Something was shifting. He could feel it in how Jessica avoided eye contact, in the way she paused before unlocking the door now, like she was bracing herself before walking into something she wasn't sure she wanted anymore.

Miles picked up his phone and hovered over her name in his messages. **Miles:** *You okay? Want me to bring dinner to the studio?* But he didn't send it.

Instead, he dropped the phone on the nightstand and stood at the window, watching the city blur in the drizzle. It wasn't just the possibility that she'd been with someone else. It was the deeper fear—that she had become someone else. Someone who didn't need him the way she used to. And that maybe... just maybe... she'd never needed him as much as he'd needed her.

The next morning, the sun crept in through the sheer curtains of their shared apartment, brushing light across the empty side of the bed. Miles woke alone. The clock read 6:42 AM. Jordan hadn't come home.

At first, Miles tried not to panic. This close to the fashion showcase, the studio was basically her second address. Maybe she crashed on the couch, maybe she lost track of time—but the silence between them was no longer comfortable. It was loud.

Miles checked his phone. Nothing. Then the pit started forming in his gut. He got up, walked past her untouched coffee mug still sitting where she left it yesterday morning, and glanced at the sewing kit on the counter—the one she always packed when she knew she'd stay overnight at the studio – Gone. *So, she* had *planned to stay.* Miles thought as he stared at the empty space where the bag had been. Still, it felt like an excuse dressed as discipline.

Meanwhile at the design studio, Jordan stood in front of the industrial sink, splashing cold water on her face. Her reflection stared back, wild-eyed and guilt-heavy. She hadn't slept. Not just because of the showcase. Because of what she'd done.

The moment with Aaron had burned through her like a fuse. Immediate. Blinding. And now? The ash of it lingered. Everything with Miles suddenly felt too bright, too fragile—like if she touched it wrong, the whole thing would shatter.

Aaron approached, fresh coffee in hand. "Did you sleep at all?"

Jordan shook her head. "I didn't mean to make things messy," Aaron said, quieter now.

Jordan didn't reply. Aaron moved closer. "That internship could give us more than a career, J. It could give us - *us.*"

Jordan blinked, stunned. "What are you talking about?"

"You felt it. I know you did. This isn't just some studio fling." Aaron insisted.

Jordan stared at him. Part of her wanted to believe him. The other part? She didn't know who she was anymore—*student, sister, liar, lover*—she was pieces of all of it and none of it at once.

"I have to go home," she whispered.

"You sure it still *feels* like home?" Aaron countered.

Jordan turned sharply. "Don't."

Aaron just nodded, quietly.

Suddenly Miles's text lit up her screen: *Another late night/early morning?*

Jordan's stomach flipped. She didn't respond. Instead, she pulled on her sunglasses, smoothed her hair, and left the studio with her heart thudding like a warning drum.

When she got back to the apartment, Jordan slipped her key into the lock and stepped inside. The lights were off, but Miles was awake—seated at the kitchen table, hoodie half-zipped, laptop closed. He didn't look at her. Just said, "I made coffee."

Jordan froze. "I didn't hear from you," Miles continued, voice too calm. "Was the sewing machine so loud you couldn't text?"

Jordan's throat tightened. "I crashed there," she said. "Didn't mean to worry you."

Miles finally looked up, his face serious and dripping with concern, his eyes steady and fixed on Jordan. He stared at her for a minute before he spoke, like he was carefully scrutinizing every word before he let it leave his lips.

"J, we live together. You not coming home, not calling—that's not nothing." He said.

Jordan opened her mouth to respond, but nothing came out. Because he was right. It wasn't nothing. And whether she was brave enough to admit it or not... a part of her had already left.

# Chapter Thirteen

(Jessica)
Bundle of Secrets

Jessica sat on the tufted bench in the club's hallway, her black dress crisp, her hands folded too neatly in her lap. She was technically off the clock—still considered *"observing,"* as Amina put it—but she was there. Present. Watching the edges of a world she'd only tasted. She'd started seeing more of it now. The coded glances between staff. The way the air shifted when certain clients walked in. The rituals. But lately, it wasn't the allure of the club that pulled her back again and again. It was Bryce.

Bryce was steady in the middle of the surreal— a rare island of calm. Always watching, always one step ahead of trouble. And lately, when he caught her eye across the room, the look he gave her wasn't just protective. It was… tender. Complicated. She hated how much she leaned into it.

*You're losing focus,* Jessica told herself as he approached.

"Everything okay?" Bryce asked, his voice low.

Jessica nodded. "I'm fine."

Bryce studied her like he could see the lie pinned behind her smile. "This place—what it does to people—it's not always about the money."

"I know." Jessica responded.

"Then why are you still here?" Bryce questioned.

Jessica hesitated. "Because of you."

The words left her before she could stop them. Bryce went still. Not cold—but shaken in a way he didn't show often.

"Jess…" His voice was soft, but it held weight.

"If I'm the reason you're getting deeper in, that's not something I'm proud of."

"You're not," she said quickly. "Not all of it. But maybe the only reason I feel grounded in this mess is because you're here."

For a second, neither of them moved. Then a voice crackled in Bryce's earpiece. He glanced away, jaw tightening.

"Duty calls," he muttered. "Stay here. Don't follow this time." But he didn't say it unkindly.

Bryce walked off, and Jessica stared after him, her heart beating in her throat. She wasn't sure if she was chasing the danger—or the person who made it feel less dangerous. Either way, she was already too far in.

Jessica wasn't supposed to be down this hallway. That was the first rule Amina had made clear. And yet, here Jessica was, standing just outside the edge of the corridor that led to the private suites—watching Bryce through a sliver between velvet curtains. He stood near Room Five, his jaw tight, his posture more rigid than she'd ever seen it. He wasn't alone. A woman leaned close to him—tall, graceful, older, dressed in crimson silk and quiet command. She said something low, her hand resting briefly on his chest. Bryce didn't flinch. He didn't even glance around. It was like he belonged to this place completely in that moment. Like Jessica had imagined the softness in him.

Jessica's stomach twisted. A voice inside said *turn around. Go back.* But her feet stayed rooted, breath shallow. Then Bryce looked up. Their eyes locked. He didn't move right away. Didn't smile. His eyes were unreadable—like he couldn't decide if he was angry… or afraid. Then, quick and smooth, he stepped away from the woman and crossed to where Jessica stood.

"What are you doing?" Bryce whispered, low and sharp.

Jessica blinked. "I saw you – With her."

"I asked you not to follow," Bryce said, voice tight. "This is the part of the club people don't wander into."

"Then tell me what this is," Jessica shot back.

"Tell me who you are in this place, Bryce. Because every time I think I know, I see something that makes me question everything."

Bryce didn't answer right away. Then he leaned in closer, his voice barely audible. "I don't want you to know. Because if you did... you wouldn't look at me the same way again."

Jessica's heart cracked a little. She hadn't come here looking for truth. Not tonight. But she realized now she'd been hoping—quietly, stubbornly—that he'd offer it anyway.

"I should go," Jessica whispered. And before he could stop her, she did, or at least she tried. Jessica had meant to leave the club that night and never look back. Everything felt too heavy, too unfamiliar—like she'd slipped beneath the surface of something far deeper than she could handle. But it was already too late. Joe, the club's owner, saw that. Older, charismatic, and always calculating, he had a way of speaking that made danger sound like an opportunity. He promised fast money, stability, even admiration—all under the guise of choice.

"Just dance," Joe said. "Nothing more... unless you decide otherwise."

There was something in his voice that hooked her. The way he made her feel seen. And maybe that's what made her vulnerable—growing up without her father, watching her mother spiral, Jessica had always craved someone who wouldn't leave. Joe read that in her before she even understood it herself. And so, she said yes.

Months later, Jessica and Bryce began having different views on the club. Bryce hated Jessica working at the club. He tried to talk her down, but once she decided to cross into that world, nothing could pull her back. So, he did the only thing he could—he made sure he worked every night she danced, watching from the shadows, not for her attention... but for her safety. But the real danger wasn't in the crowd. It was closer. Intimate. Waiting.

The music started low—more mood than melody. A heavy, deliberate bassline that vibrated through the soles of her feet as she stepped behind the curtain. Jessica stood in the half-dark, heart pounding against her ribs like it was trying to escape. The stage light washed everything in gold, warm but blinding. She could just make out the silhouettes in the audience—lounging bodies in low booths, glasses in hand, eyes trained on the stage like they were expecting something rare.

*I still have a choice*, Jessica told herself. She could turn back. Fade into the velvet quiet. Pretend none of this ever happened. But she didn't. She stepped forward.

At first, Jessica's body moved stiffly. Her arms remembered what she'd practiced, but her mind spiraled—thinking of Joe's charm, Bryce's worry, Amina's cool silence. The room grew still in response, watching, waiting. Then something shifted. Maybe it was the way the lights hit her skin, or how the music curled around her like smoke. Maybe it was the realization that—for once— everyone was quiet, and she was the center of it. Not for who she knew. Not for what she lacked. But for her.

And with that, Jessica's movement softened. She rolled her hips to the beat, let her shoulders relax. It wasn't about seduction—not really. It was about presence. Power. The quiet ache of a girl reclaiming space in a world that so often made her feel invisible.

Somewhere in the back, she saw him—Bryce. Arms crossed, jaw tight, watching her like she might shatter or set something on fire. Jessica didn't know if she was in control. But for now, she looked out over the crowd, gathered her breath—and owned the stage.

As the final note of the track faded, the lights dimmed, and the curtain eased its way closed behind her. Jessica stood alone for a moment, heartbeat rattling in her chest like a locked drawer. Then, it hit her: she'd done it.

Backstage, the atmosphere was different—less golden, more gray. The hum of conversation still bled through the walls, but back here, it was just Jessica and her nerves, thrumming high. She reached for her robe just as Bryce appeared. He didn't speak at first. Just looked at her—his expression was unreadable, torn between relief and something darker.

"You okay?" he asked finally, voice rough around the edges.

Jessica nodded, eyes searching his face. "I think so."

Bryce stepped closer, his jaw clenched. "You were good. Too good."

"What does that mean?" Jessica asked.

"It means the kind of attention you just stirred up isn't always the kind you want." Bryce answered softly, voice full of concern.

Before she could respond, a slow clap echoed from the hallway. Joe stood there, smiling like a man who already knew her answer to a question he hadn't asked.

"You've got stage presence," he said. "Didn't think you had it in you. Glad you proved me wrong."

Jessica stiffened. Bryce didn't move. Joe stepped forward and gently tucked a loose strand of hair behind Jessica's ear—too familiar. "You've got options now. We'll talk later." Then he walked away.

As Jessica watched Joe vanish into a side door, she heard another familiar voice behind her, it was Amina.

"Congratulations pussycat, now your curiosity has been answered. And you have even caught the attention of the big dog, Joe." Amina said, then leaned in and whispered, "But be careful, big dogs don't play nice with kittens, I wouldn't want that curiosity to get you killed."

Amina stared at Jessica with look that expressed pity, concern and guilt. Like she had just led a lamb to the slaughter. Then she disappeared down the hall, leaving the smell of expensive perfume and the feeling of unspoken pressure in her wake.

Jessica stood there, robe clutched at her chest, feeling the pull between the man who stood by her side… and the one who had plans for her she hadn't yet seen. She didn't know it yet but tonight had changed everything.

The change didn't happen all at once. It came in fragments—silent choices, borrowed mannerisms, glances held a bit too long in the mirror. Jessica still went to class, still took notes in her spiraled notebook, still smiled at classmates who knew nothing about the girl who slipped through velvet curtains after dark. But the lines were blurring. Fast. She started wearing heels to lectures—not loud ones, just enough to change the sound of her steps. Her laugh, once light and spontaneous, grew quieter, more measured. She no longer flinched when someone looked at her too long. She was learning how to hold stares—and when to use them.

The money came quickly. New clothes. Fresh nails. She sent a little back to her grandparents and told them tutoring had picked up. That wasn't a lie. Just not the whole truth. But beneath the poise, something inside her felt looser. Floaty. As if she'd stepped into someone else's life and was afraid that if she exhaled too hard, it might collapse. Bryce noticed. He always did.

"You don't smile the same," he told her one night, his voice low.

Jessica looked at him, mascara immaculate, lips like wine. "I smile just fine."

But she knew what he meant. Jessica joy had grown calculated—just like the steps she took on stage. She wasn't sure if she was losing herself… or building someone new from the ruins of the girl she used to be. Jessica had planned to walk away from the club and never return. That night had shaken her—too much, too fast. But walking away was never going to be easy. Not when someone like Joe was watching.

# Chapter Fourteen

## (Jordan)
## Give an Inch and Lose a Miles

The apartment wasn't cold – But it felt it. The silence that wrapped around the walls had weight now—something Jordan could feel pressing on her chest every time she walked through the door. Miles wasn't talking much, and when he did, his voice came carefully measured, as if too much emotion might crack it wide open.

Jordan dropped her sketchbook on the table and kicked off her shoes. The clink of her keys sounded like a warning.

Miles stood in the kitchen, leaning against the counter, arms folded. "You're late again."
Jordan froze. "I told you, the fabric shipment was delayed. And we—"

"We," he cut in. "You and Aaron."
Jordan's heart thumped once, loud and sharp. "It's not like that."

Aaron studied her. "Isn't it?" Jordan didn't answer.

Miles stepped forward, his voice quieter now. "You don't talk to me. You come home smelling like starch and someone else's cologne. You haven't looked me in the eye in weeks, J."

"I'm just tired—" Jordan started

"No," Miles interrupted, shaking his head. "Tired looks different on you. This isn't tired. This is... gone."

The truth landed between them like broken glass. Jordan turned away, but Miles followed.

"I'm not trying to control you," Mile said, gentler now. "I love you. But I can't be the only one standing here trying to save something you keep slipping out of."

Jordan closed her eyes. "Are you in love with him?" Miles asked in a low and desperate tone.

There was a pause, then Jordan whispered with eyes cast down and filling with tears. "I don't know."

That was enough. Miles grabbed his overnight bag—already packed. Already planned. "I'm staying with Darrell for a while. Down the hall. Just... figure out what you want. Before there's nothing left here to come home to." Miles said slamming the door behind him as he exited.

Jordan jumped at the sound, as if it was a hammer hitting fragile heart and shattering it like pieces of glass. And then he was gone. Jordan stood there, shaking, staring at the door like she was hoping it would open back up and undo the last ten minutes. But it didn't.

Later that night, the studio was near silent. Outside, the city pulsed with its usual rhythm—horns blaring, distant sirens, the occasional shout from the street below—but in the back room of the design building, the world had narrowed to a single thread.

Jordan sat at her worktable, shoulders hunched, eyes red-rimmed from exhaustion and something heavier. The soft whir of her sewing machine filled the space, but her hands betrayed her—trembling as she tried to guide the silk beneath the needle. She'd already ripped the seam out twice. Still, she kept going.

Aaron leaned against the far wall, arms crossed, watching her with the kind of stillness that made people underestimate him. He hadn't said much since she walked in—just offered her a quiet nod, a cup of tea, and space. But now, as he watched her fingers fumble again, he stepped forward. "You okay?"

Jordan didn't look up. She shook her head, her voice barely audible. "I messed up."

Aaron didn't press. He waited.

Jordan set the fabric down and rubbed her hands over her face. "I told him."

Aaron's voice was gentle. "Miles?"

Jordan nodded. "Not everything. But enough."

Aaron moved closer, still careful not to touch her. "How did he take it?"

Jordan gave a bitter laugh. "He left."
Aaron's jaw tightened, but he said nothing.

Jordan looked down at her lap. "And the worst part is… I don't know if I wanted him to stay."

That admission hung in the air like smoke—thick, unspoken, dangerous.

Aaron's voice was quiet. "What do you want now?"

Jordan looked up at him then—really looked. His face was open, steady, but there was something in his eyes. Not expectation. Not hope. Just presence. A willingness to hold whatever she gave him.

"I want to stop hiding," Jordan said. And then—before she could talk herself out of it—she reached for him. Her fingers brushed his, tentative at first. Testing the space between them. Then she closed the distance, curling her hand into his.

Aaron didn't flinch. He didn't ask if she was sure. He just let her hand find his, and when it did, he held it like it was something sacred. Jordan exhaled, the kind of breath that comes after holding too much for too long.

Aaron stepped closer, slowly, until they were inches apart. "I'm not going to ask you for anything," he said softly. "Not clarity. Not promises. Just... don't lie to yourself. Not here. Not with me."

Jordan nodded, her voice barely a whisper. "I don't want to lie anymore."

Aaron reached up, gently brushing a strand of hair from her face. "Then don't."

Jordan leaned into his touch, eyes fluttering shut for a moment. When she opened them, she wasn't crying—but she looked like she could. "I don't know what this is," she said.

Aaron smiled, just a little. "That makes two of us."

They stood there in the quiet, the hum of the machines now distant, the world outside forgotten. And for the first time in weeks, Jordan wasn't unraveling. She was beginning.

The next morning, the sun hadn't fully risen yet, but the studio's windows were already glowing with the soft, gray light of early morning. The city outside was still stretching awake—delivery trucks rumbling down side streets, birds calling from fire escapes, the occasional jogger passing by with headphones in and purpose on their face.

Inside, Jordan sat cross-legged on the floor, her back against the wall, a blanket draped over her shoulders. Her sketchbook rested in her lap, but the pencil in her hand hadn't moved in ten minutes.

Aaron sat across from her, sipping coffee from a chipped mug someone had left behind weeks ago. His legs were stretched out, ankles crossed, posture relaxed—but his eyes never left her.

They hadn't gone home. After Jordan reached for him the night before, they'd stayed. Talked. Not about Miles. Not about the show. Just about everything else. Childhood memories. Favorite movies. The first time they each realized they were good at something. It had been quiet. Easy. Real. Now, the silence between them felt different. Not heavy. Not awkward. Just full. Jordan finally broke it.

"I didn't sleep," she said.

Aaron nodded. "Me neither."

Jordan looked at him. "Do you regret staying?"

Aaron shook his head. "Not even a little."

Jordan exhaled, her fingers tightening around the pencil. "I keep thinking about what comes next. What people will say. What Miles will think. What I'll think of myself."

` Aaron leaned forward, resting his elbows on his knees. "You don't owe anyone a version of yourself that isn't true."

Jordan looked down. "I don't even know what the true version is anymore."

Aaron was quiet for a moment. Then: "Maybe that's the point. Maybe you're still becoming her."

Jordan blinked, caught off guard by the gentleness in his voice. "I don't want to hurt anyone," she said.

"You didn't set out to," Aaron replied. "But you can't live your whole life trying not to break things. Sometimes you have to choose what you're willing to fight for."

Jordan looked at him, really looked. "And what are you fighting for?"

Aaron didn't hesitate. "You."

The word landed between them like a promise. Jordan's breath caught. "You don't even know the whole story."

"I know enough," he said. "I know you're brilliant. I know you're scared. I know you're trying. And I know that when you reached for me last night, it wasn't a mistake."

Jordan swallowed hard. "It wasn't."

Aaron stood, walked over, and sat beside her. Close, but not too close. "You don't have to decide anything right now," he said. "But I'm here. When you're ready."

Jordan leaned her head against his shoulder, eyes fluttering shut. For the first time in weeks, she felt still. Not fixed. Not certain. But still. And that was enough.

# Chapter Fifteen

(Jessica)
To Be Loved

The club lights still shimmered behind her eyes as Jessica stepped out into the warm night air. Her feet ached, her makeup was smudged, and her curls were pulled into a loose bun that had started to fall apart hours ago.

Jessica was halfway through digging in her purse for money for a cab when a familiar voice called out. "You good?"

Jessica looked up. Bryce leaned against his car, arms crossed, keys dangling from one finger. He wasn't in uniform tonight—just jeans and a black tee that clung to his frame like it had been tailored for him.

Jessica blinked. "You're still here?"

Bryce shrugged. "Didn't feel right letting you leave alone. You looked tired."

Jessica raised an eyebrow. "You offering me a ride, Officer?"

Bryce smirked. "Only if you promise not to call me that, nothing about my job is about protecting and serving anyone who deserves it– except you."

Jessica hesitated, then smiled. "Alright, Bryce. Let's ride."

They ended up at a 24-hour diner on the edge of the city. Vinyl booths. Fluorescent lights. The kind of place where the coffee was always burnt and the pancakes tasted like childhood.

Jessica stirred her hot chocolate with a spoon, watching the marshmallows melt. "So," she said, "you always hang around strip clubs after hours, or am I just special?"

Bryce chuckled. "I was off-duty. Came to pick up my check. Saw you dancing, thought you were off tonight, that's why I wasn't working. You looked... like you were somewhere else."

Jessica tilted her head. "That a compliment?"

"It's an observation." Bryce answered.

Jessica smiled. "I was somewhere else. I always am."

Bryce leaned forward. "Where?"

Jessica looked out the window. "Anywhere but here."

Bryce nodded slowly. "I get that."

Jessica glanced at him. "You do?"

"My mom left when I was ten. Dad bounced in and out. I was raised by my grandmother. She used to say I had an old soul because I never acted like a kid."

Jessica's eyes softened. "Same. My grandma Zena raised me and my sister. My mom... she was around, but not really. And my dad—he was in prison most of my life."

Bryce whistled low. "Damn. That's rough."

Jessica shrugged. "It was what it was. I learned early not to expect much from people."

Bryce looked at her for a long moment. "That why you don't let anyone get close?"

Jessica blinked. "Who says I don't?"

Bryce smiled. "You just did."

They both laughed.

After that night, they were inseparable. Bryce started taking her home after shifts, even when she didn't ask. They'd grab food, drive around the city, talk about everything and nothing. He never pushed. Never judged. Just listened.

One night, they sat on the hood of his car, watching the sunrise. "You ever think about leaving all this behind?" Bryce asked.

Jessica leaned against him. "Every day."

"Then why don't you?" Bryce quizzed.

Jessica was quiet for a moment. "Because I don't know where I'd go. Or who I'd be without the fight."

Bryce nodded. "Maybe you don't have to fight alone."

When the school year ended, Jessica didn't go back to North Carolina. She packed her things and moved in with Bryce. Amina, ever the ride-or-die, got her own apartment in the same building—just across the hall. It made the story Jessica told her grandparents easier to sell.

"Me and Amina got a place together," Jessica said over the phone. "Closer to campus. Cheaper rent."

Zena had hesitated. "You sure that's safe, baby?"

Jessica smiled. "I'm sure." She didn't mention Bryce. Not yet.

Some things felt too sacred to explain.

That night in bed, Bryce traced lazy circles on her back as Jessica lay curled against him.

"You ever think this is too fast?" she asked.

Bryce kissed her shoulder. "Nope."

Jessica laughed. "That's it? No hesitation?"

"I knew the second you sat across from me in that diner," he said. "You weren't just another girl. You were the one."

Jessica went quiet. Then: "I think I'm falling for you."

Bryce smiled. "Then fall. I'll catch you."

Before long, Bryce and Jessica fell into a rhythm. Their apartment smelled like sage and cinnamon. Jessica stood barefoot in the kitchen, stirring a pot of rice while Bryce grilled chicken on the balcony. Music played low—old-school R&B, the kind that made everything feel softer. The summer heat pressed against the windows, but inside, it felt like peace.

Jessica glanced at the clock. Almost time to call Zena. She wiped her hands on a towel, grabbed her phone, and stepped into the bedroom.

"Hey, Grandma," she said, voice bright.

"Hey, baby. You sound tired." Zena responded.

Jessica smiled. "Long shift. Amina and I are still getting used to the new place."

"You girls eating right?" Zena asked.

"Of course. I'm cooking now." Jessica assured her, attempting to assuage her grandmother's worry.

Zena chuckled. "Well, that's a miracle."

Jessica laughed, but it felt tight. "I'm learning."

"Your sister called," Zena added. "She said she hasn't heard from you in a while."

Jessica's stomach twisted. "Yeah, I've just been... busy."

"You sure everything's alright?" Zena questioned.

Jessica hesitated. "Everything's fine, Grandma. Promise."

They said their goodbyes. Jessica hung up and stared at the phone for a long moment. Bryce walked in, holding a plate of grilled chicken. "You okay?"

Jessica nodded. "Yeah. Just talked to my grandma."

Bryce raised an eyebrow. "You tell her about me yet?"

Jessica looked away. "Not yet."

Bryce set the plate down. "Jess... we live together. I'm not a secret."

"I know," she said quickly. "It's not that I'm ashamed. It's just... complicated."

Bryce sat beside her. "You think they wouldn't approve?"

"I think they'd ask questions I'm not ready to answer."

Bryce was quiet for a moment. Then he said reassuringly: "I'm not going anywhere. But I need to know you're not ashamed of this—of us."

Jessica turned to Bryce, eyes soft. "I'm not. You're the only thing in my life that feels real."
Bryce kissed her forehead. "Then let's keep building something real."

Days turned into weeks. Jessica danced less and worked more shifts at the boutique Amina helped her get into. She started taking classes again. Bryce encouraged her, quizzed her on flashcards, and left notes in her textbooks.

"You're brilliant," one read. "Don't let the world convince you otherwise."

They cooked together. Laughed. Fought over what to watch. Made up before bed.

But every time her phone rang with a call from home, Jessica hesitated. She told herself she was protecting them. That they wouldn't understand. That she needed more time. But deep down, she knew the truth. She was afraid they'd see the cracks.

One afternoon, Zena called while Jessica was folding laundry. Bryce walked by in the background singing, shirtless, towel slung over his shoulder.

"Was that a man's voice I heard?" Zena asked, sharp.

Jessica froze. "What? No—that was the TV."

Zena didn't press, but her silence said everything.

After the call, Jessica sat on the edge of the bed, heart pounding. Bryce came in, drying his hair. "You okay?"

Jessica nodded. "Yeah. Just tired."

But the lie sat heavy in her chest, not just about Bryce, but about her new life.

# Chapter Sixteen

## (The Alexanders)
## Can't Fool Family

Zena sat at the kitchen table, her Bible open but unread. The morning sun filtered through the lace curtains, casting soft patterns across the wood grain. Her coffee had gone cold. Again.

Jake walked in from the porch, wiping his hands on a rag. "You talk to Jess?"

Zena didn't look up. "Yesterday. She said everything was fine."

Bryce poured himself a cup of coffee, took a sip, and grimaced. "You believe her?"

Zena finally met his eyes. "No."

Jake sat down across from her. "Me neither."

They sat in silence for a moment, the kind that only comes after decades of knowing someone too well to pretend.

"She said she and Amina got a place together," Zena said. "But I heard a man's voice in the background. She said it was the TV."

Jake raised an eyebrow. "TV don't sound like that."

Zena sighed. "I don't want to jump to conclusions."

Jake leaned back in his chair. "Zee, that girl's been lying since she was old enough to spell it. Not because she's bad. Because she's scared."

Zena nodded slowly. "She's always been the one who runs. Jordan stands and fights. Jessica disappears inside herself."

Jake's voice softened. "You think she's in trouble?"

"I think she's in something she doesn't want us to see." Zena responded.

Later that evening, Zena stood on the porch, watching the sky turn lavender. Jake joined her, two mugs in hand.

"She's hiding something," Zena said again, more to herself than to him.

Jake nodded. "You want me to go down there?" Zena shook her head. "No. Not yet. If we push, she'll just dig in deeper."

Jake sipped his coffee. "So, what do we do?"

"We wait. We watch. And we pray." Zena said.

Jake looked out at the horizon. "You think she's with someone?"

Zena's jaw tightened. "I think she's with someone she doesn't want us to know about."

Jake's voice dropped. "You think it's like last time?"

Zena didn't answer right away. Then she said: "I think we better find out before it is."

The next day, Zena sat on the edge of her bed, the cordless phone warm in her hand. The house was quiet—Jake was out back with their younger son Ronnie, helping him patch the fence—but her thoughts were loud and restless.

Zena stared at the phone for a long moment before dialing. It rang twice.

"Hey, Grandma," Jordan answered, her voice bright but stretched thin.

Zena smiled softly. "Hey, baby. You got a minute?"

"Of course. Everything okay?" Jordan asked with concern.

Zena replied sweetly, "I was just thinking about you girls. Wanted to check in."

Jordan exhaled. "I've just been swamped. The showcase is coming up, and I've barely slept."

Zena nodded, even though Jordan couldn't see her. "I figured. You always did throw yourself into your work when something was weighing on you."
Jordan gave a soft laugh. "I'm fine, Grandma. Really."

Zena let the silence stretch. "You talked to your sister lately?"

Jordan hesitated. "Not really. We've both been busy. She's got school, and I've got the show…"
Zena's voice was gentle but firm. "You sure that's all it is?"

Jordan paused. "I think so."

Zena's tone shifted, just slightly. "And how are you and Miles doing?"

Jordan's breath caught for half a second. "We're good. Just… focused on our careers right now."

Zena closed her eyes. "Jordan, I've known you since before you had teeth. I know when you're lying."

Jordan didn't respond.

Zena softened. "I'm not mad, baby. I'm just worried. About both of you."

Jordan's voice cracked. "I'm okay, Grandma. I promise."

Zena didn't push. Not yet. "Alright," Zena said gently. "But if either of you need anything—anything at all—you call me. You hear?"

"I will." Jordan promised.

"I love you, Jordi." Zena said still concerned.

"I love you too." Jordan replied.

Zena hung up and sat still, the phone resting in her lap. A few minutes later, Jake stepped inside, wiping his hands on a rag. Their younger son Ronnie followed, carrying a toolbox and a quiet concern in his eyes.

"You talk to her?" Jake asked.

Zena nodded slowly. "I did."

Ronnie set the box down. "She alright?"

Zena looked at her son—her steady, quiet Ronnie, the one who never gave them trouble, the one who stepped in when Carolyn stepped out. He'd helped raise Jordan and Jessica like they were his own, driving them to school, sitting through dance recitals, patching scraped knees and broken hearts.

"She says she is," Zena said. "But something's off. I can feel it."

Jake sat beside her. "You think it's Jessica too?"

"I know it is." Zena said turning to look Jake in his eyes.

Ronnie leaned against the doorframe, arms crossed. "You want me to drive up there? Check on them?"

Zena shook her head. "Not yet. But keep your phone close." She looked out the window, voice low. "I've already lost one child to her own choices. I'm not losing my grandbabies too."

Ronnie nodded. "Then I'll be ready. Just say the word."

Ronnie Alexander didn't believe in meddling. But he believed in showing up. When Zena hung up the phone with that worried look in her eyes—the one she used to wear when Carolyn would vanish for days—Ronnie knew what he had to do. Jordan had always been the strong one, the composed one, the one who carried the weight of her mother's legacy like it was stitched into her spine. But even strong girls crack. So, Ronnie packed a bag, filled his thermos, and hit the road for D.C.

Ronnie didn't call ahead. Jordan would've found a way to deflect, to delay, to make herself sound fine over the phone. Instead, he pulled up outside her building just after noon. Ronnie made his way up to Jordan's apartment and knocked on the door – No answer. He knocked again. Finally, the door opened a crack. Jordan stood there in leggings and an oversized hoodie, dark circles under her eyes, hair pulled into a messy bun.

Jordan blinked. "Uncle Ronnie?"

Ronnie smiled. "Hey, baby girl."

Jordan opened the door wider, stepping aside. "What are you doing here?"

"Just passing through D.C.," he said, stepping in. "Thought I'd check on my favorite niece."

"I'm your only niece in D.C." Jordan replied sarcastically.

"Still counts." Ronnie said with a smirk.

Jordan's place was clean, but lived-in. Sketches and fabric swatches covered the table. A half-eaten bowl of cereal sat on the counter.

Ronnie looked around. "You sleeping?"

Jordan shrugged. "When I can."

He sat on the couch. "You eating?"

She gave a half-smile. "That's what the cereal was for."

Ronnie nodded. "You want to tell me what's going on, or you want me to guess?"

Jordan sat across from him, arms folded. "I'm fine."

"You're not." Ronnie retorted.

Jordan looked away.

Ronnie leaned forward. "Mama's worried. Daddy's pacing. And you—you're lying to everyone who loves you."

Jordan's voice cracked. "I didn't want to worry them."

"Too late." Ronnie replied.

Jordan wiped her eyes. "Miles left. We broke up. I messed up."

Ronnie's voice was gentle. "You want to tell me how?"

Jordan hesitated. "There's someone else. It's complicated. I didn't mean for it to happen."

Ronnie nodded slowly. "You're human, Jordan. Not perfect. But hiding from the people who love you? That's how you make a mess permanent."

Jordan looked up at him. "I don't know how to fix it."

Ronnie put his hands on his niece's shoulders and looked in the eyes lovingly, "You start by telling the truth. To them. To yourself."

Ronnie's words lingered in the air like smoke, but Jordan breathed them in like oxygen.

Ronnie didn't stay long. He didn't need to. Before he left, he hugged Jordan tight.

"You're not alone, you hear me?" He said holding Jordan like she might collapse if he let her go.

Jordan nodded into his shoulder. "I hear you."

Ronnie pulled back. "And if that boy—Aaron, is it?—if he's not treating you right, you let me know."

Jordan laughed through her tears. "He's not the problem."

Ronnie smiled. "Then maybe he's part of the solution. Just don't lose yourself trying to figure it out."

# Chapter Seventeen

## (Jordan)
## Be Careful

Backstage buzzed—models checked mirrors, designers gave last-minute tugs and pins, but Jordan stood still, fingers trembling slightly at her sides. She was next. The finale. Her gown—Aaron's design, their design—was everything she'd worked toward. Crimson silk, low in the back, clean in the lines. Powerful. Unapologetic – And yet, inside, she was unraveling.

Jordan peeked through the velvet curtain, scanning the crowd under the stage lights. Zena. Jake. Ronnie. A few professors. Editors she recognized from magazine mastheads. But not Miles. His seat—third row, left aisle, the one he always chose—was empty. And somehow, she'd known it would be. Her chest clenched. The guilt spread like static under her skin. She turned away, ducked behind a display rack, pulled out her phone with shaking hands.

**Miles – mobile – Call.**
One ring. Two. Then nothing.
*Call failed.*
She tried again.
Call failed.

*Blocked?*

Jordan didn't cry - Not then. Instead, she tucked the phone away, straightened her spine, and walked toward the entrance to the runway like a general going to war. The music swelled. Her cue.

Jordan stepped into the lights. Every eye followed her as the fabric caught the air—fluid, sharp, alive. She walked like it didn't hurt, like her heart wasn't in pieces, like the man who had once kissed her sketches and memorized the way she laughed didn't just walk out of her life. She smiled—elegant. Controlled. And when she turned at the end of the runway, face lit in a halo of flashes and applause, she didn't let the heartbreak show. She finished strong. And left the stage to a roar.

Moments later, Aaron approached Jordan full of excitement and brandishing a wide smile.

"We won," Aaron said breathlessly, eyes wide with disbelief. "Jordan—we won."

Jordan nodded, trying to smile. It *was* everything she wanted. The House of Maison de Luxe internship. The applause. The validation. But it was all blurred beneath the weight in her chest.

Later, alone in the dressing room, she sat on the edge of a bench and finally let herself break. Her shoulders shook in silence. Mascara streaked. Fingers dug into the thick folds of crimson fabric still clinging to her like armor.

Jordan had reached the dream. But she left something irreplaceable in the climb. And sitting there—surrounded by everything she thought she wanted—Jordan realized with devastating clarity: She might have just lost the love of her life.

There was a soft knock at the dressing room door. Jordan quickly wiped her face with the sleeve of her robe, trying to collect herself. "Just a minute."

The door creaked open anyway. "Baby?" Zena's voice was gentle, cautious.

Jordan turned, eyes still glassy. "Grandma…"

Zena crossed the room in three quick steps and wrapped her arms around her granddaughter, holding her like she had when Jordan was small and afraid of thunderstorms. "You were magnificent," Zena whispered into her hair. "Absolutely magnificent."

Jordan clung to her. "I didn't think you'd come."

Jake stepped in behind them, his voice gruff but warm. "You think we were gonna miss our girl's big night?"

Ronnie followed, hands in his pockets, eyes scanning the room with quiet pride. "You lit that runway up, Jordi. That dress? That walk? You looked like you owned the world."

Jordan laughed softly, pulling back. "I didn't feel like it."

Zena cupped her face. "You don't have to feel it to be it. You were everything tonight."

Jake nodded. "And that dress? That was something else."

Jordan glanced toward the door. "It was Aaron's design. Well—ours. We built it together."

As if on cue, Aaron appeared in the doorway, hesitant. "Sorry—I didn't mean to interrupt."

Jordan stood, wiping her hands on her robe. "No, come in. I want you to meet them."

Aaron stepped forward, offering his hand. "Aaron Malik. I'm Jordan's design partner."

Jake shook his hand first—firm, appraising. "Jake Alexander. Her grandfather."

Zena smiled warmly. "Zena. And this is our son, Ronnie."

Ronnie gave a nod. "Nice to meet you."

Aaron smiled. "Likewise. Jordan's told me a lot about you."

Jake gave a small nod. "She's told us a lot about you too."

Aaron glanced at Jordan, then back at the family. "I'll give you all a moment. Just wanted to say congratulations again. You were… unforgettable."

Jordan's eyes softened. "Thank you."

Aaron gave a respectful nod to the family and slipped out. The door clicked shut.

Zena turned to Jordan, her voice low but steady. "He seems kind."

Jordan nodded. "He's been there. Through all of it."

Jake crossed his arms. "And Miles?"

Jordan looked down. "He left."

Zena's brow furrowed. "Because you hurt him."

Jordan's throat tightened. "I didn't mean to. I didn't plan any of this."

Ronnie stepped forward, voice calm but firm. "We're not here to judge you, Jordi. But you know better than to leave one door open while stepping through another."

Zena sat beside her. "Love isn't just about what feels good in the moment. It's about what you build. What you protect. Miles was part of your foundation."

Jordan's eyes welled. "I know. I just... I got lost."

Jake's voice softened. "Then find your way back. Or forward. But don't pretend like it didn't matter."

Zena took her hand. "We love you. No matter what. But don't confuse applause with peace. They're not the same."

Jordan nodded slowly, tears slipping down her cheeks. "I don't know what to do."

Ronnie gave her shoulder a squeeze. "Start by being honest. With yourself. With both of them."

Zena kissed her forehead. "You earned this moment. Just don't lose yourself in it. Now dry those tears and put those thoughts away for tonight. We are taking you out to celebrate your big win!"

Jordan smiled halfheartedly and grabbed her coat to go celebrate with her family.

The restaurant was warm and golden, all soft lighting and clinking glasses. A jazz trio played near the bar, their notes weaving through the low hum of conversation. Jordan sat at the head of the table, flanked by Zena, Jake, and Ronnie. A bottle of champagne had already been popped. The waiter had just brought out dessert—something chocolate and dramatic with a sparkler stuck in the middle.

"To Jordi," Ronnie said, raising his glass. "For showing the world what we already knew."

"To Jordi," Zena echoed, her eyes shining.

Jake lifted his glass last. "And for not tripping in those heels."

They all laughed, and Jordan smiled—grateful, touched, but not entirely present. She looked around the table, at the people who had shown up for her, who had always shown up. And yet, her eyes kept drifting to the empty chair across from her. The one she hadn't asked for but had quietly hoped would be filled. Miles's chair. She hadn't told her family she'd tried to call him. That she'd tried twice. That both calls had failed.

Blocked. The word still stung. She excused herself quietly, slipping away from the table and stepping out onto the restaurant's terrace. The night air was cool against her skin, the city glittering beyond the railing. She pulled out her phone, thumb hovering over his name in her contacts. Still there. Still grayed out.

Jordan tried again. Call failed. Jordan stared at the screen, her heart thudding. She tried again, this time it rang, but went straight to voicemail. She left a message. Her voice—shaky, quiet, raw.

*"Miles... I don't even know if you'll hear this. But I need to say it. I'm sorry. For hurting you. For not being honest. You didn't deserve that. You were always steady. Always good to me. And I—I let something real slip through my fingers. I don't expect you to forgive me. I just needed you to know that I see it now. I see you. I hope you're okay. I hope you're happy. I miss you."*

Jordan hung up the phone and leaned against the railing, blinking hard. Behind her, the door opened. Zena stepped out, wrapping her shawl tighter around her shoulders. "You alright, baby?"

Jordan nodded. "Yeah. Just needed some air."

Zena stood beside her, quiet for a moment. Then: "You thinking about Miles?"

Jordan didn't answer right away. "He blocked me."

Zena sighed. "That boy loved you. Deep."

"I know." Jordan whispered.

"You broke something in him, Jordi. Doesn't mean he won't heal. But it might mean he won't come back." Zena said with her arm around Jordan's shoulders.

Jordan's voice cracked. "What if I don't want anyone else?"

Zena looked at her, eyes soft. "Then you keep showing up. Not for him. For yourself. For the woman you're becoming. And if he ever looks back, make sure he sees someone worth walking toward again."

Jordan nodded, tears slipping silently down her cheeks.

Zena pulled her into a hug. "Come on. Your dessert's melting."

At that moment, Joran knew she had to end things with Aaron.

Meanwhile, back at Darrell's apartment, Miles had listened to the voicemail three times. Well—*almost* listened. Each time, he stopped somewhere around the part where Jordan's voice broke. He hadn't deleted it. Couldn't. It sat there, tucked between texts from professors and reminders to pick up almond milk, like a wound wrapped in velvet.

*"Miles... I know I don't deserve to ask anything of you. Not after how I left things. But tonight's the show. And I just—God, I wanted you there. Not for the win. Just... for me."*

The beep came too soon after that. *She never said goodbye.* He had blocked her after that message, but unblocked her shortly after, he still wanted her to be able to call, even if he still wasn't emotionally ready to answer. He sat in Darrell's apartment—bare walls, loud pipes, a couch that creaked if you breathed on it wrong—staring at the dim light blinking from his phone.

*It wasn't about the show. Not really. It was about watching someone fall in love with possibility—and realizing they'd quietly placed you behind them on the shelf.*

*Miles ran a hand over his jaw, eyes tired, throat tight. He still loved her. That was the worst part. Because how do you mourn someone who's still alive in your heart?*

A knock interrupted his thoughts. Darrell poked his head in. "You good?"

"Yeah." Miles lied.

"You sure?" Darrell questioned.

Miles gave a tight smile. "I will be."

He looked at the phone once more. The message still unsaved. Still there.

Somewhere between kept and gone. Just like her. His phone buzzed. Another message. It was her.

# Chapter Eighteen

(Miles)
So Close, Yet Still So Far

Darrell's guest room was dim, lit only by the soft flicker of a muted basketball game. Miles sat on the edge of the bed, elbows on his knees, phone in hand. The walls were bare. The air smelled faintly of detergent and takeout. It wasn't home—but it was close enough to remind him of everything he was trying to forget.

Just down the hall, in the same building, was the apartment he used to share with Jordan. He hadn't been back since he left. The first voicemail she left—he'd heard that one. A week ago. Her voice had been hopeful, nervous. She'd asked him to come to her show. Said it would mean a lot. Said she understood if he couldn't.

Miles hadn't responded. Instead, he blocked her. He told himself it was for closure. For peace. But after the show, he unblocked her. And now there was a second message. Still marked "unplayed." He stared at it for a long time. Then tapped. Jordan's voice came through, softer this time. No hope in it. Just truth.

"Miles... I don't even know if you'll hear this. But I need to say it. I'm sorry. For hurting you. For not being honest. You didn't deserve that. You were always steady. Always good to me. And I—I let something real slip through my fingers. I don't expect you to forgive me. I just needed you to know that I see it now. I see you. I hope you're okay. I hope you're happy. I miss you."

The message ended. Miles sat still, the phone resting on his knee. He didn't cry. He didn't call back. But he didn't delete it either. A knock came at the door. Darrell stepped in, holding two beers. "You good?"

Miles didn't look up. "She left another message."

Darrell handed him a bottle and sat down across from him. "You listen to it?"

Miles nodded. "Yeah."

Darrell leaned back against the wall. "You want to talk about it?"

Miles took a long sip. "Not really."

They sat in silence for a while, the kind that only exists between men who've seen each other at their lowest and stayed anyway.

Finally, Darrell said, "You know she meant it." Miles looked up. "I know."

"You still love her?" Darrell asked.

Miles didn't answer right away. Then: "I don't know what I feel. I just know it doesn't go away."

Darrell nodded. "Then don't rush it. Let it sit. Let it hurt. That's how you know it was real."

Miles looked down at the phone again. He hit play. And this time, he didn't flinch.

The next morning, the city was already humming by the time Miles stepped out onto

Darrell's balcony. The air was crisp, the sky a pale wash of blue, and the street below buzzed with early commuters and dog walkers. From here, he could almost see the corner of the building where he and Jordan stopped for coffee every morning. Everything about the life they shared was close. Too close.

Miles sipped his coffee slowly, letting the bitterness settle on his tongue. The second voicemail still echoed in his head. He'd listened to it three times now. Not because he was looking for something new in her words—but because he couldn't stop hearing what was already there – She missed him – She was sorry. – She saw him. – And still… he couldn't move.

Darrell stepped out behind him, stretching. "You sleep?"

Miles shook his head. "Not really."

Darrell leaned on the railing beside him. "You thinking about calling her?"

Miles didn't answer right away. "I'm thinking about what I'd even say."

Darrell nodded. "You don't owe her anything. But if you're stuck in the middle, that's a kind of pain too."

Miles stared out at the skyline. "I'm not angry anymore. Not like I was."

"So, what are you?" Darrell quizzed.

Miles exhaled. "Tired. Confused. Hollow, maybe."

Darrell didn't push. Just stood beside him, quiet.

"I keep thinking about the night she left that first message," Miles said. "I was sitting right here.

She said she wanted me at her show. Said it would mean something."

Darrell glanced at him. "And you didn't go."
Miles nodded. "I couldn't. I didn't want to be the guy sitting in the third row, clapping for someone who broke me."

Darrell was quiet for a minute. "But now she's not asking for applause. She's asking for grace."
Miles looked down at his coffee. "I don't know if I have it in me."

Darrell clapped a hand on his shoulder. "Then don't force it. Just don't lie to yourself about what you still feel."

Miles nodded, jaw tight. He went back inside, sat on the edge of the bed, and opened his phone. Jordan's contact was still there. So was the voicemail. He hovered over the call button. Then locked the screen. Not yet. Maybe not ever. But not today.

# Chapter Nineteen

(Jessica)
The Price of Freedom

The boutique manager didn't even look her in the eye. "I'm sorry, Jessica. We've been more than flexible, but we need someone reliable. You've called out too many times."

Jessica stood there, arms crossed over her chest, trying not to let the sting show. "I've been sick."

"I understand. But this is a business." The manager responded.

And just like that, the job Amina had helped her get—the one that made her feel like she was building something real—was gone.

Amina didn't ask questions. She just showed up at Jessica's door with a bottle of water, a granola bar, and that look that said *I'm not letting you do this alone.*

Amina took Jessica to the clinic to get checked out. The waiting room was cold. Sterile. Jessica sat with her hands in her lap, eyes fixed on the floor.

"You nervous?" Amina asked gently.

Jessica nodded. "I've been throwing up every morning for two weeks. I thought it was stress. Or food poisoning."

Amina gave her a look. "Girl, you've been pregnant since Mardi Gras."

Jessica let out a shaky laugh. "Don't say that." But when the nurse called her name and the test came back positive, she didn't cry. She just stared at the ceiling, numb.

Amina squeezed her hand. "We'll figure it out."

Afterwards, Jessica sat on the edge of her bed, hands folded over her stomach. Bryce stood across from her, still in his work shirt, sweat on his brow. "I'm pregnant," she said.

Bryce blinked. "Say it again."

"I'm pregnant." Jessica repeated slowly.

For a moment, Bryce just stared. Then he crossed the room and knelt in front of her, hands on her knees. "Jess… this is it. This is our way out." Jessica looked at him, uncertain. "Out of what?"

"The club. Joe. All of it. We've been talking about getting clean from that life—this is the push." Bryce said excitedly.

Jessica's voice was small. "It's not that simple."

"No," Bryce said. "But it's real. And it's ours."

Later that night, Bryce went to work at his second job at Fat Tuesdays in Underground Mall. The music thumped through the floor as Bryce stood at the entrance, arms crossed, eyes scanning the crowd. He'd picked up the second job fast—bouncer at Fat Tuesday, three nights a week. It wasn't glamorous, but it was clean. No backroom deals. No Joe.

Bryce still worked the club, too. For now. Until they had enough saved. He told himself it was temporary. He told himself they were almost free. Meanwhile at the club, Joe sat behind his desk, swirling a glass of bourbon, watching the security feed from the club floor. Jessica wasn't on it. He already knew why.

Bryce had told him. Straight-faced. Calm. "She's pregnant."

Joe had smiled. Congratulated him. Even offered a toast. But inside, he was calculating. He knew girls like Jessica. Knew the way the world closed in when the baby came. Knew how fast the money dried up, how fast the dreams shriveled when diapers and formula and rent started stacking up. She'd be back. Not now. Maybe not even in a few months. But eventually. And when she came back, tired and desperate, he'd be waiting. Smiling.

At home, Jessica sat on the floor of the apartment, surrounded by open windows and the soft hum of a box fan. A half-folded baby onesie lay in her lap, the tag still on. It was the first thing she'd bought since finding out. Pale yellow. Neutral. Safe. Jessica hadn't told her grandparents yet. She hadn't told Jordan. She hadn't even said the word "mother" out loud. But it was coming for her, fast. The nausea had faded, but the weight hadn't. It had just shifted—from her stomach to her chest.

Bryce came in from his shift at Fat Tuesday later that evening, smelling like sweat and fried food. He dropped his keys in the bowl by the door and kissed her forehead.

"You eat today?" he asked.

Jessica nodded. "Amina brought soup."
Bryce sat beside her, pulling off his boots. "I picked up an extra shift this weekend. We'll be alright."

Jessica didn't answer right away. She just stared at the onesie in her lap.

"Do you think I'll be good at this?" she asked quietly.

Bryce looked at her. "At what?"

"Being someone's mother." Jessica responded searching his eyes for answers.

Bryce took her hand. "I think you already are."
Jessica shook her head. "I don't even know who I am half the time. I've lied to everyone I love. I've danced for men I hated. I've made choices I can't take back."

Bryce's voice was steady. "And you're still here. Still standing. That counts."

Jessica looked at him, eyes glassy. "What if I mess this kid up?"

"You won't." Bryce assured her.

"You don't know that." Jessica replied still clutching the onesie.

"No," he said. "But I know you. And I know you won't stop trying."

Later that night, Jessica sat on Amina's couch, her feet tucked under her, a mug of tea in her hands. "I feel like I'm living someone else's life," she said.

Amina raised an eyebrow. "You mean the part where you're growing a whole human or the part where you're not dancing anymore?"

Jessica gave a tired smile. "Both."

Amina leaned back. "You're allowed to be scared, Jess. But you're not allowed to give up. You were never meant for that life Jess, and I will never forgive myself for introducing it to you."

Jessica looked down. "It was my choice. You didn't force me or introduce me, I followed you remember? I forced my way into that life, you are not responsible for my choices. I am. Just like I am responsible for this new life growing inside me, but I don't know how to do this without falling apart."

Amina's voice softened. "Then fall apart. I'll help you put the pieces back."

That night, Jessica stood in the bathroom, staring at her reflection. Her body was already changing—subtle, but undeniable. She placed a hand on her stomach, fingers splayed.

"I don't know who I'm going to be," she whispered. "But I promise I'll try to be better than I was."

Jessica didn't know if the baby could hear her. But she said it anyway.

# Chapter Twenty

(Jordan)
Something Just Ain't Right

Jordan sat at her drafting table, pencil in hand, but the lines on the page refused to cooperate. She'd redrawn the same neckline three times, each version more lifeless than the last. The fabric swatches beside her felt dull. Her playlist was on, but she wasn't listening.

*Something was off.*

Jessica hadn't returned her last two texts. Or the one before that. And the last time they spoke— really spoke—was weeks ago, after the show. Jordan had been too wrapped up in the aftermath to notice at first. But now, the silence was loud.

Jordan picked up her phone again. No new messages. She scrolled back through their thread. The last message from Jessica was short: *"I'm good. Just tired. Talk soon."*

*That was twelve days ago.* Jordan frowned. She tapped out a new message.

*Hey. You okay? Starting to get worried. Call me when you can.*

She hovered over send. Then added: *Please.* Jordan didn't wait long. She hit Amina's contact and called.

Amina answered on the third ring, her voice cautious. "Hey, Jordi."

Jordan didn't waste time. "Is Jess okay?"

A pause. Then Amina said hesitantly "She's… figuring things out."

Jordan's stomach dropped. "What does that mean?"

"It means she's going through something, and she'll tell you when she's ready." Amina responded.

"Amina." Jorden retorted.

"She's not in danger," Amina said quickly.

"She's just… processing."

Jordan stood, pacing. "Is she sick? Did something happen with Bryce?"

"No. Nothing like that." Amina said assuredly

"Then what?" Jordan quizzed.

Amina hesitated. "It's not my place."

Jordan's voice cracked. "She's my sister."

"I know. And she loves you. But she's scared. And she's trying to get her feet under her before she brings anyone else into it."

Jordan sat back down, heart pounding. "So, she's hiding."

"She's protecting herself." Amina responded.

Jordan was quiet for a long moment. "Tell her I'm here. No matter what it is."

"I will." Amina replied. Then they said goodbye.

Later that night, Jordan sat on her bed, phone still in her hand, staring at the ceiling. She thought about all the times she and Jessica had fought as kids—over clothes, over secrets, over who got the bigger slice of cake. But they always came back to each other. Always.

This silence felt different. Heavier. She opened her text messages and started typing.

*Dear Jess,*

*I don't know what's going on, but I feel it. I feel the distance. And I hate it. You don't have to be perfect. You don't even have to be okay. Just let me in. Please.*

*Love, Jordi.*

Jordan didn't send it. Not yet. But she saved it. And hoped her sister would come back to her before the silence grew too wide to cross.

Jordan couldn't sleep. She lay in bed, staring at the ceiling, the city's glow bleeding through the blinds. Her flip phone rested on the nightstand, its small green screen dark. No new messages. No missed calls.

She'd tried to distract herself—sketching, reorganizing her portfolio, even flipping through old issues of *Vibe* and *Elle*—but nothing held her attention. Her mind kept circling the same question: *What could be so big that Jess wouldn't tell me?*

Jordan thought back to their last conversation. Jessica had sounded tired. Guarded. Like she was holding something in her mouth she couldn't swallow. Jordan sat up, flipped open her phone, and scrolled to Amina's number again. She typed slowly, thumbs clumsy on the tiny keypad.

*Are you sure Jess is okay?* She hit send. Waited.

A few minutes later, her phone buzzed. *She's safe. Just going through something. She'll talk when she's ready.*

Jordan stared at the screen. Then typed: *Is she pregnant?*

The reply took longer. *I can't say.*

Jordan didn't need a yes. She already knew. That afternoon, Jordan sat in her studio, sketchbook open but untouched. She stared at the blank page, pencil hovering. Jordan was in deep thought.

*Pregnant.* The word echoed in her mind like a dropped pin in a cathedral. She thought about Jessica's silence. The boutique job. The missed calls. The way Amina had been circling her like a bodyguard. It all made sense now. And it broke her heart. Not because Jessica was pregnant. But because she hadn't told her.

Jordan flipped open her phone again. This time, she typed slowly, deliberately. *I miss you.* She hit send. Then set the phone down and waited.

# Chapter Twenty-One
(Jessica)
The Message

Jessica sat on the edge of the bed, one hand resting on her stomach, the other holding a glass of ginger ale that had long since gone flat. The apartment was quiet—too quiet. Bryce was at work, and Amina had gone to work at the club. For the first time in days, Jessica was alone. She didn't like it. The silence made space for thoughts she'd been trying to outrun: *What if I'm not ready? What if I mess this up? What if I become my mother?*

The cordless phone sat on the nightstand. The answering machine blinked once—an old message from Jordan she hadn't had the courage to replay. She reached for it, then stopped. Instead, she picked up her cell phone. The screen lit up with a single unread text. *I miss you.*

Jessica stared at it, her throat tightening. Jordan. She hadn't responded to the last few messages. Hadn't called back. Hadn't explained. Because how do you explain something like this? How do you tell the person who's always seen you as the wild one, the reckless one, that you're about to become someone's mother?

She read the message again. Short. Simple. No pressure. But it cracked something open. She typed a reply. Then deleted it. Then typed again. *I'm sorry I've been quiet. I didn't know how to say it.*

Jessica stared at the blinking cursor. Then added: *I'm pregnant.* Her thumb hovered over "Send." Then she set the phone down. Not yet.

She stood and walked to the window, arms wrapped around herself. The city moved below her—cars, buses, people with places to be. She felt like she was standing still while the world kept spinning. Behind her, the phone buzzed again. Another message. *Whatever it is, I'm here. Just say the word.*

Jessica turned back to the phone. She picked it up. And this time, she hit "Send."

Jessica sat on the couch, the apartment dim except for the soft flicker of the TV playing something she wasn't watching. The message had been sent. Her phone sat on the coffee table, screen dark, but she could feel it like a weight in the room. She'd told Jordan. Three words: *I'm pregnant.* No explanation. No backstory. No apology. Just the truth. Her stomach churned—not from morning sickness this time, but from the fear that Jordan wouldn't respond. Or worse, that she would.

Jessica stood and paced the room, arms folded tightly across her chest. The silence stretched. She glanced at the clock. Almost 10 p.m. Jordan was probably still in her studio, maybe just getting home. Maybe reading the message right now. The phone rang. Jessica froze. She stared at it, heart pounding. The caller ID blinked: **Jordan.** She didn't move. It rang again. And again. Then stopped.

Jessica exhaled, her whole-body trembling. A minute later, the answering machine clicked on. Jordan's voice filled the room—steady, soft, and unmistakably hers.

*"Jess... I got your message. I don't know what to say except—I'm here. I love you. And I'm not going anywhere. Call me back when you're ready. Or don't. I'll still be here."*

The machine beeped. Silence returned. Jessica sat down slowly, tears slipping down her cheeks. She hadn't realized how tightly she'd been holding herself together until now. She reached for the phone. Paused. Then pulled her hand back. Not yet. But soon. Jessica curled up on the couch, one hand resting on her stomach, the other clutching a throw pillow to her chest. Jordan knew. And she hadn't run. That was enough—for tonight.

The apartment was quiet again, but the silence felt different now—less like isolation, more like space. Space to breathe. Space to think. Space to begin.

Jessica sat on the floor, back against the couch, a notebook open in her lap. Not the kind she used to scribble dance sets or shift schedules in. This one was new. Blank. She bought it on a whim at the corner store last week, not knowing why. Now she did.

At the top of the first page, she wrote: *What kind of mother will I be?* She stared at the question for a long time. Then, slowly, she began to write.

*I want to be the kind who listens. Who doesn't flinch when the truth is ugly. Who shows up, even when she's tired. I want to be the kind who doesn't lie to herself. Who doesn't run when things get hard. Who doesn't disappear like mine did.*

Jessica's pen paused. She thought about her own mother—Carolyn. The way she'd drifted in and out of their lives like a ghost with a key. The way Zena had stepped in, filled the gaps, held the line. Jessica had always told herself she was nothing like Carolyn. But lately, she wasn't so sure. She flipped to a new page.

*Things I'm afraid of:*
– Not being enough
– Needing help
– Becoming her
– Losing myself
– Loving this baby too much
– Not loving it enough

Jessica set the pen down and pressed her palms to her face. The tears came quietly this time. Not from panic. Not from shame. From release. From the slow, aching realization that she was already changing. Not because she had to. But because she wanted to.

Later, Jessica stood in front of the mirror, lifting her shirt just slightly. Her belly was still flat, but she could feel the difference. A tightness. A tenderness. A beginning. She placed her hand there, fingers splayed.

"I don't know what I'm doing," she whispered. "But I'm going to try."

Jessica didn't know if the baby could hear her. But she said it anyway.

Meanwhile, Jordan was preparing to take a break from her own drama to check on her sister. She stood at the kitchen counter, a half-eaten bagel growing stale beside her coffee. The answering machine light blinked once—Jessica hadn't called back. But she had sent the message. And that was enough to crack something open.

Jordan had replayed her own voicemail three times since leaving it. Each time, she listened for signs—did her voice sound too calm? Too desperate? Too much like a sister trying not to fall apart? She finally stopped second-guessing and pulled out her planner. The next few days were packed with fittings, fabric orders, and a meeting with the Maison de Luxe rep. But none of it mattered. Not right now.

Jordan sat at her drafting table, the crimson gown still hanging in the corner like a ghost of triumph. The final showcase was behind her. The applause, the internship offer from Maison de Luxe, the photo in the campus paper—it had all happened. She'd done it.

Graduation was in a month. One month until she walked across that stage. One month until she packed up her studio and stepped into the next chapter. She should've been riding the high. But instead, her eyes kept drifting to the small green screen of her flip phone, where a single message sat frozen: *I'm pregnant. I'm scared. I miss you.*

No punctuation. No explanation. Just truth. Jordan had stared at it for ten minutes before responding. *I'm here. Always.*

Jessica hadn't replied. Jordan looked at her calendar. Maison de Luxe onboarding in two weeks. A reception next Friday. A dozen things she could reschedule. She didn't hesitate. She picked up the phone and called her advisor and informed her that she needed to leave town.

"You're going to Atlanta?" Professor Langston raised an eyebrow. "Jordan, you're in the final stretch."

"I know," Jordan said. "But I have time. Graduation's a month away. And my sister needs me."

Langston studied her. "You're not walking away from Maison de Luxe, are you?"

"No," Jordan said. "Just… pressing pause. I'll be back in time."

Langston nodded slowly. "You've earned the right to take a breath. Just don't lose your momentum."

Jordan smiled faintly. "I'm not. I'm just shifting it."

That evening, Jordan stood on the platform at Union Station, a small duffel slung over her shoulder. She hadn't told Jessica she was coming. She didn't want to give her the chance to say no. The conductor called for boarding. Jordan stepped onto the train, found her seat, and pulled out her phone again. The message was still there. *I'm pregnant. I'm scared. I miss you.* She read it one more time. Then closed the phone and tucked it into her bag.

The sun was low when the train pulled into the station in Atlanta. Jordan stepped off, the heat wrapping around her like a memory. She hadn't been back in months. Not since before the showcase. Not since before everything shifted. She didn't have Jessica's new address, and her phone was dead. But she knew who to call. She stepped into the payphone booth and dialed Amina's number from memory. It rang twice.

"Hello?" Amina answered.

"Amina. It's Jordan."

A pause. "You're here." Amina asked.

"I need to see her." Jordan replied.

Another pause. Then Amina responded: "I'll come get you."

The ride from the station was quiet. Amina's Mercedes purred down the expressway, windows cracked just enough to let in the warm Atlanta air. The leather seats were cool against Jordan's skin, the dash spotless, the stereo low—Sade humming something smooth and unbothered.

Jordan glanced around the interior, eyebrows lifting slightly. She hadn't remembered Amina driving anything like this the last time she visited.
A college senior in college with a car like this? She didn't ask, but the question lingered: *What exactly does Amina do?*

Amina caught her looking and smirked. "It's not stolen, if that's what you're thinking."

Jordan smiled faintly. "I wasn't thinking that."

"You were thinking something." Amina quipped.

Jordan shrugged. "Just wondering how a college student pulls off a Mercedes with leather seats and a six-CD changer."

Amina laughed. "Let's just say I know how to keep my side hustles clean, and my receipts organized. And let's not forget I am slightly older than most college seniors, in fact I am older than you."

Jordan didn't press. She never had to with Amina—she always gave just enough to keep you curious, never enough to pin her down. When they pulled up outside Amina's building, Jordan finally opened her phone. The screen lit up with a message:
*Where'd you disappear to? Thought we were celebrating this week. Everything okay?*
*Aaron.*

Jordan stared at it for a moment, thumb hovering. She could still hear his voice after the showcase—bright, breathless, full of belief. *"We won."* And they had. But somewhere between the runway and the silence that followed, Jordan had realized something she hadn't wanted to admit – she couldn't carry both. Not the internship and the relationship. Not the future and the weight of what she hadn't said. Not him and the truth. She typed slowly.

*Hey. Sorry for the sudden exit. I had to leave town for a bit—family stuff. I'll explain when I'm back.*

Jordan hesitated. Then added: *We should talk when I return.* She hit send before she could change her mind.

The reply came quickly. *Talk? Everything okay?* Jordan didn't answer. Not yet.

Later that night, Jordan sat on the pullout couch at Amina's apartment, her duffel at her feet, the hum of the ceiling fan overhead. Amina had gone across the hall to check on Jessica, promising to bring her back in the morning. Jordan had offered to come, but Amina had gently said, "Let me ease her into it."

Jordan understood. She opened her planner and flipped to the back, where she'd tucked the letter from the internship coordinator. Her request had gone through. The new Maison de Luxe location in Georgetown was opening in the fall. She'd asked to be reassigned there. Closer to home. Closer to Jessica. Closer to herself. She hadn't told Aaron. Not yet.

Jordan closed the planner and leaned back, staring at the ceiling. She wasn't running. She was choosing. And tomorrow, she'd start telling the truth.

Meanwhile, back in D.C., Aaron sat on the edge of his bed, the light from his desk lamp casting long shadows across the sketchpad in his lap. The page was blank. Had been for an hour. His pencil hovered, but nothing came. His phone buzzed again. Still nothing from Jordan. He scrolled back to her last message:

*Hey. Sorry for the sudden exit. I had to leave town for a bit—family stuff. I'll explain when I'm back. We should talk when I return.*

*We should talk.* The phrase sat heavy in his chest. It wasn't a breakup text—not exactly—but it wasn't nothing either. It was the kind of message that came before a shift. Before the door closed. He tossed the phone onto the bed and stood, pacing the room. The studio was quiet. His roommate was out. The silence made everything louder.

Aaron thought back to the night of the showcase—Jordan in that crimson gown, the crowd on their feet, the Maison de Luxe rep shaking her hand. He'd waited near the back, hoping to catch her afterward. But she'd left with her family—her grandparents, and that uncle she always talked about, Ronnie.

Jordan had texted him later that night: *Sorry I disappeared. My folks pulled me out fast. Rain check?*

Aaron told himself it didn't mean anything. That she was just caught up in the moment. But now she was gone again. No warning. No details. Just *family stuff.* Aaron sat back down and opened his sketchpad again. This time, he didn't try to draw. He just stared at the paper. He hadn't told her yet, but he'd turned down another offer to take the Maison de Luxe placement with her. He'd rearranged his summer. He'd made space.

And now? Now she was somewhere else, making decisions he wasn't part of. His phone buzzed again. A message from his best friend, not Jordan.

*You still on for studio hours tomorrow?* Aaron didn't answer.

Aaron noticed he still had one of Jordan's sketch books. He flipped it open and saw one word scribbled in the corner: *Georgetown?* He didn't know why she wrote it, he was aware that there was new location opening up there for Maison de Luxe, but Jordan never mentioned being interested in staying in D.C. – But something told him Jordan hadn't told him everything.

# Chapter Twenty-Two

### (Jordan & Jessica)
### Two Sisters, One Heart

Jordan stood in Amina's bathroom, hands braced on the edge of the sink, staring at her reflection. The morning light filtered through the blinds in soft stripes, catching the edges of her curls and the tension in her jaw. She hadn't slept much. Her body was in Atlanta, but her mind was still pacing the length of her studio in D.C., still replaying Jessica's message over and over. *I'm pregnant. I'm scared. I miss you.*

Jessica read it again that morning, as if the words might have changed overnight. They hadn't. She splashed cold water on her face and dried it with a towel that smelled like lavender and something faintly citrusy—Amina's signature. The apartment was quiet except for the low hum of the fan and the occasional creak of the floorboards.

Jordan dressed slowly: jeans, a soft white tee, the same denim jacket she'd worn the night of her showcase. She didn't know why she reached for it—maybe because it still smelled like home. Like Zena's hug. Like the moment before everything

155

shifted. She was tying her sneakers when Amina knocked gently on the doorframe.

"She's ready," Amina said.

Jordan stood. "How is she?"

Amina gave a small, unreadable smile.

"Nervous. But she didn't say no."

Jordan nodded, heart thudding. "Okay."

The walk across the hall felt longer than it should have. Jordan's palms were damp. She kept smoothing them down the sides of her jeans, trying to steady her breath. Amina knocked once, then stepped back. The door opened slowly. Jessica stood there, barefoot, wearing an oversized T-shirt and leggings. Her hair was pulled into a loose bun, and her eyes—though tired—were clear.

For a moment, neither of them spoke. Then Jessica said, "You came."

Jordan nodded. "Of course I did."

Jessica looked down, then stepped aside. "Come in."

The space was small but clean. A few dishes in the sink. A folded blanket on the couch. A half-finished glass of ginger ale on the coffee table. Jordan took it all in quietly, her eyes landing on a small notebook on the armrest—open to a page that read: *What kind of mother will I be?*

Jessica noticed. "Don't read that."

Jordan looked away. "Sorry."

They sat on the couch, a careful space between them.

"I didn't know how to tell you," Jessica said.

Jordan nodded. "I figured."

"I thought you'd be disappointed."

Jordan blinked. "Why?"

Jessica shrugged. "Because you're out there winning internships and walking runways and I'm... here. Starting over."

Jordan's voice was soft. "Jess, I'm not disappointed. I'm scared for you. But I'm proud of you, too."

Jessica's eyes welled. "Even now?"

"Especially now." Jordan responded.

They sat in silence for a moment, the kind that only exists between people who've known each other's worst and stayed anyway. Then Jordan reached over and took her sister's hand.

"I'm here," she said. "And I'm not going anywhere."

Jessica nodded, tears slipping down her cheeks. "I know."

The days passed in a quiet rhythm—meals shared in Amina's kitchen, long walks through the neighborhood, whispered conversations between sisters that stitched old wounds closed. Jordan had planned to stay only a few days. But when Jessica asked her to stay "just a little longer," she didn't hesitate. She pushed her return ticket back once. Then again. Graduation was still weeks away. There was time. And then, without warning, time ran out.

It was early—barely light outside—when Jordan heard the knock on the door. She sat up, heart already racing.

Amina stood in the hallway, eyes wide, phone in hand. "It's Jess," she said. "Her water broke." Jordan was already pulling on her jeans.

The waiting room at Grady Memorial Hospital was a blur of fluorescent lights and too-cold air. Jordan paced. Amina sat with a vending machine coffee, trying to look calm. Bryce arrived not long after, breathless and wide-eyed, still in his work shirt from Fat Tuesday.

"She's early," Bryce said, voice cracking. Jordan nodded. "But the doctor said the baby's strong. They're watching her close."

They waited. And waited. And then—A nurse stepped into the room, smiling. "He's here," she said. "And he's healthy."

Jordan let out a breath she didn't know she'd been holding. Bryce sat down hard, hands over his face.

Amina grinned and whispered, "Told you she's tougher than she looks."

In the recovery room, Jessica looked pale but radiant, her hair damp, her eyes glassy with exhaustion and something deeper—something fierce. She held a tiny bundle in her arms, wrapped in a blue-striped blanket.

Jordan stepped in slowly, unsure if she should speak.

Jessica looked up. "Come meet him."

Jordan crossed the room, her throat tight. She looked down at the baby—his skin soft and warm, his tiny fist curled against Jessica's chest.
"He's perfect," Jordan whispered.

Jessica smiled. "His name's Bryce Anthony Jr. We're calling him BJ."

Jordan looked at her new little nephew and smiled. "Hi BJ, I am your auntie Jordi and so happy to meet you little one." She said sweetly.

Jessica's voice was quiet. "I couldn't think of a better way to honor the man that has always shown up for me and loves me beyond reason.

Jordan reached out and touched BJ's hand. "He's going to be so loved Jess."

Jessica looked at her sister. "He already is." The morning Jordan left Atlanta, the air was thick with that slow, Southern heat that made everything feel like it was happening in slow motion. Jessica stood outside the building she and Bryce now called home—just across the hall from Amina—BJ tucked into the crook of her arm, his tiny face half-hidden beneath a soft cotton cap.

Jordan adjusted the strap on her duffel, heart tight. "You sure you're okay?"

Jessica nodded. "We're figuring it out. One day at a time."

BJ stirred, letting out a soft sigh. Jessica smiled down at him, then looked up at her sister. "Promise me something?"

Jordan hesitated. "What?"

"Don't tell Grandma and Grandpa. Not yet. I want to do it myself. When I'm ready." Jessica asked.

Jordan blinked. "Jess…"

"I will. I swear. I just… I need to do it in my own time. On my terms." Jessica promised.

Jordan looked at her sister—tired, determined, holding her son like a shield and a promise—and nodded slowly. "Okay. I promise." But the words sat wrong in her mouth.

When Jordan arrived back in D.C., she stepped off the train and back into the rush of Union Station, the noise and motion jarring after the quiet of Atlanta. She had a week until graduation. Her Maison de Luxe reassignment to Georgetown was confirmed. Everything was moving forward. But part of her felt like she'd left something behind. Jordan kept her promise. When their grandma called to check in, Jordan said Jessica was "doing okay." When their grandpa asked if she'd seen her, she said, "Yeah, we talked." She didn't lie. But she didn't tell the truth either. And every time she hung up, she felt it—like a thread pulling tighter.

Jordan sat at her desk, flipping through a stack of graduation announcements. One was addressed to Grandma Zena and Grandpa Jake. She hadn't mailed it yet. She stared at the envelope, then picked up her phone.

*You tell them yet?* She hit send.

A few minutes later, Jessica replied:

*Not yet. I will. Just... not tonight.*

Jordan sighed, setting the phone down. She'd kept her promise. But it was getting harder.

A month later, Jessica stood in the tiny kitchen of her apartment, rocking BJ gently in one arm while scribbling a grocery list with the other. The baby was growing fast—already outgrowing the onesies Amina had bought in a flurry of excitement. Formula wasn't cheap. Diapers even less so. Bryce was still working nights at the club and picking up extra shifts at Fat Tuesday. But it wasn't enough.

So, Jessica applied at IHOP, she was only a sophomore in college at this point, so her occupational choices were limited.

The manager had been skeptical—"You just had a baby?"—but Jessica convinced him. She needed the hours. The tips. The distraction. BJ stayed across the hall with Amina during her shifts. Sometimes Bryce was home, sometimes not. They were scraping by. Just barely. The building had become their little ecosystem: Amina's door always open, Jessica and Bryce's always one knock away. Bottles warmed in borrowed microwaves. Diapers passed between units like sugar. Every day, Jessica told herself: *Tomorrow I'll call Grandma. Tomorrow I'll tell them.* But tomorrow kept passing.

# Chapter Twenty-Three

### (Jessica)
### What's New Pussycat?

The club was already humming by the time Amina walked in—bass thudding through the walls, lights low and pulsing, the scent of sweat and cologne thick in the air. She moved through the crowd with practiced ease, nodding at the regulars, ignoring the ones who stared too long.

Amina didn't like being back here tonight. Not with everything going on across the hall. Jessica was barely holding it together, and BJ had been fussy all day. But bills didn't wait, and Amina's shifts at the club still paid better than anything else she could pick up on short notice.

She was halfway to the dressing room when she heard his voice. "Amina." She turned. Joe stood in the hallway near the back office, arms crossed, gold watch catching the light. He looked like he always did—calm, pressed, and dangerous. Amina didn't stop walking. "I'm on the clock."

Joe fell into step beside her. "You always are." Amina didn't respond. They reached the dressing room door. She reached for the handle, but he spoke again. "How's Jessica?"

Amina froze. She turned slowly. "She's fine."

Joe raised an eyebrow. "Haven't seen her around. Thought maybe she moved."

"She's across the hall from me. She didn't move."

He nodded, like he already knew that. "She still with that boy? Bryce?"

Amina's jaw tightened. "They're doing what they need to do."

Joe smiled, but it didn't reach his eyes. "You know, I always figured she'd come back. Girls like her usually do. Especially when things get tight." Amina stepped closer, voice low. "She's not coming back here, Joe."

He tilted his head. "You sure about that?"

"I'm sure." Amina retorted through clinched teeth.

Joe studied her for a moment, then shrugged. "Alright. Just checking in. You know I like to keep tabs on my people."

"She's not your people." Amina shot back, never breaking his stare.

Joe's smile widened. "Everyone's someone's people. Until they're not."

Amina didn't flinch. She just turned and walked into the dressing room, the door clicking shut behind her. But her hands were shaking. Joe was handsome in a rough around the edges sort of way. Older and wiser, with a predator's patience – He had been keeping his distance, biding his time and awaiting his opportunity.

When Joe learned Jessica began dating Bryce, he didn't object—he waited. He knew the hunger she'd developed for the money, the lifestyle, the illusion of control. And he also knew eventually Bryce would try to pull her off the stage, away from the spotlight and the cash that once felt so easy. Joe had offered safety, indulgence, admiration. And Jessica, raised with an empty chair where her father should've been, was drawn to the attention. His voice reminded her of what she thought she'd missed.

Bryce wanted out—badly. Especially when he saw Jessica getting in too deep.

"We can leave all this behind," he told her. But Jessica kept one foot in both worlds, unwilling to let go of the comfort she'd found in the chaos.

For a whole year, Jessica lived in two worlds. One wrapped in the quiet love she shared with Bryce—warm, steady, hopeful. The other cloaked in velvet shadows and half-spoken lies. Bryce grew even more disenchanted with the lifestyle and wanted out. When he found out Jessica was pregnant, Bryce saw it as their moment of escape. Their do-over.

A baby meant leaving the club for good, starting fresh with clean hands and late-night feedings. But Joe had never been the kind of man to surrender what he believed he owned. When he heard the news, he didn't argue. He waited. Patient, watchful. He knew how far Jessica had already fallen—for the money, the attention, the illusion of power. He knew pregnancy would push her off the stage, out of the light. All he had to do was give her time to miss it.

Jessica continued to hid that she had a child from her family, she made up excuses why she couldn't come to Jordan's graduation or come home. She told them she'd been offered a coveted research position—traveling the globe with a professor. Madrid. Cairo. Rome.

In truth, Jessica's international experience came with pancakes and graveyard shifts. She clocked in at IHOP while her dreams sat cooling in the window. She made up cheerful stories for her grandparents and smiled through the phone, but each call left her emptier. She was learning that hiding didn't always feel like protection. Sometimes, it just meant you were slowly disappearing.

After BJ was born, it didn't take long for the weight of it all to bear down. The bills. The missing scholarship. The baby cried at night while the world demanded rent. Bryce worked. Two jobs. No sleep. Endless hustle. But they were slipping fast. Then Joe reappeared. He slid into a booth at IHOP like he owned the place, like he still owned her. Ordered a black coffee, handed her a hundred-dollar tip, and spoke like he already knew her answer.

"You look tired," he murmured. "Let me help." That was his opening. He pitched her promises like fairy tales. "You only have to dance," he said. "Unless you want more. Come on, I know you could use the money – Do it for your son, your family." That was the bait, and he was the hook.

Jessica's love for her son was fierce. Her need to shield Bryce from more pressure, just as real. But she knew he'd never let her return to the club. So, she lied. Joe arranged it all—shifts that wouldn't overlap with Bryce's, doors that stayed closed, money that slid into her purse before she could feel the shame. But then came the next hook.

"You've lost your spark," Joe said one night backstage. "The customers are starting to notice." He dropped two pills into her hand. "Just vitamins. For nerves." They weren't.

Soon, they were routine. Easier than guilt. Easier than silence. And when Joe told her sleeping with him was just for the money—just for her family—she didn't ask questions. She just closed her eyes.

It started with a lie so small she barely noticed it leave her mouth. "I picked up an extra shift at IHOP," Jessica said, brushing a kiss across Bryce's cheek. She didn't flinch. Didn't fumble. She's said it so many times by now, it felt like second nature. But she didn't go to IHOP. She went to the club. To Joe. To dim lights and fast cash and that little white pill that lets her float above it all. At first, it worked. Bryce was too busy juggling classes, work, and BJ to ask too many questions.

Jessica moved between worlds like smoke— slipping out, slipping back in, unmarked. Until the baby's blanket smelled like vanilla perfume she never wore at home. Until she said she worked a closing shift—but her manager stopped by the house to drop off some paperwork and casually mentions Jessica had been off all week. Until Bryce found glitter in their son's crib. That's when Bryce started noticing more.

Jessica was edgy when she was home. Her sleep was fractured. Her body was there, but her mind was always... somewhere else. Her hands trembled when she poured formula. She cried in the shower and lied about why her lips were bruised. Bryce doesn't want to believe it at first. Then everything falls apart. That night, he waited up for her. He held BJ in his lap like a shield, like a question, but Jessica never came home. Eventually he put the baby to bed, called Amina and left to work his second job.

The next morning, the door creaked open, and Jessica stepped into the apartment—mascara streaked like warpaint, heels dangling from her fingers, eyes dazed and shadowed. The space was quiet, too quiet. BJ was napping peacefully in his playpen. Amina sat nearby on the couch, legs tucked beneath her, cradling a lukewarm mug of coffee. She looked up as Jessica entered, her gaze unreadable.

Jessica didn't speak. She dropped her purse with a dull thud and drifted into the kitchen, resting both hands on the counter as if it were the only thing keeping her upright. Her reflection stared back at her from the microwave door—hollow, unfamiliar. Something spilled from her bag. A club pass, bold and smug. And beside it, a folded envelope with two white pills pressed against the laminate counter like a threat.

Amina rose quietly and approached. "Jess," she said softly, "Are you okay?"

Jessica didn't turn around. Her knuckles tightened against the counter. "Define okay."

Amina glanced at the items on the counter but didn't touch them. "Do you want to talk about last night?"

Jessica exhaled sharp, shaky. "I don't even remember most of it. I just wanted to feel something other than lost."

"Bryce hasn't come home yet. He asked me to watch BJ last night when you weren't home before he had to leave for his shift." Amina offered, not accusing, just anchoring the silence.

Jessica winced. "I didn't expect him to. Hell, I wouldn't want to be around me either."
Amina's voice was firmer now, warm with quiet strength. "That's not fair. You're going through something, Jess. But disappearing like this… it's not just hurting you."

Jessica finally turned to face her. "I know. I saw BJ asleep just now and I felt… I felt like I didn't deserve to be his mother."

Amina stepped forward, placing a hand gently on Jessica's shoulder. "You're still here. That means something. Let's figure this out, together. No shame, just truth."

Jessica's eyes glossed over, but she nodded. "Okay… yeah. Together."

Just then Bryce stepped inside, keys in hand, eyes already scanning her face. He didn't say anything at first. Just looked. And in that look, everything shifted. No anger. No shouting. Just heartbreak.

Amina gave Jessica a hug, kissed BJ, and gave Bryce a reassuring pat on the shoulder and exited to give them time to talk.

Jessica's voice cracked before it even reached her throat. "Bryce…"

Bryce closed the door behind him. "Where were you last night?"

"I—" She swallowed. "I picked up a double. IHOP was short-staffed."

Bryce didn't blink. "I called. They said you've been off all week."

Jessica's mouth opened, then closed.
Bryce stepped forward, voice low. "There was glitter in BJ's crib."

Jessica's breath caught.

"I thought maybe it was from Amina," he said. "But then I found this." He reached into his pocket and pulled out the club flyer she'd left in her coat. "You left it in the laundry."

Jessica's knees buckled. She sank to the floor, tears already spilling. "I didn't mean for it to get this far."

Bryce didn't move. "How far is it, Jess?"
She looked up at him, mascara streaking her cheeks. "I was trying to help. I thought—if I could just make enough to get us ahead—"

"By going back to him?" His voice cracked. "To Joe?"

She sobbed. "I didn't want you to know. I didn't want you to see me like this."

"I see you," he said. "I've always seen you. Even when you were trying to disappear."

Jessica reached for the envelope on the floor, opened it, and stared at the pills. "I don't even know when it started. One night turned into two. Then I couldn't sleep without them. Couldn't dance without them."

Bryce knelt beside her. "You don't have to do this anymore."

She shook her head. "I already promised you I wouldn't go back. But I lied. I'm still lying."

"Then stop." His voice was quiet. "Right now. Tell me the truth."

Jessica looked at him, eyes raw. "I'm scared."

"I am too," he said. "But I'd rather be scared with you than lose you to this."

Jessica broke then—completely. Collapsed into his arms, sobbing into his shoulder. "I'm sorry. I'm so sorry."

He held her. Not tightly. Just enough to keep her from falling apart.

After a long silence, she whispered, "I'll quit. I'll go back to IHOP. I'll flush the pills. I'll never see Joe again."

Bryce didn't answer right away. Because they both knew. As soon as the words left her lips, she'd lied again.

# Chapter Twenty-Four

(Jordan)
Old Flame vs Twin Flame

The morning of graduation was bright and too hot even for June, the kind of heat that made everything feel a little more fragile. Jordan stood in front of the mirror in the apartment she shared with Miles, smoothing the front of her gown, trying to ignore the hollow space beside her.

Jessica wasn't coming. She'd sent a cheerful voicemail the night before:

*"Hey, I'm so proud of you, Jordi . I wish I could be there, but this professor I'm shadowing is flying out early. Madrid first, then Cairo. I'll call you when I land, okay? Love you."*

Jordan had stared at her phone long after the message ended. She knew she left that message so she wouldn't have to lie to their grandparents when they ask if she had heard from Jessica, but she knew the truth, and it was getting harder to keep.

And Carolyn? Not even a message. Not since she married Evan and moved to Charlotte. Just a few scattered postcards and a birthday card that still smelled like someone else's perfume.

Jordan adjusted her cap and turned as a knock came at the door.

"You ready, baby girl?" Uncle Ronnie peeked in, beaming. "You're about to make us all cry in public."

Jordan smiled. "I'm ready."

Zena and Jake were already waiting in the hallway, Jake holding a bouquet of sunflowers and Zena dabbing her eyes with a tissue she pretended not to need.

As they stepped out into the hallway, Jordan nearly collided with someone coming from the opposite direction – Miles. He was with his family—his mother, his little sister – and Darrell, his best friend, trailed behind them holding a camera bag.

Jordan froze. So did Miles.

"Hey," she said, voice soft.

"Hey," Miles replied, eyes scanning her face. "You look... good."

"So do you." Jordan said nervously.

There was a pause. A long one. The kind that held everything they hadn't said.

Then Zena's voice called from behind her. "Jordan, come on, baby! We don't want to be late!"

And Miles's mother tugged his sleeve. "Let's go, sweetheart. We'll miss the shuttle."

They both turned away at the same time.

At the graduation ceremony, the crowd was a sea of caps and gowns, camera flashes, and proud families waving from the bleachers. Jordan had just crossed the stage, heart pounding. She scanned the crowd once, twice—no sign of Miles.

Then she saw him as she was walking back to her seat. He was across the aisle, already seated, staring straight at her. Their eyes locked, but were interrupted, by the President of Howard pronouncing them all the graduating class of 1999.

As everyone began mingling with their families, Jordan and Miles caught eyes again. This time, Miles began to approach her, Jordan opened her mouth—just slightly. But before she could move, Aaron appeared beside her, grinning.

"There she is!" he said, pulling her into a hug. "Top of the class and still the most beautiful woman here." He kissed her cheek—too close to her mouth. Jordan stiffened. Across the aisle, Miles turned away.

"Aaron," she said, pulling back. "Wait."

He blinked. "What's wrong?"

"I need to talk to you. Now." Jordan said, pulling him away from the crowd.

Jordan and Aaron stood beneath a tree near the edge of the quad, the sound of happy graduates and proud families echoing in the distance.

"I'm not going to New York," Jordan said.

Aaron stared. "Wait…What?"

"I asked to be reassigned. I'm taking the Georgetown placement."

Aaron stepped back. "You didn't even tell me you were thinking about that."

"I know. I should have. But I needed to make the decision for myself." Jordan responded looking down at her shoes and away from his eyes.

Aaron folded his arms. "So, what does that mean for us?"

Jordan hesitated. "I think… I think we've been holding onto something that doesn't fit anymore."

Aaron's jaw tightened. "You mean me."

"I mean us," she said gently. "You're brilliant, Aaron. And you're going to thrive in New York. But I can't follow you there. Not when I know I'm supposed to be here."

Aaron looked away. "Is this about Miles?"

"It's about me," Jordan said. "But yeah... maybe it's also about what I haven't let myself feel."

Aaron nodded slowly. "Okay. I wish you'd told me sooner."

"I know." Jordan replied, now looking in his eyes. "I'm really sorry Aaron, you are wonderful man, and you are going to be an amazing man for an incredibly lucky woman – I'm just not that woman."

Aaron wiped a tear from his eye, gave Jordan a kiss on the forehead and said, "I know we are meant to be together, but I will give you the space to figure that out as well, you will be back, and I will be waiting". Then he walked away without another word.

Jordan returned to her waiting family and searched the crowd, scanning every face. She checked the reception tent, even the parking lot. But Miles was gone. She stood on the sidewalk, cap in hand, the sun beginning to dip behind the trees. She whispered, "I should've said something." But the wind didn't answer. And neither did Miles.

The reception had thinned out. Folding chairs were being stacked, balloons deflated, and the last of the punch had gone warm in its bowl. Jordan stood near the edge of the lawn, her cap in one hand, her phone in the other, screen dark.

Jordan had already checked the tent. The parking lot. Even the side alley where the food trucks had been parked. No sign of Miles. She ran into to Darrell, who was packing up his camera gear near the steps of the arts building.

"Hey," Jordan said, trying to sound casual. "Did Miles leave already?"

Darrell looked up, surprised. "Yeah. Right after the ceremony. Said he had somewhere to be."

Jordan's heart sank. "Did he say where?"

Darrell shook his head. "Nah. He didn't really say much. Just dipped."

Jordan nodded, trying to hide the disappointment. "Okay. Thanks."

Darrell paused, then added, "He saw you, though. I know he did."

Jordan gave a tight smile. "Yeah. I saw him too."

Jordan left to rejoin her family. They went out to eat to celebrate, Jordan didn't have much of an appetite. Still, she pressed on through dinner, then returned to her apartment alone. Her family were staying at Zena's baby sister Jackie's house while they were in town.

The next morning, Jordan awoke to a quiet apartment again. Her gown hung over the back of a chair, and the bouquet from her grandpa Jake sat in a large mason jar on the windowsill. Jordan sat on the edge of her bed, still in her dress, phone in her lap. She opened her messages. Scrolled to Miles's name and typed: *"I saw you today. I wanted to talk. I should've said something sooner."*

Jordan stared at it. Deleted it. Typed again: *"I'm not going to New York. I stayed. I thought maybe you should know"*. She hovered over send. Then the door buzzed.

Jordan jumped, heart leaping. But when she opened it, it was Uncle Ronnie, holding a bag with breakfast and grinning.

"Figured you hadn't eaten," he said. "And I know you don't cook when you're stressed."

Jordan smiled, even as her chest ached. "You know me too well."

Ronnie handed her the bag. "You okay?"

Jordan hesitated. "I don't know."

Ronnie nodded. "That's alright. You don't have to know everything right now." Then gave her a hug and told her they were all having dinner later that day at Aunt Jackie's before they headed out in the morning.

Jordan promised she would be there and thanked her uncle again for the breakfast, then closed the door behind him and sat back down, the silence pressing in again. She opened her phone one more time and typed: *"If you ever want to talk... I'm here."*

This time, she hit send. The message went through. No reply. Not yet, but Jordan was not going to stop trying to undo one of the biggest mistakes of her life.

# Chapter Twenty-Five

## (Jessica)
## What You Won't Do for Drugs

Two months had passed since Jessica promised she was done with the club. She'd looked Bryce in the eye, held his hand, and said the words like she meant them.

"I'm done. I swear. Just IHOP and home. That's it."

But something in her had shifted. She was more distracted. Forgetful. Her stories didn't line up. She'd say she worked a double but come home without tips. She'd forget what night she said she was off. And BJ—he'd started waking up crying when she came home, like he could smell the lie on her skin.

Bryce tried to believe her. He wanted to. But the doubt kept growing. And then came the night he stopped by IHOP. The manager blinked at him, confused. "Jessica? She hasn't worked here in over a month."

Bryce didn't speak. He just turned and walked out, his hands shaking. When he arrived at the club, the parking lot was full. The bass thudded through the walls like a pulse. Bryce parked crooked, didn't lock the door. He didn't care. Amina was watching BJ.

The bouncers at the front froze when they saw him. "Yo, Bryce—"

Bryce didn't stop. Just shoved past them and stormed down the hallway, past the velvet curtain, past the dressing rooms, straight to the back office. He didn't knock. He kicked the door open. And there she was – Jessica. High. Naked and straddling Joe.

Jessica gasped and tried to cover herself, scrambling off Joe's lap and falling to the floor. Her eyes were glassy, her lipstick smeared. She looked up at Bryce like she didn't recognize him. Joe didn't flinch. He leaned back in his chair, puffing on a cigar, smoke curling around his grin.

"I know you're not scheduled tonight," Joe said calmly. "Why don't you head home? I'll send Jessica along when I'm done."

Bryce's vision went red. He lunged. Joe was faster. The .9mm was already in his hand, aimed steady.

"Easy now," Joe murmured. "You wouldn't want that boy of yours growing up without a father, would you?"

Jessica sobbed, clutching her clothes to her chest. "Bryce, please… I did this for us."

Bryce's voice cracked, raw and furious. "You call this love? You're high, naked, screwing my boss—and that's for us?"

Joe chuckled, slow and cruel. "She made her choice, son. You weren't enough. She needed someone who could really take care of her."

Bryce stared at Jessica, his heart breaking in real time. She couldn't meet his eyes. He backed away slowly, hands raised, chest heaving.

"I loved you," he whispered. "I would've done anything for you."

Jessica's sobs deepened. "I know."

But it was too late. Bryce turned and walked out, the door swinging shut behind him.

Joe exhaled a long stream of smoke and looked down at Jessica. "You want to keep lying to yourself, or are you ready to admit what you are?"

Jessica didn't answer. She just curled into herself on the floor, shaking.

That night, something in Jessica broke. She didn't go home. She didn't call. She stayed with Joe. Jessica showed up at the club the next night, and the next, and the next. She kept dancing. Kept taking the pills. Kept telling herself it was temporary. That she was in control. That she could stop whenever she wanted. But Joe knew better. And before long, he had her entirely. She returned to the apartment when Bryce wasn't home and grabbed her clothes. She left Bryce. Left BJ. And followed Joe to Miami.

Jessica stood at the departure gate at Hartfield airport, sunglasses hiding the bruises beneath her eyes. Joe's hand rested on the small of her back, firm and possessive.

"You sure about this?" she asked, voice barely above a whisper.

Joe didn't look at her. "You already made your choice."

Jessica nodded, swallowing the lump in her throat.

"Where's my phone?" she asked.

Joe smiled without warmth. "You won't need it where we're going."

When Bryce returned home and saw that Jessica's clothes were missing, he headed back to the club and stormed through the front doors, fists clenched. The bouncers didn't stop him this time. They just looked away. He found Joe's second-in-command behind the bar.

"Where is she?" Bryce demanded.

The man didn't blink. "She's gone."

"Gone where?" He quizzed.

The man stopped wiping down the bar and said bluntly, "Miami."

Bryce's voice cracked. "She left her son?"

The man shrugged. "She left a lot of things."

That night, Bryce packed a bag and headed to Jessica's grandparent's house in North Carolina. BJ slept in the back seat, his tiny fists curled against his chest. Bryce gripped the steering wheel, eyes burning from the long drive. The highway stretched ahead, dark and endless. He hadn't stopped since Atlanta. He couldn't. Not until he got to them.

Bryce rehearsed the words in his head, over and over. *She's gone. She left. I didn't know what else to do.* When Bryce arrived at Zena and Jake's house in North Carolina, it was early in the morning. He paused outside the door, contemplating his decision to drive hundreds of miles to show up unannounced on the doorstep of his missing girlfriend's grandparents.

Bryce knocked softly at first, then harder. He didn't want to startle them, but he had come all this way, he couldn't turn back now. Zena opened the door in her robe, startled to see a young man standing there, holding a baby carrier.

"Can I help you?" she asked cautiously.

Bryce's voice was hoarse. "You don't know me. I'm Bryce. I'm... I'm Jessica's—was Jessica's boyfriend."

Jake appeared behind Zena, frowning. "What's going on?"

Bryce took a breath. "I need to talk to you. Please. It's about Jessica."

Zena stepped aside slowly. "Come in."

Bryce entered, gently setting the carrier on the floor. BJ stirred, blinking up at the unfamiliar room.

Jake's voice was sharp. "Where is she?"

Bryce looked down. "She's gone. She left two weeks ago. With a man named Joe. Her boss. They went to Miami."

Zena's hand flew to her mouth. "What do you mean, gone?"

"She left everything. Me. Our son." Bryce replied.

Jake's eyes narrowed. "Your son?"

Bryce nodded. "His name is Bryce Jr. We call him BJ."

Zena stared at the baby, stunned. "She had a baby. And didn't tell us?"

"I wanted her to," Bryce said quickly. "I begged her to. She said she would. She kept saying she needed more time."

Jake's voice was tight. "And you're just now coming to us?"

"I didn't know what else to do," Bryce said. "I thought she'd come back. I thought she just needed space. But she's not coming back. And I can't do this alone."

Zena knelt beside the carrier, tears in her eyes. "He looks just like her."

BJ reached for her finger, and she let him wrap his tiny hand around it.

Jake sat down slowly, processing. "Tell us everything."

Bryce did. The club. The pills. The lies. That night he found her. The gun. The silence that followed. When he finished, Zena was crying.

"She's our granddaughter," she whispered. "And we didn't even know she was a mother."

Jake looked at Bryce. "You did the right thing coming here."

Bryce's voice cracked. "I just want her to be okay. I want her to come home."

Zena lifted BJ into her arms, holding him close. "We'll help you raise him. And we'll find her."

Jake nodded. "Whatever it takes."

Bryce sat back, exhausted. "Thank you."

Zena kissed BJ's forehead. "You're not alone anymore."

# Chapter Twenty-Six

## (Carolyn)
## Don't Wake Me I'm Dreaming

Evan had become even more dangerous than before—agitated by the smallest perceived offense, and far more calculated in his fury. One day, Carolyn had gone to the country club for a spa day, a rare indulgence after weeks of walking a careful line. Afterward, she slipped into the pool, to cool off. The sun was high, the pool glinting like a jewel set into the manicured lawn of the club.

Carolyn stretched out on a lounge chair, her skin warm, her limbs loose from the massage she'd just indulged in. She wore the red bikini Evan had bought her in St. Barts—barely-there fabric, gold accents, the kind of thing that made her feel like a woman in a perfume ad. For a moment, she let herself enjoy it.

Compliments floated her way like petals.
"Looking good, Mrs. Mitchell." The waiter said, bringing her a cocktail. "Red's your color."

Carolyn smiled, polite but distant. She didn't notice Evan watching from the edge of the golf course, his club frozen mid-swing, his jaw clenched so tight it looked carved from stone. He saw the way men looked at her. Heard the laughter. The way she tilted her head back, carefree. He was there with friends, halfway through the back nine when the mask slipped instantly. He stormed across the deck, rage boiling beneath his skin.

"Get up." He barked.

Carolyn blinked, startled. Evan stood over her, eyes blazing. "What—Evan, I—"

"I said get up." He demanded again, this time with more force.

Before Carolyn could even react, Evan grabbed her arm, yanking her off the chair so violently her sunglasses flew off. Gasps echoed around the pool deck. A few staff rushed forward, but Evan blew past them, dragging Carolyn through the club.

"Evan, stop! You're hurting me—" Carolyn pleaded.

"You think this is a game?" Evan hissed, dragging her toward the parking lot. "You think you can flaunt yourself like that? Let men drool over what's mine?"

"Evan, please—" Carolyn pleaded again.

A staff member stepped forward. "Sir, I'm going to have to ask you to—"

Evan shoved him aside like a rag doll. "Touch me again and I'll bury you."

Carolyn stumbled, trying to keep up, her arm burning where his fingers dug in. "You're making a scene—". She whined.

"You made the scene. Now you're going to pay for it." he snapped, tossing her into the car like a discarded bag.

The car peeled out of the lot, tires screaming.

"Evan, slow down—please—" Carolyn begged.

Evan didn't speak. His knuckles were white on the wheel. His silence was worse than shouting. It was the silence of a man who had already decided what came next. He drove recklessly—swerving through tight curves, tires screaming, Carolyn's heart lodged in her throat.

Her voice cracked. "Let's just talk. Pull over, we can—"

"Shut up." He retorted.

Carolyn flinched.

"You think I don't see what you're doing?" Evan growled. "You think I don't know what you are?"

"I haven't done anything—" Carolyn responded in a voice dripping with fear.

"You behave like a whore and wonder why men look at you." Evan spat between clenched teeth.

Tears welled in Carolyn's eyes. "Evan, please—" Carolyn begged.

Evan slammed on the brakes in front of the house. The door flew open. Before Carolyn could move, he was at her side, dragging her out by the hair.

Mrs. Greene was on her porch when Evan dragged Carolyn out of the car like she weighed nothing. She had lived next door to Evan's property for nearly twenty years. She was the kind of woman who never missed a garbage day, never let her garden go wild, and never failed to notice when something felt *off*.

When Evan first bought the house next to her, she was just glad to see the old place restored.

Evan's return had brought fresh paint, manicured hedges, and a flashy car that glinted like a warning. And his new wife—Carolyn—she was elegant, polished, the kind of woman who could make heads turn in church, even if she never stepped inside. But Mrs. Greene had seen too much in her lifetime not to recognize the warning signs.

The stiff smile. The bruises hidden under cardigans, even in the heat. The way Carolyn flinched at loud noises. The silence that fell over the house like a curtain after the sun went down. Then came the night she heard the screaming. She knew then that this day would come. And when it did, she was ready.

"Evan Mitchell, you let go of that woman right now!" Mrs. Greene shouted.

Evan didn't even blink. Carolyn's knees scraped the pavement as she pleaded for help. "Please—someone—".

Phones were out. Neighbors shouted. But Evan didn't stop. He dragged her through the front door and slammed it shut behind them. Mrs. Greene had called 911 before he even crossed the threshold.

"911, what's your emergency?" the operator asked.

"It's happening. He's going to kill her. You need to get here now." Mrs. Greene screamed into phone.

Inside the House, the silence was thick. Carolyn tried to crawl, but he kicked her hard in the ribs. Carolyn's cries were muffled, broken. The neighbors had shouted for him to stop, phones in hand, but Evan didn't care. Didn't even hesitate. He had stormed inside with Carolyn in tow, as if none of them were even there.

The moment the door shut, the violence had begun. Evan didn't yell. He didn't threaten. He simply broke. His fists landed hard and without pause—punches, kicks, stomps. He flung Carolyn like an object, her body crashing into walls, over tables, into silence. When she tried to crawl, he dragged her by her hair across the floor.

"You humiliated me," he said, voice eerily calm.

Carolyn tried again to reason with him "Evan" He punched her again. Once. Twice. Carolyn hit the other wall, then the floor. Her vision blurred.

"You think you're smarter than me?" he snarled, dragging her by her arms now. "You think I don't know about the phone? The pictures?" Carolyn's heart stopped. He knew. He tore the bikini from her body, twisting the fabric tightly around her neck.

"You want to be looked at?" he hissed. "Let's see how they look at you now."

As Carolyn lay gasping, broken, and stripped of everything but pain, a strange calm settled in. She wasn't thinking of herself. She thought of her girls—the ones she'd wounded with coldness and pride. She thought of Jesse. Her parents. All the people she'd cut down in the name of survival.

*Is this what I deserve?* she wondered. *Is this my penance for the mess I made of every life I touched?* Carolyn's world narrowed to sound: the thud of fists, the crack of bone, the rasp of her own breath. The darkness came for her like an old friend. Then nothing. Just a whisper in her mind: *God forgive me. And please take care of my babies.*

Moments later, the police arrived, and flashing lights painted the street in red and blue, Mrs. Green stood on her porch, hands trembling—not with surprise, but fury. Because she had known. And this time, she had made sure *someone* was listening. She just hoped that they were not too late. The door burst open.

"Police! Get down!"

Evan turned, wild-eyed, blood on his hands. Officers tackled him to the ground.

Paramedics rushed in. "She's not breathing!"

"Start compressions—now!"

The defibrillator whined. Carolyn's body jerked. Flatline.

"Again."

Carolyn's body jerked with another jolt…nothing.

"Again."

Then—faint. A pulse.

"Let's move!" One the paramedics shouted rushing Carolyn to the ambulance waiting outside. Somehow, they got a pulse. They rushed her to the hospital, machines breathing for her, but no one expected her to survive the night. Doctors feverishly worked to try to repair Carolyn's broken body, while she lingered in between life and death.

*It feels like I am sinking through the bed, and everything is getting further away.* Carolyn thought floating somewhere between the sterile beep of machines and a silence too vast to hold.

Carolyn couldn't move—she didn't feel pain exactly, only the suggestion of her body outlined in bruises and shame. Thoughts drips slowly, like water off a faucet no one remembers to shut off. There's no time here. Just fragments.

*A red bikini. The smell of cheap perfume and fried shrimp from that beach bar in Curaçao. Evan's hand. Her mother's hands. The sound of her own laugh—back when it was easy.* And then: *the girls.*

Faces flash behind her eyes—her daughters, wild and small, running barefoot across porch steps she can't quite place anymore. One turns to look at her—angry, maybe. Or afraid. Carolyn wants to speak, but her mouth doesn't work here. Still, the guilt pulses. Heavy and rhythmic. *What kind of mother...*

Carolyn sees Jesse's silhouette, hands trembling, holding a letter he never opened. Her parents' eyes filled with something harder than disappointment—something like sorrow edged with steel. And somewhere beneath it all, the version of herself she used to be, before control became a game and love felt like leverage.

*Is this penance?* She's not sure if she's speaking to God or to herself. Doesn't matter. It echoes the same. And still... the smallest flicker inside her refuses to dim. A question, a tether: *Am I too far gone? Or is there still something left worth crawling back for?*

The monitor continues its lonely chant. Somewhere, someone is willing to wake her up.

And deep in the folds of her broken mind, a whisper stirs—*not yet*

# Chapter Twenty-Seven

## (Carolyn)
## From Dreams to Nightmares

The machines beeped steadily, indifferent to the wreckage they surrounded. Tubes snaked from Carolyn's arms. Her face was swollen, lips split, one eye still sealed shut. Her body was a map of bruises and brokenness. But she was alive. Barely.

The nurse at the front desk made the call. "Next of kin. Parents. Jake and Zena Alexander."

The call came in to Zena and Jake's home in late afternoon. The house was unusually full. Bryce was in the den, bouncing BJ gently on his knee while Ronnie stirred a pot of gumbo in the kitchen, humming low. Zena sat at the table folding laundry, and Jake was outside, trimming the hedges before the sun dipped too low.

The phone rang. Zena answered on the second ring. "Hello?"

"Mrs. Alexander? This is Presbyterian Hospital. Your daughter, Carolyn Mitchell, has been admitted. She's in critical condition."

Zena's hand flew to her chest. "What happened?"

"She was assaulted by her husband. She was found unresponsive. She's stable now, but… it was severe." The nurse answered.

Zena's voice cracked. "We're on our way." She stood abruptly, the phone still in her hand.

Ronnie turned from the stove. "Mama? What is it?"

Jake stepped in from the porch, wiping his hands on a rag. "Everything alright?"

Zena looked at them both, her voice trembling. "It's Carolyn. She's in the hospital. Critical condition. They said… it was an assault."

Jake's face darkened. "Who?"

Zena hesitated. Then said : "It was him. Evan."

Jake's jaw clenched. "That son of a—" He stopped himself, but the fury in his eyes said everything. "I should've killed him the first time," he muttered. "I knew he'd come back around. I knew."

Ronnie's voice was low, steady. "Let's not waste time talking about what we should've done. Let's go."

Bryce stood, holding BJ close. "Do you want me to stay here with the baby?"

Zena shook her head. "No. You come too. You're family now."

Bryce blinked, surprised—but nodded. "I'll pack a bag for the baby," he said, already moving.
Jake grabbed the keys. "Let's go get our daughter."

Inside her hospital room, Carolyn didn't wake. But inside her mind, something stirred. She stood barefoot in a hospital gown, surrounded by a flickering wall of television screens. Each one played a different scene—some soft and golden, others jagged and gray.

On one screen: a beach in Curaçao. Evan laughing, handing her a drink. Her daughters building sandcastles nearby. The life she wanted. She smiled. Then the screen went black.

A second version of herself stepped into view— dressed in black leather, eyes sharp, mouth curled in something between pity and contempt. "Let's not lie to ourselves," the other Carolyn said, and changed the channel.

Now: a memory. Carolyn at the door, suitcase in hand. Jordan silent, arms crossed. Jessica screaming, sobbing, reaching for her mother.

"Don't go, Mommy! Please!"

Carolyn didn't turn back. She just kept walking.

The real Carolyn—watching—sank to her knees.

"No," she whispered. "I didn't mean to—"

The other Carolyn clicked the remote again.

Now: Jordan, older, wiping blood from her sister's nose after a fight. Jessica curled up on the couch, eyes hollow.

"You left them," the other Carolyn said. "You chose men. You chose escape. You chose yourself."

"I didn't know how to stay," Carolyn whispered.

"You didn't try." The other one shot back.

In the waiting room, Jake paced. Zena sat with her hands clasped so tightly her knuckles were white. Ronnie stood by the window, arms crossed, watching the parking lot like he expected Evan to show up.

Bryce sat quietly in the corner, BJ asleep in his arms.

"She's going to pull through," Zena said, as if saying it enough would make it true.

Jake didn't answer.

"She's still our daughter." Zena continued.

"She was our daughter the first time he hit her," Jake snapped. "And she went back."

Zena's voice broke. "She thought he changed."

Jake turned away, fists clenched. "I should've dragged her out of that house myself."

Ronnie spoke, calm but firm. "You can't carry that. Not now."

Jake's eyes filled with tears he refused to let fall. "I just want her to come back."

Bryce looked up. "She's lucky to have you. Both of you."

Zena turned to him, her voice soft. "We're lucky to have you, too."

Inside Carolyn's mind, the screens flickered faster now—memories colliding.

Jessica's                                    sadness.
Jordan's                                     silence.
Jesse's                                      arrest.

Her parents' disappointment.

And then—one final screen. Carolyn, older. Alone. Watching her daughters from a distance as they laugh with someone else. A family she's no longer part of.

The other Carolyn turned to her. "You can still change the ending," she said. "But you have to wake up."

Carolyn reached for the screen. And somewhere, in the real world, her fingers twitched. She couldn't open her eyes. Couldn't move. Couldn't speak. But she was awake. Somewhere between pain and paralysis, she hovered—listening. The steady beep of the monitor beside her, the low hum of machines doing what her lungs couldn't. And the voices.

Her parents. Jake's voice was thick, low with worry. Zena's was gentler, brittle in the way only heartbreak could make it. They were on the phone, speaking softly—too softly to know she was listening.

*Jessica had vanished. Gone off with that man from the club. Left Bryce. Left the baby. And Jordan... Jordan had ruined the only real love she'd known. Sabotaged it out of fear. Out of pain.*
The tears came silently, slipping from Carolyn's eyes and soaking into her pillow.

*My babies...*

So much damage. So many consequences planted with her own hands. When she and Jesse were together, raising those girls—that was the truest peace she'd ever known. But it wasn't enough. She had wanted more. More sparkle, more power, more everything. She'd urged Jesse to keep pushing—to keep selling. To chase a dream that wasn't theirs to catch. And when the walls caved in, he went to prison. She went chasing fantasy.

She married a monster. And now, her girls were lost in their own spirals.

*God,* she thought, *don't let this be the end of the story. If You bring me back,* she prayed, *I swear I'll spend what life I have left making it right. For Jessica. For Jordan. For Jesse. For Mama, Daddy and Ronnie. Just give me a chance to try.*

And in that moment, surrounded by the sterile hush of machines, Carolyn made her first promise in years that she truly meant.

It was strange, this in-between place—like drifting underwater in a body she barely recognized. Carolyn couldn't open her eyes. Couldn't move. But her thoughts pressed in sharp and unrelenting, louder than the machines hissing beside her.

Her chest ached—not just from the broken ribs or the weight of tubes, but from the ache of *knowing.* She'd heard everything. *Jessica is missing.* Caught in the gravity of the same hunger Carolyn once wore like perfume. And Jordan— sabotaging her own happiness out of fear she'd been taught, not born with. *What have I passed down to them?*

A cry Carolyn couldn't voice curled in her throat. She thought about Jesse. About how he'd wanted out. He had begged her—*let's just build something real, raise our girls, stay clean.* But she wasn't ready to give up the shine. And because of her, he'd gone deeper into the game. Because of her, he was locked up. Because of her, their family had shattered. And now their daughters were lost. One vanished into someone else's control. The other pushing away the one person who might have loved her whole.

Carolyn wanted to scream, but all that came were tears. Quiet ones. Hot and steady. They slipped from beneath lashes that wouldn't open and soaked into bandages that had become her second skin. If she ever opened her eyes again, it couldn't be to more pretending.

*God,* she thought, *I don't deserve another chance. But if You give it to me—if I wake up and speak again—I'll spend what time I've got left making it right. For them. For Jesse. For Mama and Daddy. I swear it. Just don't let this be how it ends.*

And somewhere deep beneath the drugs, the pain, the breath machines, a flicker stirred in her chest. A promise trying to become a heartbeat.

# Chapter Twenty-Eight

## (Jordan)
## The Call That Split the Sky

Jordan was halfway through unpacking a box of books when her phone rang. She'd just moved into her new apartment near Georgetown's campus—bare walls, fresh paint, a stack of unopened mail on the counter. The sun was setting outside, casting long shadows across the floor.

She didn't recognize the number. "Hello?"

"Jordan?" Bryce's voice was tight. Raw.

She froze. "Yeah. What's wrong?"

There was a pause. Then: "I'm in North Carolina. At your grandparents' house."

Jordan sat down slowly. "Wait—what? Why?"

"It's Jessica," he said. "She's gone."

Jordan's heart dropped. "Gone where?"

"Miami. With Joe." Bryce stated.

She blinked. "Joe? The club owner?"

"Yeah." Bryce replied.

Jordan stood, pacing. "I thought she quit. She told me she was done."

"She told me that too," Bryce said. "But she never stopped. She just got better at hiding it."

Jordan's voice cracked. "She left BJ?"

"She left both of us." Bryce

198

Silence. Then Bryce added, "I told your grandparents everything. About the baby. About the club. About the pills. They didn't even know she had a child."

Jordan closed her eyes. "They didn't know because she made me promise not to tell them. She said she'd do it herself. I didn't know about the club, Bryce. I swear."

"I believe you," he said quietly. "But it's all out now."

Jordan sank onto the couch, her voice barely a whisper. "How's BJ?"

"He's okay. Ms. Zena's holding him right now. Mr. Jake's… trying to hold it together."

Jordan nodded, tears stinging her eyes. "I should've told them. I should've done something."

"You did what you could," Bryce said. "We all did."

There was a pause. "There's more," he added.

Jordan braced herself. "What?"

"It's your mom. Ms. Carolyn. She's in the hospital. Critical condition. Her husband Evan beat her. Bad."

Jordan's breath caught. "What?"

"She's in a coma. They found her unresponsive. Ms. Zena and Mr. Jake got the call while I was here."

Jordan's voice broke. "Jesus Christ."

"I'm sorry," Bryce said. "I didn't know who else to call."

Jordan wiped her face. "No, you did the right thing. Thank you."

"I also called Amina when Jessica disappeared," he added. "Asked if she'd heard from her. She hadn't. She's worried too."

Jordan nodded, her voice hollow. "Call her again and see if there is any news. Tell her what happened to our mother."

"Okay." Bryce said.

They sat in silence for a moment, the weight of everything pressing down.

Then Bryce said, "I don't know what happens next."

Jordan looked out the window, the sky darkening. "Neither do I." "But I'm coming home."

Meanwhile, Bryce called Amina to fill her in on what was going on. Amina answered on the first ring. "Bryce?"

"Yeah. I just wanted to check in. See if you've heard from Jess." Bryce asked.

"No," Amina said, her voice tight. "Not since she left for that 'extra shift' two weeks ago. I knew something was off."

"She's in Miami," Bryce said. "With Joe."

Amina cursed under her breath. "That bastard."

"She left BJ. Left me. Just disappeared." Bryce snapped.

Amina was quiet for a moment, the responded softly. "I'm so sorry."

"There's more," Bryce said. "Ms. Carolyn's in a coma. Her husband Evan put her in the hospital."

Amina gasped. "What?"

"I'm in North Carolina with her parents. With BJ. It's… a lot."

Amina's voice softened. "You're not alone, Bryce. Whatever you need—say the word."

"Thanks," he said. "I might take you up on that."

Say less, I am on my way. Send me the address. Amina said, jotting down the address. After getting the ok from Zena and Jake, Amina headed to North Carolina.

Meanwhile, back in D.C., Jordan sat on the floor, knees pulled to her chest, phone still in her hand. Her mother was in a coma. Her sister was missing. Her nephew was in North Carolina with a man she barely knew, and yet somehow trusted more than most. She had stayed behind to build a life. And now everything she'd left behind was unraveling.

Jordan opened her messages. Scrolled to Jessica's name and typed: *Where are you? Please come home. We need you.* She hit send. No reply. Just silence. Jordan stared at the screen, then whispered to the empty room: "Don't disappear on me too."

Jordan sat on the edge of her bed, suitcase open but untouched. Her hands trembled as she typed the message to Miles, the weight of everything pressing down on her chest like a stone.

*Hey. I know it's late, and I don't even know if you'll want to hear from me. But I wanted to tell you what's going on.* She paused, then continued: *Jessica's missing. She left for Miami with someone dangerous. She left her son behind. And... my mom—Carolyn—she's in a coma. Evan beat her. She's at Presbyterian Hospital in Charlotte. I'm heading to North Carolina to be with my family. I just… thought you should know.*

Jordan stared at the message, then added: *I'm sorry for everything. I never should've let you go the way I did.* She hit send. Then she packed.

In North Carolina, the house was heavy with grief and motion. Jordan arrived just after midnight, Amina arrived at the same time. They hugged and exchanged greetings, before walking in the house together. Zena met them at the door, pulling Jordan into a long, silent hug, and giving Amina a welcome hug as well. Jake stood behind her, his eyes tired but warm.

Bryce was in the living room, BJ asleep on his chest. Ronnie sat nearby, flipping through a notebook filled with names and numbers—contacts, leads, anything that might help them find Jessica.

Jordan knelt beside Bryce. "Hey."

He looked up, eyes red. "Hey."

She gently touched BJ's back. "He's gotten so big."

"He asks for her in his sleep," Bryce whispered. "He doesn't know what's happening, but he knows something's wrong."

Jordan nodded, swallowing the lump in her throat. "We'll find her."

The next morning, the family made the drive to Charlotte. Carolyn lay motionless in the hospital bed, machines humming softly around her. Her face was still bruised, her body still broken—but she was alive.

Jordan sat beside her, holding her mother's hand.

"I'm here," she whispered. "We're all here."

Behind Jordan, Zena stood with Jake and Ronnie. Amina helped Bryce with BJ in the hallway, rocking him gently. Then the door opened. Jordan turned. Miles stood there. She blinked, stunned.

"You came." She said softly.

Miles nodded, stepping inside. "You said your family needed you. That means they need me too." Jordan's eyes filled. "I didn't expect—"

"I know," Miles said softly. "But I'm here." Jordan stood and walked into his arms. He held her without asking for anything in return.

The next day, the family visited Jesse in prison. The visiting room buzzed with quiet tension. Jesse sat on one side of the glass, arms crossed, jaw tight. He hadn't seen Jordan in months. When she walked in, he stood before he even realized it, eyes scanning her face. She looked older. Tired. Like she'd been carrying something too heavy for too long.

Jordan picked up the phone. Jesse did the same.

"Hey, baby girl," he said, trying to smile.

"Hi, Daddy." Jessica replied, attempting the same.

Jesse studied her. "What's going on?"

Jordan hesitated. Then said, "It's Jessica."

Jesse's brow furrowed. "What about her?"

"She's missing." Jordan blurted out, not being able to hold anything any longer.

Jesse stood up. "Missing?"

"She left two weeks ago. Took off to Miami with a man named Joe." Jordan responded.

Jesse's eyes narrowed and he sat down hard in his seat. "Joe who?"

"Joe—the club owner. She was working for him." Jordan answered, fearing having to tell him the rest of the story.

Jesse blinked. "Working how?"

Jordan's voice dropped. "She was dancing. Stripping."

Jesse stared at her, stunned. "Jessica? My Jessica?"

Jordan nodded. "She didn't tell anyone. Not even me. She said she was working at IHOP. But she was living a double life."

Jesse's voice was hoarse. "Why would she do that?"

"She was trying to help. To survive. But she got in too deep. Pills. Lies. Joe had her wrapped around his finger." Jordan answered, information now flowing out of her like a waterfall.

Jesse leaned back, shaking his head. "I didn't even know she was in trouble."

"There's more," Jordan said, her voice trembling. "She had a baby. A son. His name is Bryce Jr. We call him BJ."

Jesse's mouth fell open. "She had a child?"
Jordan nodded. "With her boyfriend, Bryce. He's here. He brought BJ to Grandma Zena and Grandpa Jake."

Jesse's hands trembled. "I didn't even know she had a boyfriend."

"I know," Jordan whispered. "None of us did. Not really. Her friend Amina came up from Atlanta to help out as well."

Jesse stood, pacing behind the glass, dragging his hand down his face. "She had a baby. She was stripping. She's missing. And I'm sitting in here like a damn ghost."

Jordan's voice cracked. "You couldn't have known."

"I should've known something," he snapped. "I should've been there. I should've—" He stopped, breathing hard.

"There's more," Jordan said quietly.

Jesse turned slowly. "What now?"

"It's Mama. Evan beat her. Bad. She's in a coma. They found her unresponsive. She's at Presbyterian in Charlotte."

Jesse's face twisted in rage. "That bastard. I told her. I told her he'd do it again."

Jordan nodded. "We all did."

Jesse slammed his fist against the glass. "And now my daughter's missing, my grandson's been abandoned, and my ex's in a hospital bed fighting for her life?"

Jordan's eyes filled. "Yes."

Jesse sat down slowly, the fight draining from his face. "I failed all of you."

"No," Jordan said. "You're still our father. And we need you to know what's happening. We need your strength."

Jesse looked up, with glassy eyes. "Where's the baby now?"

"With Grandma Zena. She and Amina are helping Bryce take care of him."

Jesse nodded slowly. "Good. That boy's got guts, showing up like that."

Jordan hesitated. "Miles is here too."

Jesse blinked. "Miles?"

"He came to be with me. With us. He's helping look for Jessica."

Jesse studied her. "I thought you broke that boy's heart."

"I did," she whispered. "And he came anyway."

Jesse leaned forward, voice low and fierce. "Then don't make the same mistake twice." He looked past her, locking eyes with Miles, who stood quietly behind the glass.

"You," Jesse said, pointing.

Miles stepped forward and picked up the receiver.

"You take care of my daughter. You hear me?" Jesse instructed

"Yes, sir. I will." Miles promised.

Jesse nodded, jaw tight. "Good. Because I may be in here, but I'm still their father. And I don't care how far-gone Jessica is—we don't give up on family."

Jordan wiped her eyes. "We won't."

Jesse leaned back, voice thick. "You find her. You bring her home. And when she walks through that door, you tell her, her daddy's waiting."

# Chapter Twenty-Nine

## (Jordan)
## The Search Party

The drive to Atlanta was quiet, heavy with unspoken fears. Jordan sat in the backseat of Jake's truck, staring out the window as the miles blurred past. Miles sat beside her, their hands brushing but not quite holding, Zena sitting in front beside her husband. In the car behind them, Bryce and BJ rode with Ronnie and Amina.

They arrived just after sunset. Bryce's apartment was small, but clean. Amina's was just across the hall. Between the two, they made space—air mattresses, borrowed blankets, and the kind of closeness that only grief and desperation can forge.

The Next Morning, they went to the authorities for help. The fluorescent lights buzzed overhead as the family sat in a row of plastic chairs in the Atlanta Police Department, waiting. Amina had called ahead, explained everything. A missing woman. Dangerous man. History of drug use. A child left behind.

Finally, a detective stepped out. Mid-forties, tired eyes, badge clipped to his belt.

"Jessica Alexander?" he asked.

Jordan stood. "Yes. She's my sister."

He nodded. "Come with me."

They crowded into a small interview room—Jordan, Miles, Ronnie, Zena, Jake, and Amina. Bryce had stayed behind at the apartment to take care of BJ.

The detective sat across from them, flipping open a notepad, then asked "When was the last time anyone saw her?"

"Two weeks ago," Jordan said. "She left with a man named Joe. He owns a club here. She was working for him."

"She left her child behind," Zena added, voice trembling. "She didn't take anything. No phone calls. No contact since."

The detective scribbled something down. "Any indication she was in danger when she left?"

"She was high," Amina said. "She'd been using. Joe had her wrapped around his finger."

"She didn't leave because she wanted to," Jordan said. "She left because she didn't think she had a choice."

The detective sighed. "Look, I understand you're worried. But Jessica's an adult. If she left of her own free will, there's not much we can do."

Jake's voice was sharp. "She left her baby. That doesn't sound like free will to me."

"She's vulnerable," Ronnie added. "And she's with a man who's known to exploit women."

The detective held up a hand. "I get it. I do. But unless there's evidence of a crime—proof she's being held against her will—we can't open a formal investigation."

Jordan's voice cracked. "So, we just wait? Hope she turns up?"

"I can file a welfare check," the detective offered. "But if she tells us she's fine, that's the end of it."

Zena stood, her voice steel. "If something happens to my granddaughter, and you could've helped—her blood is on your hands."

The detective didn't respond.

That Night, back at the apartments, the family gathered in Amina's living room, maps and notepads spread across the coffee table. Ronnie had already started compiling a list of clubs Joe was known to frequent. Amina was texting old coworkers. Miles was scrolling through social media, looking for any trace of Jessica.

"She's out there," Jordan said quietly. "I can feel it."

Jake nodded. "Then we keep looking. With or without the police."

Zena placed a hand on Jordan's shoulder. "We're not leaving this city without knowing what happened to her. Someone here knows where he took her in Miami."

Miles looked up. "Then let's start tomorrow. Club by club. Door by door. Whatever it takes."

Jordan met his eyes. "Thank you. For being here."

He reached for her hand. This time, she didn't pull away.

The next morning, Atlanta was already sweating under the weight of summer. The family split into teams—Jordan, Bryce, and Miles took the east side, Ronnie and Amina the west. Zena and

Jake stayed behind to make calls, coordinate, and care for BJ. "He needs to be close," Zena had said. "He needs to be here when she comes home."

They started with the clubs. Jordan stood outside a narrow brick building with blacked-out windows and a flickering neon sign that read *Velvet Room*. She hesitated.

"You okay?" Miles asked.

She nodded. "Yeah. Just... I hate that I'm looking for clues about my sister in places like this."

Miles opened the door. "Then let's find out where he took her and get her out."

Inside, the air was thick with stale perfume and last night's regret. A woman behind the bar looked up, suspicious.

"We're not here for trouble," Bryce said. "We're looking for someone. Jessica Alexander. She used to dance at Club Lux, but we think she might've been brought here."

The woman's eyes narrowed. "You cops?"

"No," Jordan said. "Family."

The woman studied them for a minute, then shook her head. "Haven't seen her. But if she's with Joe, she's not coming here. He keeps his girls close."

Jordan's stomach turned. "Do you know where he might've taken her?"

The woman hesitated. "He's got a place in Buck head and another in Decatur. Private. Real quiet. But I didn't tell you that."

Jordan nodded. "Thank you."

They left a flyer with Jessica's photo and their contact info, then stepped back into the heat.

Miles looked at her. "Buckhead?"

Jordan nodded. "Let's go."

Meanwhile Ronnie and Amina were also looking for clues. Ronnie leaned against the hood of his car, watching Amina argue with a bouncer outside a club called *The Den*. The man was stone-faced, arms crossed.

"She's not here," he said. "And even if she was, I wouldn't tell you."

"She's missing," Amina snapped. "She's not just some girl who skipped town. She left her baby. She's in danger We know Joe took her to Miami, we just need an address or potential places to look."

Ronnie stepped forward, voice calm but firm. "Look, man. I know how this works. I know about Joe. I know what he does. We're not trying to blow up your spot. We just want to bring my niece home."

The bouncer looked at him, then at Amina. Something in his expression shifted.

"She was here. A few weeks ago. Looked rough. Joe picked her up himself. Said he was taking her out of town."

"Where?" Amina asked.

"Didn't say. But he had a driver. Black Escalade. Georgia plates. That's all I got."

Ronnie nodded. "Thanks."

They walked back to the car in silence.

"She's slipping through our fingers," Amina said.

Ronnie shook his head. "Not yet. We're getting closer."

Back at the Apartment that night, the family reconvened to share what they found, exhausted but determined. Maps were marked, notes compared. Jordan sat on the floor, BJ asleep beside her, his tiny hand curled around her finger.

"She's out there," she whispered.

Miles sat beside her. "And we're going to find her."

Ronnie looked up from his notes. "Tomorrow, we hit Decatur."

Zena nodded. "And we don't stop until we bring her home."

The sun was sinking low as Bryce, Jordan, Miles, Ronnie, Amina, and Jake pulled up to the address in Decatur. Zena stayed behind to watch BJ. The building was nondescript—faded brick, boarded-up windows, and a rusted-out metal gate that groaned when Ronnie pushed it open.

"This can't be the place," Miles said quietly, glancing around the empty lot. "It looks abandoned."

Jordan checked the note again, scribbled in sharp handwriting by the bartender at the Velvet Room: *Decatur. Joe's place. Careful.*

They stepped inside. The air was stale, heavy with old cigarette smoke and something else—something sour.

"What the hell happened here?" Ronnie muttered.

Then a voice spoke from the back hallway. "I wouldn't go much further if I were you."

The woman stepped into view wearing scrubs and carrying a mop. She looked tired, worn, but her eyes were sharp.

"I clean here twice a week. Ain't much left to clean anymore."

Jordan stepped forward. "We're looking for someone. A young woman. Jessica Alexander."
The housekeeper raised an eyebrow. "You family?"

"She's my sister," Jordan said. "We were told this was Joe's property. That she might've been here."

The woman's expression shifted. "She was. A few weeks ago."

Bryce stepped beside Jordan. "Did you speak to her?"

The woman hesitated. "Not really. She didn't look like she could talk. She was...out of it. Blank. Like someone turned the lights off behind her eyes."

Amina closed her eyes, heart breaking.

"She say anything?" Ronnie asked.

"No. But I heard Joe in the back on the phone. He was talking about getting out of Atlanta. Miami, he said. Said it was time to get her 'somewhere quieter.' That's all I heard."

Miles stepped forward. "You know where in Miami?"

"No clue. He was being careful. But he took her. I know that much."

Jordan nodded, swallowing hard. "Thank you."

The housekeeper looked around. "If you're trying to find her, I hope you do it fast. I've seen what happens to girls who stay too long with men like him."

The family returned to North Carolina with heavy hearts and only one concrete truth: Jessica was in Miami. Everyone gathered around the kitchen table, the tension thick as Jesse called to check in.

Jordan answered. "Hey, Daddy."

"You hear anything?" Jesse asked, with his heart pounding in his chest.

Jordan exhaled. "Yeah. We found the house in Decatur. Empty. But the housekeeper saw her."

Jesse's voice sharpened. "She okay?"

Jordan hesitated. "She said Jessica looked drugged. Out of it. Joe was there. Took her to Miami."

Silence. Then Jesse said, "Okay. Thank you."

Jordan's voice cracked. "We don't know where in Miami. We don't have anything else."

"That's enough," Jesse replied. "You did good."

Later that night, Jesse sat in silence for a long time after the call. Miami. He stood, crossed the cell, and pulled out the slip of paper Juan had given him months ago—the number for Arturo Delgado, the man with reach, resources, and a debt owed to Jesse Braxton.

The next day, Jesse made a phone call. When Arturo picked up, Jesse didn't bother with pleasantries.

"I need your help," he said. "A man named Joe took my daughter. Took her to Miami. I don't know where. She's not safe. I need her found."

Arturo paused, then said simply, "She's yours?"

"She's mine." Jesse said.

"Then she's mine too. I'll find her." Arturo replied.

And with that, the wheels turned. The hunt for Jessica had truly begun.

# Chapter Thirty

## (Jesse)
### Karma is a Bitch

The prison walls had never felt so thin. Jesse sat on the edge of his bunk, fists clenched, jaw tight. Since the visit from Jordan, since hearing about Jessica's disappearance and Carolyn's coma, something inside him had cracked wide open. He wanted to tear the walls down with his bare hands. He wanted to find his baby girl. He wanted to hold his grandson. He wanted to look Carolyn in the eye and tell her she wasn't alone anymore. But he had weeks left.

Just a few more weeks until release. And he wasn't about to throw that away. Not now. Not when his family needed him more than ever. Still, that didn't mean he had to wait to act. Two days later in the recreation yard, Jesse sat at a worn metal table, nodding to Juan as he approached. The younger man dropped into the seat across from him, eyes sharp.

"You good?" Juan asked.

Jesse didn't answer right away. He reached into his shirt pocket and pulled out a folded slip of paper.

"I need you to get this to your father."

Juan took it, unfolding it carefully. Inside was a photo of Jessica—one Jordan had left behind—and a note in Jesse's tight, deliberate handwriting:
Her name is Jessica Alexander. My daughter. She's in Miami. She's in trouble. With a man name Joe – dangerous. You said if I ever needed anything, all I had to do was ask. I'm asking.

Juan looked up. "You sure?"

Jesse's eyes were steel. "I already put the call in to your father. If she's down there, I want her found. I want her safe. And I want the man who took her to know he just made a mistake he won't live long enough to regret."

Juan nodded. "I'll get it to him, my cousin is in town and coming to see me today on his way back to Miami. I will send it by him."

Meanwhile at his estate in Miami, Arturo Delgado read the note in silence, his thumb brushing the edge of the photo. He recognized the look in the girl's eyes—lost but not broken. Not yet. He turned to his lieutenant. "This girl is Jesse's daughter. She's under our protection now. Find her. Quietly. Bring her home."

The man nodded. "And the one who took her?"

Arturo's voice was calm. "Make sure he understands what it means to touch someone in Arturo Delgado's family.

Back in prison, the guards moved differently that morning. Jesse noticed it immediately. A glance here. A nod there. Then one of them passed by his cell and murmured, "He's here."

Jesse didn't need to ask who – Evan. Convicted. Sentenced. And now transferred to the same facility. It didn't take long. That night, two guards approached Evan's cell. "You've got laundry duty."

"I didn't sign up for—" Evan's words were interrupted.

They didn't wait for him to finish. A black bag went over his head. Hands grabbed his arms. He was dragged down a hallway, feet scraping the floor. The laundry room was empty. Dimly lit. Silent.

When the bag was removed, Evan was face to face with Jesse. Barely conscious, Evan's head slumped to one side.

"Oh, don't go to sleep yet sunshine, the fun is just getting started." Jesse said slapping Evan awake.

Evan looked at Jesse through now visibly swelling eyes and laughed. "Well look at who it is, my dead wife's baby daddy. You want a piece of me pussycat? Bring it on. You ain't bad nigga, you had to have your boys tie me down because you know I woulda whooped your high yella ass".

Gritting his teeth, Jesse told his friends to let Evan go.

Wiping the blood from his lip and smiling, Evan stood up and said "Boy I'm about to beat you like I did my whore of a wife and like I shoulda beat those uppity little bitches you call daughters. But I have to say, they have turned into some fine little hookers. Maybe I should have traded in their mama for the younger versions. Maybe when I get outta here I still will."

Never flinching Jesse looked at Evan and began to laugh. The sadistic smile on Evan's face was replaced by a look of confusion, and he asked, "What the hell is so damn funny?"

Still laughing Jesse replied "Cuz, you aint never gettin outta here."

Evan smiled and shot back, "Boy things have changed. I have enough money to buy one of them Jew lawyers to get me outta here by tomorrow."

Jesse stepped up and looked Evan right in his eyes and said calmly "You aint gonna see tomorrow...boy."

The smile left Evan's face as he felt a sharp pain in his side followed by the feeling of his blood gushing out of his body. He looked down and saw Jesse had plunged a shank into his rib cage, but before he could react, another prisoner came up behind him and slit his throat. While the life seeped slowly out of Evan, Jesse leaned over and whispered, "And you thought Carolyn was a bitch, meet Karma nigga."

As the light in his eyes dimmed, Evan's last sight was of Jesse smiling over his dying body. Jesse went back to his cell and left the laundry room as if he was never there. An inmate who was in for life took credit for the entire crime and the guards backed the story.

With one part of his plan to avenge his family taken care of, Jesse focused on finding Jessica, and he didn't have to wait long, before gaining success on that front as well. The call came in just after midnight.

A soft ring. A long pause. Then a voice Jesse hadn't heard before—low, confident, wrapped in Cuban cadence. "We found her."

Juan's father hadn't broken his word. From the moment Jesse made the call, the wheels had turned. Quiet money passed in back rooms. Photos exchanged. A whisper here, a discreet inquiry there. Miami had ears, and this man had pull in all the right corners.

Jessica wasn't dancing anymore—not exactly. She was being *kept*. Joe had tucked her into a luxury condo high above Biscayne Bay, far from the strip where the girls still hustled under neon lights. She was guarded, rarely left alone, and never without the haze of something in her system. He had turned her into a prized possession. Or maybe a prisoner.

The intel came from a pair of twin cousins— Raúl and Mateo—discreet, sharp-eyed men with tattoos that told old stories and patience that made others nervous. They shadowed Joe's crew for days, clocked Jessica's movements, and confirmed what Jesse feared: she wasn't just staying—she was stuck.

"She's not in shape to run," Raúl said. "But she looks like she's waiting for someone to come get her."

And Jesse was. He just couldn't go yet. So, the plan shifted. Not a smash-and-grab, but a lift. Mateo posed as a driver for one of Joe's associates. He started running errands to the building. Always respectful. Always quiet. Until Jessica noticed him.

The second week, he slipped a note inside her cup of tea.

*"Your father sent us. If you want out, nod tomorrow morning when you see me. We'll handle the rest."*

The next morning, she nodded. And in that split second, the course of her life bent toward home. They'd need precision. Patience. And a window. And come hell or high water, they would find it.

Back in North Carolina, Jesse prepared himself to rejoin his family. Two weeks left. That was all that stood between Jesse and the open air. He marked time in heartbeats now—each day a slow march toward the gate, toward his daughters, toward everything lost and broken waiting to be made whole.

He'd spent years turning stone into silence, violence into control. And now, all that discipline had narrowed into a razor's edge. Jessica was still out there—vulnerable, caged in a life she wasn't built for. Carolyn was alive, but barely. And Jordan... his baby girl was flailing, torching the good in her life because she thought pain was easier than hope.

Jesse sat in his bunk that morning with a letter in one hand, a phone call still echoing in his ears. Mateo and Raúl had made contact. Jessica was reaching—quietly, cautiously. And Jesse had learned long ago that caution was survival. He didn't push. Just waited. Listened. She was alive. And that was enough—for now.

In his cell, beneath the cracked cinderblock walls, Jesse started making lists. Not just names and favors. But vows. He'd bring Jessica home. He'd be what Jordan needed. And somehow, if Carolyn opened her eyes again, if the woman he once loved could rise from what Evan left her with—he'd be there too. Not to lecture. Not to blame. But to own his part and begin again, if she'd let him. He folded the list, tucked it inside the back of his worn Bible—next to the photo of Jessica and Jordan taken the week before the trial.

And then he whispered to himself, "Time to come home."

# Chapter Thirty-One

(Jessica)
Sucker Punched for Love

Miami was hot in all the wrong ways. The salt air didn't taste like freedom—it clung to Jessica's skin, thick and unforgiving. The apartment Joe brought her to was nothing like the glossy penthouse he'd hinted at back in Atlanta. It was cramped, windowless in the bedroom, and smelled faintly of bleach and old perfume. The locks clicked loudly when the door shut behind her. She didn't realize, at first, how final that sound would become.

At first, Joe was gentle. He fed her promises: "Just rest while you settle in," "We'll get you back to yourself," "You're not alone here, baby." She wanted so badly to believe it. That this was still her choice. That BJ would be better off with her gone for a little while until she got back on her feet.

But then the routines began. Joe controlled Jessica's phone. Watched her walk to the corner store from the car. Introduced her to the other girls like she was just another transaction. The pills came more often—little blue ones, then white ones when she said her nerves were too shot to sleep.

Jessica stopped asking for Bryce. Stopped asking for her baby. Every time she tried to bring up going home, Joe's mouth would tighten, his voice sweeten in just the wrong way. "You want to go back to that IHOP life? Back to struggling? I thought you were smarter than that."

Joe said he loved her. Jessica started saying it back because it hurt less than silence. Nights blurred. Her skin bruised more easily now. Her laugh—when it came—sounded like someone else's.

The girl who'd once danced because she wanted to prove something now dressed up for strangers and called it survival. But somewhere inside the haze, something still flickered. A memory. A name. A chubby-cheeked smile she hadn't kissed in weeks – BJ.

Jessica didn't know how long she could go on like this. But she did know this: if there was even the smallest chance she could find her way back to him, she'd take it. Even if she had to crawl.

The night Jessica decided to try again, the Miami rain was coming down in sheets, turning the street outside into a glimmering blur of red tail lights and broken dreams. Joe had passed out on the couch, a half-empty bottle on the floor and his phone loosely clutched in his hand. The bruises on her thigh were still fresh, but numb. She was tired of nursing them in the mirror like they were part of her.

Jessica sat in the bathroom, barefoot on the cold tile, staring at the strip of light beneath the door. Her body hurt. Her head ached. But her spirit—that part of her she thought was dead—was beginning to twitch.

BJ's name was scrawled on the back of an old envelope she kept under the sink. She'd written it on a night she was afraid she might forget. Bryce Jr. Her baby. Her boy. His eyes, soft and wide, had started to fade in the clouded recesses of her memory. That's when she knew she couldn't stay.

Jessica waited until dawn, slipped Joe's phone from under his hand, and crept back into the bathroom. She didn't even know who she was calling—her fingers moved on instinct. When the line picked up, her breath caught.

It was Bryce's voice. "Hello?"

Silence.

"…Jess?" Bryce asked in a voice dripping with desperation and hope.

A quiet gasp.

"I want to come home," Jessica whispered, voice raw.

Bryce didn't ask how she got the phone. Didn't lecture. Didn't yell. There was only silence for a moment… and then: "Where are you?"

That was the beginning of something that might still break. Might still burn. But for the first time in what felt like forever, Jessica reached toward the edge of the hole she'd fallen into—and felt someone reaching back.

The sun hadn't fully risen when Jessica slipped the phone back under Joe's fingers, his slow, rhythmic snoring still steady beside the empty bottle. She crept quietly to the kitchen, barely breathing, every movement measured. She had enough cash to make it a few blocks—maybe to a station, maybe to a friend of a friend who owed her a favor. Bryce was coming. He had to be.

But fifteen minutes later, a floorboard creaked. And the air in the apartment changed. "Jess ?" Joe's voice was groggy—raspy with sleep and bourbon—but laced with suspicion.

Jessica froze.

Joe sat up slowly on the couch, rubbing his face before looking around. His brows furrowed. "Where's my phone?"

Jessica turned from the sink. "You dropped it last night. I plugged it in."

His eyes found her, a little too sharp now. "You never do that."

A pause.

"Why are you dressed?" Joe quizzed.

Jessica shrugged, her voice careful. "Just… needed air. Coffee."

Joe stood. The creak of the floor beneath his feet sounded like thunder in her chest. "Jess… what did you do?"

Jessica shook her head, but her face gave her away. Her hands trembled just slightly. She backed up an inch without meaning to. And that's when he knew. Joe's jaw clenched, slow and deliberate. "You called him."

Jessica said nothing.

Joe's voice was calm. Too calm. "What—did you think he'd ride in here with a cape on and scoop you up like a damn fairytale?"

Joe moved closer. Jessica reached for the counter, hands finding a knife drawer—then hesitated. Joe laughed bitterly. "Look at you. Thinking you've still got choices."

For a moment, nothing moved but the clock on the wall. Then a car horn blared from outside. Both of them looked toward the window. Jessica moved first but was met with a blow from Joe's fist that sent her flying across the room, and landing in a corner, where she lay sobbing until she cried herself to sleep.

Jessica woke to the sound of waves. Not the kind that soothed. These were distant, hollow—filtered through thick windows and a luxury she hadn't asked for. Jessica blinked into the gauzy morning light spilling across cold marble floors.

The air smelled like ocean salt and stale perfume. She was alone in the condo. Joe had flown out on "business"—something about a club expansion in Brickell—and left her with an overstocked fridge, a credit card she wasn't allowed to use without permission, and a security guard in the lobby who never looked her in the eye.

Jessica crept barefoot into the bathroom, stared at herself in the mirror. Bruises mostly faded. Eyes ringed in sleepless hollows. Hair that no longer held curl. There was no sparkle. No stage. No lies left to lean on.

The pills were the only thing that made the days soft enough to survive. Except she hadn't taken one last night. And now, raw and hollow, her brain felt like static. But then her eyes caught it—on the side table, barely tucked beneath yesterday's takeout menu.

The note. *"Your father sent us. If you want out, nod tomorrow."*

It had been four days since Jessica slipped that note into her pocket and nodded through the morning haze. Four days since that driver—Mateo—handed her tea with trembling hands and eyes that looked nothing like Joe's.

Jessica didn't know if help was coming. But today, for the first time in months, she didn't feel entirely invisible. Jessica opened the window, let the wind slap her skin awake, and whispered, "Come get me."

# Chapter Thirty-Two

(Carolyn)
Daddy is Home

The automatic doors of the hospital slid open with a soft hiss, but for Jesse Braxton, it felt like the ground itself had shifted. He was free. Released early for good behavior and overcrowding, Jesse hadn't told anyone. No celebration. No detour. No delay. He went straight to her. Room 214. Carolyn.

Jesse stepped into the room quietly, but his weight filled the space. The machines beeped steadily. The air smelled of antiseptic and lavender—Zena's touch. Carolyn lay still, her face bruised, her jaw wired shut, but her chest rose and fell. She was alive.

Jesse walked to her bedside, took her hand, and brushed a trembling kiss on her forehead. "Don't worry, baby," he whispered. "I'm home. And I'm gonna bring our daughter back, just like I promised. But you've gotta hold on for me, alright? No checking out. Not now."

Carolyn's eyelids fluttered. Then—movement. Carolyn's eyes opened. Tears welled immediately, tracing down her cheeks as she met his gaze for the first time in what felt like lifetimes. She couldn't speak. But her eyes said everything—remorse, relief, and a pain that had waited far too long to be seen.

Jesse leaned in, steady but soft. "We've both got a lot to make up for. For the girls. For us. But I'm here now. For good."

Carolyn's hand tightened around his. Zena stepped into the room, followed by Jordan, Ronnie, Bryce, Amina, and Miles. BJ was asleep in Bryce's arms.

Zena's voice was gentle. "She's been waiting for you."

Jesse turned, nodding. "I know. I've been waiting for this too."

Jordan stepped forward, her voice cautious. "You're really out?"

"Walked out this morning," Jesse said. "Didn't even stop to breathe. I had to see her first."

Ronnie crossed his arms. "What now?"

Jesse looked at each of them. "Now I go to Miami. Juan, Raúl, and Mateo are already in place. Arturo Delgado's got eyes on Jessica. They know where she is."

Jordan's voice cracked. "Is she okay?"

"She's alive," Jesse said. "That's all I know. But I'm not coming back without her."

Bryce stepped forward, voice low. "You're not going alone, are you?"

"I've got backup," Jesse said. "And I've got something else to tell you."

He looked at Carolyn, then at Zena and Jake. "Evan went to prison. Same one I just left."

Zena's eyes narrowed. "And?"

Jesse's voice dropped. "He won't be hurting anyone ever again."

Ronnie's jaw tightened. "What did you do?"

Jesse didn't blink. "What needed to be done. He paid for what he did to her. And he knows now—this family isn't unprotected."

Carolyn's eyes filled again. A single tear slipped down her cheek.

"I'm sorry I wasn't there to stop it," Jesse whispered. "But I'm here now. And I'm not letting anyone else take from us again."

Jordan stepped forward, her voice soft. "Be careful, Daddy."

"I will," Jesse said. "But I need you all to hold it down here. Be strong for your mama. Be strong for BJ. When I bring Jessica home, I want her to see what she's coming back to."

He kissed Carolyn's forehead again, then turned to the door. "I'll call when I land. And when I have her, you'll be the first to know."

Zena reached for his arm. "Bring our baby home."

Jesse nodded. "I will." And then he was gone— out the door, down the hall, into the fight to bring Jessica home.

The hospital waiting room had taken on the rhythm of a second heartbeat. The family moved through it like a tide—quiet, steady, always circling back to Room 214. No one said it aloud, but they were all waiting for two things: for Carolyn to heal, and for Jesse to call.

Zena sat by the window with her Bible open but unread. Jake stood at the coffee machine, staring into his cup like it might offer answers. Ronnie paced. Jordan hadn't let go of her phone in hours. Amina scrolled through news alerts and club rosters in Miami, just in case. Bryce sat on the floor with BJ, building towers out of plastic blocks and knocking them down again.

Miles stood behind Jordan, his hand resting gently on her shoulder.

The silence was thick until the elevator dinged. Carolyn's nurse stepped into the waiting room. "She's asking for you."

Zena stood first. "All of us?"

"She nodded when I asked. I think she wants her people." She is in Room 214.

Carolyn looked stronger today. Her eyes were clearer, her skin less pale. The swelling had gone down, and though her jaw was still wired shut, her presence filled the room in a way it hadn't before.

Zena sat beside her, brushing a hand over her daughter's hair. "You're doing so good, baby."

Carolyn blinked slowly, then looked at Jordan. Jordan stepped forward, voice soft. "Daddy came. He saw you before he left. He's in Miami now. He's going to bring Jessica home."

Carolyn's eyes welled.

Ronnie leaned against the wall, arms crossed. "He's got people down there. Real ones. They know where she is."

Amina added, "They're not going in blind. They're watching her. Making sure she's safe until they move."

Carolyn's gaze shifted to Bryce, who stepped forward with BJ in his arms.

"He's been asking for her," Bryce said. "He doesn't understand, but he knows she's gone. He misses her."

BJ reached out, babbling softly. Carolyn's hand trembled as she reached toward him. Bryce gently lowered BJ to the edge of the bed, letting him curl into her side.

Carolyn closed her eyes, tears slipping free.

Zena whispered, "She's coming home, baby. You just keep healing."

Jake finally spoke, his voice low and steady. "And when she does, we'll be ready. All of us."

Carolyn opened her eyes again and looked at Jordan.

Jordan nodded. "We're not going anywhere."

Miles stepped forward. "We've got you. All of you."

Carolyn's gaze swept the room—her mother, her father, her brother, her daughters' partners, her grandson. Her family. She couldn't speak, but her eyes said it all: I'm sorry. I'm grateful. I'm still here.

Later that night at Jake and Zena's House, the family had returned to the house in shifts. Carolyn was resting. The nurses said she'd made more progress in the last 48 hours than they'd expected in a week. In the kitchen, Zena stirred a pot of soup while Amina chopped vegetables beside her.

"She's fighting," Zena said. "I can feel it."

"She's got something to fight for now," Amina replied.

In the living room, Jordan sat curled up on the couch, phone in hand. Miles sat beside her, his arm around her shoulders.

"You okay?" he asked.

She nodded. "I just keep thinking… what if she doesn't want to come back?"

"She will," Miles said. "And if she doesn't know how, we'll show her."

Ronnie walked in from the porch. "Still no word?"

Jordan shook her head. "Not yet."

Bryce came down the stairs, BJ asleep on his shoulder. "He finally knocked out."

Jake looked up from his recliner. "He's gonna need his mama."

Bryce nodded. "We all do."

The house was quiet, but no one was sleeping. Carolyn was resting at the hospital, sedated and stable. The rest of the family had returned to Zena and Jake's home in North Carolina, trying to settle into something like stillness—but the air was thick with waiting.

Jordan sat on the couch, phone in hand, eyes fixed on the screen. Miles sat beside her, his hand resting on her knee. Ronnie stood at the window, arms crossed, watching the wind stir the trees. Bryce paced the hallway with BJ in his arms, whispering lullabies that sounded more like prayers. Amina sat at the kitchen table with Zena, both of them nursing mugs of tea that had long gone cold.

Then Jordan's phone buzzed. She jumped. Everyone turned. She answered quickly. "Daddy?"

Jesse's voice came through, low and steady. "I'm on my way to the airport now. Arturo just called."

Jordan stood, heart pounding. "Did they find her?"

"They did," Jesse said. "She's in Miami. They've confirmed it. She's alive."

Jordan's knees buckled slightly. Miles caught her.

Zena stood from the table. "What else did he say?"

"They're putting a plan together now," Jesse continued. "They're watching her. Making sure she doesn't get moved. But they haven't gone in yet."

Ronnie stepped closer. "So, she's not safe yet."

"Not yet," Jesse said. "But she will be. I'm going down there to make sure of it."

Jordan's voice cracked. "Did they say what kind of shape she's in?"

"No details yet," Jesse said. "Just that she's alive. That's all I've got."

Zena took the phone from Jordan, her voice trembling. "You be careful, Jesse Braxton. You hear me?"

"I will Mama Z," Jesse said. "I'll call again when I land."

Zena handed the phone back to Jordan and sat down slowly, her hands shaking.

"She's alive," Jordan whispered. "They found her."

Bryce stepped into the room, BJ asleep on his shoulder. "But she's not home yet."

"No," Ronnie said. "But now we know where to look."

Amina stood, her voice quiet but firm. "Then we hold the line. We stay ready. And we pray."

Jake walked in from the porch, having heard enough to understand. "We've waited this long. We can wait a little longer. But not one second more than we have to."

Jordan looked at her family—tired, bruised, but standing.

"She's coming back," she said. "And when she does, she's going to see all of us here. Still fighting. Still hers."

Miles nodded. "We're not going anywhere."

# Chapter Thirty-Three

(Jesse)
Have you seen Her?

Jesse stepped off the plane in Miami just as the sun began to bleed gold across the skyline—too beautiful, he thought, for what he came to do. Mateo was waiting. Slick car, quiet nod. No small talk. Just respect.

They drove in silence until they reached a discreet house tucked in Little Havana, where Raúl met them at the door. Inside, maps and photos were spread across the table—surveillance stills of Jessica stepping out onto the condo balcony, of Joe's men posted by the elevators, of security shift changes logged with precision.

"She's ready," Mateo said simply. "We just need your blessing to move."

Jesse scanned every detail. That father's instinct—sharpened by absence and guilt—knew better than to rush in blind. But it also told him time was running out. Jessica's eyes in the photos were vacant. She wasn't just trapped—she was *fading*.

"How clean can we keep it?" Jesse asked.
Raúl shrugged once. "As clean as she lets us. We can get her out fast and quiet. But she might not walk easy."

"She will," Jesse said. "When she sees me, she'll remember she was never lost. Just waiting to be found."

Mateo handed him a phone. "We'll call when we're in place. She trusts me now. She'll come."
Jesse nodded. He wasn't a killer looking for revenge anymore. Not today. He was a father—armed with grace, guilt, and the weight of a promise.

"Let's go get my daughter," Jesse said.
The signal came just after dusk. Raúl watched from the alley across the street, eyes fixed on the glowing balcony ten stories up. Jessica had stepped outside exactly as planned, arms wrapped around herself, gazing unfocused.

Mateo's text came through one minute later: *"She's ready. Elevator's ours. Two on the door, but lazy."*

Inside, the building's doorman barely glanced up as Mateo walked through the lobby in a linen shirt and delivery cap. Third time this week—his face already familiar. He gave a small nod to the security guard, handed over a fake clipboard, and used the moment to tap twice on his left wrist: *Now.*

Jessica waited by the door. Heart hammering, she held the note in her pocket like a lifeline. No pills today. Not since dawn. She needed to *feel* this.

Mateo knocked once. "Housekeeping."

Jessica opened the door. No hesitation. No questions. She just stepped into the hallway and followed him. Seconds later, the service elevator swallowed them whole. On the tenth floor, Joe's guards were too busy arguing over a baseball bet to notice she'd vanished. By the time they did, she was already in the car—Raúl behind the wheel, Mateo beside her, doors locked, tires spinning toward the causeway.

In the back seat, Jessica stared ahead, frozen, shaking. Mateo reached over and gently offered her a phone. "Your father's waiting on the other end."

Jessica took it like it might disappear, stared at the screen. Her thumb hovered. Then—she pressed the call button. "Hello?"

There was a minute of silence. Then Jesse's voice, steady and thick with emotion: "Jess?" And for the first time in a long, long time—she exhaled.

The safe house was tucked away in the quieter edges of Little Havana—sunlight slipping through slatted blinds, the kind of place meant for laying low, not healing wounds. But for Jessica, it might as well have been the first room with air she'd breathed in months. She sat on the worn sofa, fingers fidgeting with the hem of a borrowed T-shirt, eyes locked on the door. Mateo had made her tea. Raúl had kept a lookout. They were kind, in the way quiet men sometimes are when violence has shaped their lives.

And now... her father was coming. Jessica hadn't seen him since the trial. Since the screaming. The cuffs. The walls that swallowed him whole. She was a child then—angry, frightened, tired of being the one left behind. And now she was the one returning.

The knock came soft. Then the door creaked open. Jessica sat on the edge of a stained mattress in a dimly lit room that smelled like old perfume and newer fear. Her arms were wrapped around herself, her eyes hollow. She didn't look up at first—she didn't expect kindness anymore.

But then she heard the voice. Low. Familiar. Steady. "Jess."

Jessica looked up. Jesse Braxton stood in the doorway—older than she remembered, with more gray in his beard, more weight on his shoulders. But the storm in his eyes was still there. So was the quiet fire that had always lived behind his silence.

He didn't speak at first. Neither did she.

Then Jessica stood up on shaking legs. Her voice cracked through the air. "Daddy?"

Jesse crossed the space in two strides. Wrapped her in arms that held like home. Jessica collapsed into him, breath hitching, tears hot and wordless. Her fingers clutched the back of his shirt like she was afraid he'd disappear.

For a long moment, neither of them tried to explain. There was too much. Too many years. Too many fractures. But in that silence, forgiveness started to bloom—not perfect, but possible.

Jesse pulled back just far enough to hold Jessica's face in his hands. "We're going home," he said. "You hear me? Not just back. Home."

Jessica nodded, her voice barely a whisper. "I didn't think anyone would come."

Jesse's jaw tightened. "You're my daughter. I don't care how far you fall—I'll always come."

Jessica looked down. "I messed up."

"We all did," Jesse said. "But you're still breathing. That means you get to start again."

Jessica wiped her face. "Does Mama know?"

Jesse hesitated. "She's in the hospital. Evan…
he put her in a coma."

Jessica's knees buckled. Jesse caught her.
"No," she whispered. "No, no, no—"

"She's alive," Jesse said quickly. "She's
fighting. And she's waiting for you."

Jessica sobbed into his chest. "I didn't know. I
didn't know he—"

"I know," Jesse said. "And he won't ever touch
her again."

She looked up, eyes wide. "What do you
mean?"

Jesse's voice was low. Cold. "He was in prison.
Same one I just left. And let's just say… he paid for
what he did."

Jessica stared at him, stunned. "You…?"

"I made sure he understood what it feels like to
be powerless," Jesse said. "He won't hurt anyone
again."

Jessica nodded slowly. "Thank you."

Jesse reached into his pocket and pulled out his
phone. "There's someone who wants to talk to
you." He dialed.

Zena answered on the first ring. "Jesse?"

"I've got her," Jesse said. "She's safe."

There was a pause. Then Zena's voice cracked.
"Thank you, Lord."

Jesse handed the phone to Jessica. "It's
Grandma."

Jessica took it with trembling hands.
"Grandma?"

"Oh, baby," Zena said, her voice thick with tears. "We've been praying for you every day. Every hour."

Jessica broke. "I'm so sorry."

"You don't have to be sorry," Zena said. "You just have to come home. We'll take care of the rest."

Jessica nodded, even though Zena couldn't see her. "I want to come home."

"Your mama's waiting. She's getting stronger. She's holding on for you."

Jessica wiped her face. "I'll be there soon."

Zena's voice softened. "There's someone else who wants to talk to you."

Jessica heard a shuffle, then a new voice. "Jess?"

Her breath caught. "Bryce?"

"Yeah. It's me." Bryce answered.

Jessica started crying again. "I didn't think you'd ever want to hear my voice again."

"I didn't think I would either," Bryce said honestly. "But I do. And so does someone else."

There was a pause.

Then: "Mama?"

Jessica's knees gave out. She sank to the floor, clutching the phone.

"BJ?" Jessica whispered.

"He's right here," Bryce said. "He's okay. He's safe. He misses you."

Jessica sobbed. "I miss him so much. I didn't mean to leave him. I just... I didn't know how to stay."

"You don't have to explain right now," Bryce said. "Just come home."

"I will," Jessica whispered. "I promise."

Jesse knelt beside her, wrapping an arm around her shoulders. "We've got a flight in the morning," he said. "Tonight, you rest. Tomorrow, we go home."

Jessica looked at him, eyes red but clear. "Okay." And for the first time in a long time, she meant it.

# Chapter Thirty-Four
(Joe)
The Devil's Wake

The door slammed open so hard it cracked the drywall. Joe stormed into the penthouse, his gold chain swinging, cigar clenched between his teeth like a fuse waiting to be lit. The air reeked of stale cologne, sweat, and fear. Two of his men—Reese and Tino—stood frozen near the kitchen island, mid-conversation, eyes wide as their boss stormed in like a hurricane.

"Where is she?" Joe barked, voice like gravel dragged across steel.

Reese blinked. "Boss, we thought she was still in the back. She—she was asleep when we checked"

"She's gone," Joe snapped. "Gone. And you two were supposed to be watching her."

Tino stepped forward, hands raised in defense. "We didn't hear anything. No one came in or out. We were right here the whole time—"

Joe didn't wait for the rest. He moved fast for a man his size. The first punch landed square in Tino's gut, folding him in half with a sickening grunt. The second cracked across Reese's jaw,

244

sending him sprawling into the counter, blood splattering across the marble.

"You think I'm stupid?" Joe roared. "You think I don't know what this is?"

He grabbed Tino by the collar and slammed him against the wall, the man's feet barely touching the ground.

"You let someone take her. You let someone walk into my house and take what's mine."

"She was drugged!" Reese gasped from the floor, wiping blood from his mouth. "She could barely stand—how the hell did she get out?"

Joe turned, eyes wild. "She didn't get out on her own. Someone came for her. Someone who knew what they were doing."

He let go of Tino, who crumpled to the floor, coughing. Joe paced the room like a caged animal, fury radiating off him in waves. He pulled out his phone and dialed.

"Yeah," he said when the line picked up. "She's gone. I want every camera pulled from the last 24 hours. Street, lobby, alley—everything. And I want names. Anyone who's been asking about her. Anyone who's been watching."

He paused, listening. "No. I don't care who they are. I want them found. I want faces. I want license plates. I want to know what they had for breakfast."

Joe hung up and turned back to his men, both of them groaning on the floor. "You two better pray I find her before they get her out of the city," he said coldly. "Because if I don't—what I just did to you will feel like a love tap."

Reese coughed, blood on his teeth. "Boss... you think it was that guy? The one from the club? The one who came looking for her?"

Joe's eyes narrowed. "What guy?"

"Tall. Black. Built like a linebacker. He came by a few weeks ago asking questions. Said he was family."

Joe's jaw clenched. "You didn't think to tell me this before?"

"We didn't think he was a threat," Tino wheezed. "He didn't come back."

Joe's voice dropped to a dangerous whisper. "He didn't need to. He was watching. Waiting."

He turned and walked to the window, looking out over the Miami skyline, the city glittering like a lie.

"She was mine," Joe muttered. "I gave her everything. And she ran." He turned back to them, eyes burning.

"Find out who he is. Where he's staying. What he drives. I want him followed. I want his phone tapped. I want to know what he breathes."

Reese nodded weakly. "Yes, boss."

Joe lit his cigar again, the flame dancing in his eyes. "She thinks she can disappear?" Joe said, "more to himself than anyone else. "She thinks she can just walk out and go back to her little family like none of this happened?"

Joe exhaled a long stream of smoke. "She's not going home. Not until I say so."

He turned to his men one last time. "And if anyone gets in my way—family or not—I'll bury them."

The next morning, the Miami heat clung to the city like a second skin. Joe sat in the back of a blacked-out SUV, the leather seats creaking beneath his weight, his cigar burning low between his fingers. The driver didn't speak. No one did. Not unless Joe asked a question—and even then, they answered carefully.

Joe's phone buzzed. He answered on the first ring. "Talk."

A voice on the other end—sharp, efficient. "We pulled the footage. Two men. One matched the description of the guy who came by the club a few weeks ago. Tall. Broad. Ex-military type. He was with another man—Latino, younger. They came in through the service alley. Knew the blind spots."

Joe's jaw tightened. "License plates?"

"Stolen. But we got a partial. Already running it."

Joe exhaled slowly. "They knew what they were doing."

"They were in and out in under four minutes. No noise. No struggle. She didn't scream."

"She wouldn't," Joe muttered. "She's too scared of me for that."

There was a pause.

"We also traced a burner phone that pinged near the building an hour before the grab. It's been turned off since. But we're working on it."

Joe hung up without another word. He turned to the man in the passenger seat—his enforcer, a quiet brute named Malik. "Start checking bus stations, airports, private airfields. I want eyes on every exit out of this city."

Malik nodded. "You think they're still here?"
Joe's eyes narrowed. "If they're smart, they're already gone. But if they're sentimental? They'll try to say goodbye. Tie up loose ends."
He leaned forward. "And that's when we'll catch them."

Later that day, Joe walked into a small café near the water, sunglasses low on his nose. The hostess smiled nervously.

"Table for—" She began before Joe interrupted her.

"I'm not here to eat," Joe said. "I'm looking for someone."

Joe pulled out a photo of Jessica—one from her early days at the club, before the bruises, before the pills dulled her eyes. "Seen her?" he quizzed.
The hostess hesitated. "She looks familiar, but—"
Joe leaned in. "She came in here with two men. One Black, one Latino. Big guys. She looked scared. You'd remember."

The hostess swallowed. "I—I think they were here yesterday. They didn't stay long."

Joe smiled, but it didn't reach his eyes. "That's all I needed." He turned and walked out, dialing as he went. "They were here," he said. "They're still in the city."

Meanwhile at Arturo Delgado's compound, Juan stepped into Arturo's office, and phone in hand. "We've got a problem."

Arturo looked up from his desk. "Joe?"

Juan nodded. "He's moving. Fast. He's already retracing our steps. He knows she didn't leave alone."

Arturo stood, his voice calm but deadly. "Then we move faster."

That night at his penthouse, Joe stood at the window, staring out at the city like it owed him something.

"She was mine," he said quietly. "I made her. I fed her. I gave her everything."

Malik stood behind him. "What do you want to do when we find them?"

Joe turned, eyes cold. "I want the man who took her to bleed. I want her to see it. And then I want her to remember who she belongs to." He crushed the cigar in the ashtray.

"Start with the airports. Then the bus terminals. Then the hospitals. If she's trying to run, she'll need help. And help leaves a trail."

Malik nodded and left. Joe poured himself a drink, the ice clinking like a countdown. "She's not going home," he whispered. "Not unless it's in pieces."

# Chapter Thirty-Five

(Joe)

## Blood in the Water

The city pulsed beneath Joe's feet like prey sensing the hunter. Miami was loud, hot, and fast—but Joe moved through it with a cold, deliberate calm. Every step he took was calculated. Every breath was a warning. He wasn't chasing Jessica out of love. He was chasing her because she had the audacity to leave. And no one left Joe.

In downtown Miami, Joe stood in a darkened room above a pawn shop he owned on paper but used for far more. Screens lined the walls—traffic cams, airport feeds, bus terminals, facial recognition software scraping every corner of the city.
Malik stood beside him, arms crossed, watching the footage roll.

"We've flagged three possible sightings," Malik said. "One at the Greyhound station. One at a private airstrip in Opa-locka. And one at a motel near Little Havana."

Joe's eyes narrowed. "The motel?"
Malik tapped the screen. "Check-in under a fake name. Paid in cash. But the clerk said the girl looked like she hadn't slept in days. Said she was with two men—one older, one younger. Fit the description."

Joe leaned in. "That's them." He turned to another man seated at a laptop. "Pull the footage. I want timestamps. I want to know how long they were there, what they were driving, and which direction they went when they left."

The man nodded and got to work.

Joe lit a fresh cigar, the flame flaring in the dark. "They think they're ghosts," he muttered. "But ghosts don't leave footprints." Joe gathered his henchmen and headed to the motel. The SUV cut through traffic like a blade. Joe sat in the back, phone pressed to his ear. "Yeah," he said. "I want eyes on every exit route out of the city. I want every toll booth watched. If they're still here, they're boxed in. If they're gone, I want to know where they're headed."

He paused, listening. "North Carolina?" he repeated. "You sure?"

The voice on the other end replied, "We traced a burner phone to a call made to a landline in a rural area outside Charlotte. Belongs to a Zena Alexander."

Joe's eyes narrowed. "Family."

"Looks like it. The call was short. Less than two minutes. But it was her."

Joe hung up and leaned forward. "They're trying to get her home. To her family."

Malik glanced back. "You want to intercept?"

Joe's voice was ice. "No. Not yet. Let them think they're safe. Let them get comfortable. Then we remind them who she belongs to."

Thirty minutes later, they were at the motel, busting into the room the clerk told them he rented to the men he described. The room was empty. The bed was stripped. The air smelled faintly of cheap soap and fear. Joe stood in the center of the room, staring at the dent in the mattress, the half-empty water bottle on the nightstand, the faint imprint of a woman's body in the sheets.

"She was here," Joe said.

Malik nodded. "They left this morning. Early. Clerk said they were in a rush."

Joe turned slowly, taking it all in.

"She's running to something," Joe said. "Not just away from me. That's the mistake." He pulled out his phone and dialed again. "Put someone on that house in North Carolina. I want eyes on every person who walks through that door. And if she shows up—don't touch her. Just call me."

He hung up and looked at Malik. "She thinks this is over," Joe said. "She thinks she's free." He smiled, slow and cruel. "She's about to learn what it really means to be hunted."

Jessica and Jesse were on the way to the airport. The sun hadn't yet risen over Miami, but the city was already awake—buzzing with tension, with heat, with the quiet hum of something about to break.

Jesse and Jessica sat in the back of a black SUV, parked just outside a private terminal. Arturo Delgado had arranged everything: a chartered flight, a discreet escort, and a security detail that blended into the background like shadows. But Jesse wasn't relaxed. Not yet.

Jessica sat beside him, her hands trembling in her lap. She hadn't said much since they left the safehouse. Her eyes were distant, haunted.

"You okay?" Jesse asked gently.

Jessica nodded, but her voice was barely a whisper. "I just want to see Mama."

"You will," he said. "Soon."

She looked at him. "Do you think she'll forgive me?"

Jesse reached over and took her hand. "She already has. She's just waiting to hold you."

Jessica blinked back tears. "I don't deserve it."

"You're alive," Jesse said. "That's enough."

Just then, Jesse's phone buzzed. It was Arturo. He answered quickly. "Yeah?"

Arturo's voice was calm, but sharp. "We've got a problem. Joe's moving. He knows you're flying out this morning. He's trying to intercept."

Jesse's jaw clenched. "How?"

"He's got people watching the terminals. But don't worry—we've got people watching him."

Jesse looked at Jessica. "We're not backing down."

Arturo's voice dropped. "He's not just coming for her, Jesse. He's planning to go after her family. Burn everything down. I've seen this before. He wants to make an example out of her."

Jesse's voice turned to steel. "Then we make an example out of him."

Arturo paused. "I'm already ahead of you. If he shows up, I'll handle it personally."

Meanwhile at the Miami International Airport, the private terminal was quiet, nearly empty. Jesse sat near the gate, watching the hallway like a hawk.

Jessica had gone to the restroom to splash water on her face, try to calm the storm inside her. She leaned over the sink, hands shaking, water dripping from her chin. She stared at her reflection—sunken eyes, bruised soul. But she was still standing.

Then she saw him. In the mirror. Joe. Standing behind her. Her breath caught in her throat. She turned, but before she could scream, Joe's hand clamped over her mouth.

"Shh," Joe hissed. "You didn't think I'd let you go that easy, did you?"

Jessica struggled, but Joe was strong. He dragged her backward through a side door, down a maintenance hallway.

"You think you can run from me?" he growled. "You think you can hide behind your little family? You're mine, Jessica. You'll always be mine."

Jessica kicked and thrashed, but Joe shoved her forward, toward a waiting SUV parked just outside the terminal. He opened the door, shoved her inside. And froze. Because someone was already sitting in the back seat. A man in a tailored suit, calm as still water, with eyes like razors. Arturo Delgado.

Joe blinked. "Who the hell are you?"

Arturo didn't move. "Sit down, Joe."

Joe's hand twitched toward his waistband.

"You got about two seconds to tell me—"

"Arturo Delgado," the man said simply.

Joe's face drained of color. His mouth opened, but no sound came out.

Arturo leaned forward slightly. "You've been playing gangster in my city. Stealing girls. Beating women. Threatening families."

Joe stammered, "I—I didn't know she was—"
"You didn't know she was under my protection," Arturo finished. "But you do now."

Jessica sat frozen, pressed against the opposite door, eyes wide.

Arturo turned to her, his voice softening. "You're safe now, Mija. He won't touch you again."

Then he looked back at Joe. "If you so much as look at her—or anyone in her family—there won't be enough of you left for your own mother to recognize."

Joe swallowed hard. "I didn't mean—"

Arturo raised his hand. "You meant everything. And now you're going to disappear. Quietly. Because if I hear your name again, I'll erase it."

Joe nodded quickly, sweat pouring down his face.

Arturo opened the door. "Get out."

Joe scrambled from the SUV like a man who'd just seen death.

Arturo turned to Jessica. "You okay?"

She nodded, still shaking. "Thank you."

Arturo gave Jessica a small, reassuring smile. "Go home. Heal. Your family's waiting."

Back at the terminal, Jesse stood when he saw Jessica walking back toward him, escorted by one of Arturo's men.

"You good?" Jesse asked, rushing to her.

Jessica nodded, tears in her eyes. "He tried. But Arturo was there."

Jesse pulled her into a hug. "It's over now."
She looked up at him. "Let's go home."

255

# Chapter Thirty-Six

(Jessica)
Homecoming

The Alexander home in North Carolina was alive with motion, but no one dared call it celebration. Not yet. It was something quieter. More sacred. A kind of reverent anticipation that hummed through every room like a heartbeat.

Zena stood at the stove, stirring a pot of chicken and dumplings with one hand while holding her phone in the other. She'd already checked it five times in the last hour. No new messages. But she knew the call was coming.

Jake was outside, sweeping the porch for the third time that morning. He didn't say much, but the way he kept glancing down the road said everything.

Inside, Jordan was folding fresh sheets in the guest room. The same room Jessica used to sleep in when she was little, curled up with her stuffed rabbit and a nightlight that played lullabies. Jordan paused, smoothing the pillowcase with trembling hands.

"She's really coming back," Jessica whispered.

Miles leaned in the doorway, watching her. "Yeah. She is." He agreed.

Jordan turned to him, eyes glassy. "I keep thinking about what she's been through. What she's seen. What she's had to survive just to get back here."

Miles stepped forward, wrapping his arms around her. "She doesn't have to survive anymore. She just has to come home."

In the living room, Ronnie sat on the couch, flipping through a notebook filled with names, addresses, and notes from their search in Atlanta. He hadn't let himself stop moving since they got back. But now, with Jessica on her way, he finally closed the book.

Amina walked in, carrying a basket of folded laundry. "You okay?"

Ronnie nodded. "Yeah. Just… trying to believe it."

"She's alive," Amina said. "That's enough for now."

Ronnie looked at her. "You think she'll want to talk about it?"

Amina shook her head. "Not at first. But she'll need to know we're here. No judgment. Just love."
He nodded. "We can do that."

Meanwhile, in Carolyn's hospital room, Carolyn was awake, propped up slightly with pillows. The swelling had gone down. Her eyes were clearer. She couldn't speak yet, but she could write.

Zena sat beside her, holding her hand.
"She's on her way," Zena said softly. "Jesse called. They're flying in this afternoon."

Carolyn's eyes filled with tears. She reached for the notepad on her tray and scribbled: *Will she want to see me?*

Zena read it, then looked at her daughter. "She's your baby. Of course she will."

Carolyn wrote again, slower this time: *I wasn't there.*

Zena squeezed her hand. "You're here now. That's what matters."

Carolyn closed her eyes, a tear slipping down her cheek.

Zena leaned in, brushing her hair back. "You hold on, Carolyn. You hold on and be ready. Because when she walks through that door, she's going to need her mama."

Later that morning, Bryce was playing with BJ. The toddler sat on the floor, babbling to himself, stacking blocks and knocking them down.

"You ready to see your mama, little man?" Bryce asked.

BJ looked up and grinned. "Mama!"

Bryce smiled, but his eyes were wet. "Yeah. She's coming. She's really coming."

In the kitchen, the table was set. The food was warm. The house was spotless. But no one sat down.

They were all standing near the front windows, watching the driveway.

Then Jordan's phone buzzed. She answered quickly. "Daddy?"

Jesse's voice came through, steady and full of something she hadn't heard in a long time—peace. "We just landed."

Jordan's breath caught. "Okay. We're ready." She hung up and turned to the others. "They're here. They landed and are on the way now."

Zena pressed her hand to her chest. Jake stepped onto the porch. Ronnie stood tall. Amina took BJ from Bryce and held him close. And Jordan? She opened the front door and stepped outside, the wind catching her hair, her heart pounding. Because her sister was finally coming home.

The car ride from the airport was quiet. Not tense—just full. Every mile that passed seemed to press more weight into Jessica's chest. She sat in the passenger seat beside Jesse, her fingers twisting the hem of her sleeve, her eyes locked on the road ahead. She hadn't seen this stretch of Carolina highway in years. The trees looked the same. The sky looked the same. But she didn't feel the same.

"Almost there," Jesse said, his voice low but steady.

Jessica nodded, her throat tight. "Do they... do they know everything?"

"They know enough," Jesse replied. "They know you're coming home. That's what matters."
Jessica looked down. "I don't know if I can face them."

"You don't have to be perfect," Jesse said. "You just have to be honest. And you've already done the hardest part—you survived."

She turned to him, eyes glassy. "I'm scared."
Jesse reached over and took her hand. "So was I. But you're not alone anymore."

The SUV turned onto the gravel path leading to Zena and Jake's house. The porch came into view—familiar, weathered, and lined with faces. Jessica's breath caught.

Jordan stood at the top of the steps, hands clasped in front of her. Ronnie was beside her, arms crossed but eyes soft. Amina held BJ on her hip, and Bryce stood just behind them, his face unreadable. Zena and Jake stood in the doorway, side by side, like sentinels of something sacred.

Jessica froze. "I can't," she whispered.

Jesse put the car in park and turned to her. "Yes, you can. You already did."

She opened the door slowly, her legs trembling as she stepped out. The gravel crunched beneath her feet. The air smelled like pine and home.

Jordan was the first to move. She stepped down the stairs, slowly at first, then faster.

Jessica stood frozen. Then Jordan wrapped her arms around her sister and held her like she was trying to stitch the years back together.

Jessica broke. "I'm sorry," she sobbed. "I'm so sorry."

Jordan held her tighter. "You don't have to be sorry. You just have to be here."

Ronnie stepped forward next. He didn't say anything—just pulled her into a hug that said everything he couldn't.

Amina came next, tears in her eyes. "You're safe now. That's all we wanted."

Jessica looked at Bryce, her breath catching. "I didn't think you'd want to see me."

Bryce stepped forward slowly. "I didn't think I did either."

Then he looked at BJ, who reached out and squealed, "Mama!"

Jessica dropped to her knees as BJ squirmed out of Amina's arms and reached for her.

She grabbed him, holding him close, sobbing into his tiny shoulder.

"I missed you," she whispered. "I missed you so much."

BJ patted her face, touching her tears with his small hands. "Mama"

Jessica laughed through her tears. "Yeah, baby. Mama's crying. But she's okay now."

Zena and Jake stepped down the stairs last. Zena opened her arms. "Come here, baby."

Jessica stood, still holding BJ, and walked into her grandmother's embrace.

Jake placed a hand on her shoulder. "Welcome home, sweetheart."

Jessica looked at her grandfather with her eyes full of tears, she loved her family so much, especially her grandfather. In the absence of her father, her grandfather was the only father figure she and Jordan had. He loved them, protected them, and tried to fill the void left by Jesse when he went to prison, so the thought of him being disappointed in her was overwhelming and something she was afraid to face. When she looked in his eyes and saw nothing but the same love she had always seen, her heart filled with joy and relief.

Jessica looked around at the faces surrounding her—faces that had searched for her, prayed for her, waited for her. She was home. And for the first time in a long time, she believed she could stay.

# Chapter Thirty-Seven

(Carolyn)
The Second Chance

The room was quiet when they first walked in—warm sunlight streaming through the window, the scent of lavender soap lingering from Zena's last visit. Carolyn lay propped up in bed, pillows behind her, her face thinner but glowing in a way no one had seen in years. The wires were gone. The bruises had faded. Her voice—her own voice—was back.

Jessica stopped in the doorway.

Carolyn looked up. Her lips parted, trembling. "Baby..."

Jessica blinked hard, then rushed to her mother's bedside, dropping to her knees. "Mama?"

Carolyn lifted her hand, brushing trembling fingers through Jessica's hair. "Oh God, thank You."

Jesse stepped in behind his daughter and stood tall. Carolyn's eyes welled instantly.

"You really came," she whispered.

Jesse nodded, voice thick. "And this time, I'm staying."

Zena moved beside the bed, placing her hand over Carolyn's. "Look what love does," she said gently. "It brought us all back."

Jake stood at the foot of the bed, eyes shining. "You gave us a scare, sugar."

Carolyn laughed through her tears. "That's all I've ever done—scare the people who love me."

Ronnie chuckled softly. "True. But we're still here."

Carolyn took a deep breath, steadying herself. "I need to say some things," she said, her voice soft but sure. "To all of you."

Everyone gathered around. Carolyn looked at Jake and Zena first. "I put y'all through hell. All those nights y'all stayed awake praying I'd come to my senses... I didn't. And I'm sorry."

Zena squeezed her hand. "You're here now." "And that's enough," Jake added.

Carolyn turned to Jesse. Her eyes softened, but her words were deliberate.

"I used you. I manipulated you into staying in the life because I liked the money, the flash. I let you become someone you weren't so I could pretend I was someone better. And somehow... you still loved me through it."

Jesse stepped closer. "I still do. That's why I asked you to marry me again."

Carolyn smiled, tears slipping down her cheek. "This time, I'm going to deserve it."

Then her gaze shifted to Jordan. Her voice cracked. "You grew up too fast because I wouldn't sit still. I left you and your sister so I could chase empty love. I took your childhood, Jordan. And I didn't earn your grace."

Jordan sat beside her mother and grabbed her hand. "I didn't need you to be perfect. I just needed you to come back. And you did."

Carolyn turned to Jessica next. Her voice faltered. "And you... my baby girl. You missed your daddy because I made choices that shut him out. I told you lies. I didn't protect you from that hole inside. And you paid for it."

Jessica shook her head. "We both did."

Carolyn touched her cheek. "But look at you. You came back. And I swear to you, I'll spend every day making it up to you."

BJ stirred in Bryce's arms.

Carolyn smiled and looked at Bryce. "You didn't have to stay. But you did. You loved my daughter, and you protected her when I didn't. Thank you."

Bryce nodded. "She's worth it."

She turned to Miles. "And you—thank you for loving Jordan. For standing beside her when I made her believe love couldn't last."

Miles smiled quietly. "She showed me how strong love could be."

Finally, she reached for Amina. "You came when we needed you. You housed us. Fed us. Looked for our baby girl like she was yours. Thank you, sweetheart."

Amina gripped her hand. "Family doesn't always share blood. Sometimes it shares purpose. You're mine."

Carolyn exhaled deeply. "And one more."

Jesse pulled out his phone and dialed. After a few moments, he handed it to her.

"Arturo Delgado," he said. "He's listening."
Carolyn lifted the phone to her ear. "Mr. Delgado," she said, her voice steady. "Thank you. I don't know how you did it, or why you did it. But you saved my daughter. You gave me back a chance I didn't deserve. And I'm grateful. From every inch of my soul."

Arturo's voice came smooth through the line. "You're welcome, señora. Some debts are paid in silence. Some with love. Yours was paid the moment Jessica came home."

Carolyn closed her eyes. "Thank you." She handed the phone back and looked around at her family. "I'm going to be the best mother. The best sister. The best daughter. The best wife. You all deserve that. And God gave me another chance—so I won't waste it."

Zena kissed her forehead. "Then let's start today." And for the first time in years, the whole family stood together. Not broken. Just healing.

It was quiet in the hospital room. The afternoon light had gone soft, casting long shadows across the floor as the IV pump hummed faintly beside Carolyn's bed. The rest of the family had stepped out to give them a moment alone.

Jesse pulled a chair close and sat beside her, his hand covering hers with gentle weight. "You scared me," he said quietly.

Carolyn looked over at him, a mix of exhaustion and gratitude painting her face. "I scared myself," she whispered.

He smiled, but it didn't quite reach his eyes. "You know I came straight here the minute I got out. Couldn't breathe right until I saw you."

"And I couldn't heal until I saw you," she said, turning her palm to squeeze his.

They were silent for a moment, remembering years wasted, words never said, and promises too long deferred.

Then Carolyn spoke again. "Jesse... I know I've hurt you. I know I ruined what we had. You were always the one who loved steady, and I—I just loved recklessly."

Jesse exhaled. "You didn't ruin it. You just lost sight of it. And so did I."

"I chased men. I chased parties. I chased everything but you and the girls." Her voice cracked. "And it cost all of us."

"You were broken," Jesse said softly. "So was I. But we're here. That means something."

Carolyn wiped her eyes, then chuckled through the tears. "When you proposed to me again in this hospital room... you know what I thought?"

"What?" Jesse quizzed.

"That you're either a fool or a saint." Carolyn replied through happy tears.

Jesse leaned in. "I'm a man who knows what matters now. And that's you. It's the girls. It's this crazy, messy life that we can still choose."

"I want to choose it," she whispered.

"Then we start over," he said. "We start right here. In this room."

She nodded. "And this time... I show up. For you. For them. For all of it."

He leaned in and kissed her forehead, lingering just long enough to promise he wasn't going anywhere.

After months of praying and rehab, Carolyn was finally coming home. Zena and Amina moved gracefully around the kitchen, stirring, plating, stacking warm cornbread into baskets and tossing salads into deep bowls. Jake sliced ham with his favorite carving knife. Ronnie set out glasses while Miles and Bryce chased down BJ, who was determined to run off with a spoon like it was treasure.

Jordan finished lighting the last candle, just as the front door creaked open. Jesse entered first, helping Carolyn through the doorway. The whole room stood. Jessica ran over, wrapping her arms around her mother carefully, mindful of the healing ribs.

"You look so good," she said, voice wobbling.

Carolyn smiled, brushing a curl from Jessica's cheek. "Because I've never been this loved."

Jordan walked up next. "We made dinner. Like… an actual meal."

Carolyn laughed. "That might be the most emotional part of all."

They all gathered around the table—one long, beautiful mess of cousins, partners, grandparents, brothers, sisters, love, loss, hope.

Jesse raised a glass of sweet tea. "To the woman who came back to us," he said, looking at Jessica. "To the woman who fought to find her again," he added, looking at Jordan. "And to the woman who chose all of us when she could've given up," he finished, eyes locking with Carolyn.

Jake cleared his throat. "To second chances."

Zena added, "And answered prayers."

Ronnie nodded. "And survival. Cause that's what we do."

Amina raised her glass. "To every person at this table who held someone else up when they couldn't stand."

Miles smiled. "To family. The real kind."

Bryce kissed BJ's forehead. "And to coming home."

Jessica looked around the table and wiped a tear from her cheek. "To peace," she whispered. "For once... peace."

They clinked glasses.

And for the first time in years, dinner wasn't just food. It was healing. It was witness. It was the beginning of everything they thought they'd lost— and what they finally dared to hope for.

# Chapter Thirty-Eight

(Jessica)
The Quiet After

The sun had dipped low behind the trees, casting soft amber light through Zena and Jake's backyard. The cicadas had started their slow hum, and the sounds of family laughter—BJ chasing Ronnie with a toy truck, Zena scolding Jake for sneaking a second slice of pie—filtered through the open windows like a lullaby.

Jordan sat on the porch swing, barefoot, her curls damp from a long-overdue shower. Miles sat beside her, one arm draped across the backrest, quiet and steady like he always was when her world began to unravel and piece itself back together. Jessica was home. Carolyn was healing. They were breathing again.

Jordan leaned her head against Miles' shoulder. "This doesn't feel real yet."

He turned slightly, brushing his thumb along her wrist. "She's upstairs, fast asleep. BJ curled into her side like nothing ever happened."

Jordan smiled softly. "That boy forgave her before she could ask. Kids are like that."

"Still," Miles said, "she's gotta carry it. That's going to take time."

Jordan sighed, her voice small. "We all carry it."

Miles nodded. "You've carried the most."

Jordan looked up at him. "I used to resent it. Being the one who had to keep things together when Mama couldn't. When Daddy was locked up. When Jessica started drifting."

"You didn't just keep it together," Miles said. "You held it down."

Jordan laughed gently, almost sadly. "You make it sound heroic."

"It is," he said. "You were the glue, even when no one knew they were falling apart."

She blinked away sudden tears, the kind she hadn't had space to feel until now. "I'm tired."

Miles pulled her closer. "Then let yourself rest. You're not the only one holding it now."

There was a long pause—comfortable, calm. "Do you think she'll stay?" Jordan asked quietly.

"I do," Miles said. "She wants to. You can see it."

Jordan nodded. "I want to believe she's really free."

"She is," he said. "Because this time, someone caught her."

Jordan glanced up. "And us?"

Miles smiled. "What about us?"

"You still want a future with me?" she whispered. "After all this?"

He leaned in, forehead gently pressing to hers. "Jordan, I never stopped."

Jordan closed her eyes. "I just want peace. For all of us."

Miles kissed her softly. "Then let's build it."

That evening, the chaos had softened into quiet. The porch light glowed just enough to throw a warm shimmer across the front steps where Jordan sat with two cups of chamomile tea in hand. She glanced over her shoulder through the open screen door—everyone inside was finally starting to unwind. Carolyn had dozed off with BJ curled up beside her. Ronnie was teaching Miles how to play spades. Zena and Amina were giggling in the kitchen over a pot of leftovers, and Jesse was finishing the crossword Jake couldn't solve.

Jessica stepped outside, blanket draped over her shoulders, eyes tired but calm.

Jordan scooted over, patting the seat beside her. "Come sit with me. Before someone drags you into a round of dominoes."

Jessica sank into the cushion. "If Uncle Ronnie starts trash talking, I'm leaving."

They both laughed—soft, surprised at how easy it felt again.

Jordan handed her the tea. "Grandma Z says chamomile helps heal the soul. I think it just makes people sleepy enough to forgive."

Jessica took a sip. "Does it work?"

Jordan shrugged. "I forgave you before I knew I would."

Jessica looked down, voice quiet. "I wasn't sure you'd speak to me. After everything…"

Jordan tilted her head. "You're here. That's all I wanted."

A long pause settled between them—not uncomfortable, just honest.

Jessica whispered, "I didn't know how to ask for help. I kept telling myself I could fix it. That I didn't need anyone."

Jordan nodded slowly. "Mama used to say that too. That she didn't want to be a burden."

"She was scared," Jessica said. "And I was too."

Jordan reached out, laced her fingers through her sister's. "You're allowed to be scared. You just don't get to stay lost."

Jessica's throat tightened. "I left BJ…"

Jordan squeezed her hand. "He forgave you the moment you stepped out of that car. Kids remember hugs, not absences."

Jessica blinked back tears. "You're really something."

Jordan smiled. "You helped raise me too, you know. In your own wild way."

They sat in silence a while, watching fireflies blink between the trees.

Jessica leaned her head on Jordan's shoulder. "I feel like I don't deserve this."

Jordan whispered, "None of us deserved what we got. But we survived it. And that means we get to make what comes next."

Jessica looked out over the yard. "So, what comes next?"

Jordan chuckled softly. "Breakfast that doesn't come in a Styrofoam box. Therapy. Mama's wedding. Maybe BJ finger painting on your favorite blouse."

Jessica laughed. "He's already done that."

Jordan turned to her, serious now. "Next is rebuilding. And you won't do it alone. Not this time."

Jessica nodded slowly. "Okay. I'm ready."
Jordan placed her head gently atop Jessica's. "Then let's walk the rest of this together."

The stars blinked low over Zena and Jake's property. Inside, laughter echoed from the kitchen, BJ babbled out words as he played under the dining table, and Carolyn dozed beside Jessica on the couch. But out on the front porch, Jordan and Jesse stood under the old hanging light, side by side, saying nothing at first.

Jesse leaned against the railing, arms crossed. His eyes were scanning the tree line, as if expecting movement. Jordan knew that look—it meant his mind hadn't left Miami yet. She handed him a bottle of sweet tea and broke the silence. "It's okay to breathe now, Daddy."

Jesse took it with a nod but didn't drink. "Is it?"

Jordan leaned beside him. "Jessica's back. Mama's healing. This—" she gestured toward the house— "this is the miracle."

Jesse exhaled through his nose. "Yeah. But peace needs protection."

Jordan turned toward him, studying his face. "You still think he'll come back?"

"Men like Joe don't disappear unless somebody makes them disappear." Jesse paused. "And Arturo made it clear—that man's life belongs to silence now."

Jordan hesitated. "Do you trust Arturo?"

"With my daughter's life. Because I know what kind of man he is. And I know what kind of man Joe isn't."

She nodded slowly. "I still can't believe you know him."

Jesse gave Jordan a small smile. "When I was inside, I saved Juan from a beat-down that would've put him out permanently. I didn't do it for favor—I did it because it was right. Arturo found out. And in his world, honor means something."

Jordan looked down. "Do you think we'll ever be able to stop looking over our shoulders?"

Jesse's voice was low but full of promise. "You don't have to anymore. Not while I'm standing. Not while this family's still got breath."

Jordan swallowed hard, emotions swirling in her chest. "You're different now."

"I had time to think," he said. "A lot of time. And I thought about you girls more than anything."

Jordan turned fully to face him. "You missed a lot."

"I did," Jesse said, voice thick. "And I'll carry that. But now—I want to build something better. Not just make up for what I lost. Make something that lasts."

Jordan nodded. "Me too."

They were quiet again. Then Jesse spoke once more, quieter this time.

"I'm proud of you, Jordi."
Jordan blinked quickly. "You've never said that to me before."

"I should've," Jesse said. "You became the woman I should've been around to help raise.

Instead, you raised yourself—and your sister—and this whole damn house."

Jordan looked away to hide the tears. "I just did what had to be done."

"And you did it with grace I didn't earn," Jesse said. "But I see you now. And you've got every ounce of your mother's fire—and something stronger. Your own."

Jordan smiled faintly. "I'm proud of you too."

They stood there a moment longer—two generations of resilience, finally sharing quiet.

"Tomorrow," Jesse said, "we start securing things. New locks. Security cams. Legal follow-ups. I want to make sure this house never sees danger again."

Jordan nodded. "We'll make it a fortress."

"No," Jesse said with a small smile. "We'll make it a home."

# Chapter Forty
## (Zena Jake)
## The Long View

The front porch creaked beneath Jake's boots as he eased into his rocking chair, a plate of cobbler balanced on his lap. Zena followed behind him, tucking a knitted shawl around her shoulders, clutching a mug of chamomile tea. The summer air was warm, heavy with the scent of honeysuckle and baked ham lingering from dinner. Inside, the house pulsed with laughter and the muffled rhythm of dominoes hitting the kitchen table. But out here—it was quiet. Gentle. Home.

Zena took one long sip and sighed. "You hear that, Jake?"

Jake nodded, chewing slowly. "Sounds like peace."

Zena smiled. "That sound? We prayed for it. We begged God for it."

Jake leaned back, glancing up at the stars. "I was starting to wonder if we'd ever get it."

Zena reached for his hand. "You remember how many nights we stayed awake? Waiting on Carolyn to come home? Then praying Jordan wouldn't grow up too fast. Then praying Jessica wouldn't follow the same path."

"Every single one," Jake said. "And when Jesse got locked up, I figured things couldn't fall any further."

"But they did," Zena whispered. "And now look."

Jake turned his gaze toward the living room window, where Jessica was curled on the couch beside her mother. BJ giggled as Jordan tickled his feet. Ronnie stood behind Miles, talking smack over a game of spades. Jesse laughed at something Carolyn said, his hand resting gently over hers.

"They came back," Jake murmured. "All of them."

Zena nodded, eyes welling. "And not just in body. They came back in spirit."

Jake wiped his mouth and looked over at her. "You ever think we were gonna lose her?"

Zena swallowed hard. "I didn't think—I knew. There were nights I could feel it. Like her soul was drifting so far I couldn't reach it with prayer."

Jake's voice cracked. "And when Carolyn got hurt—when we saw her in that hospital—I saw every bad choice coming home to roost."

"But then Jesse walked in," Zena said, smiling through tears. "Straight from prison. Went right to her bedside like no time had passed. Like love never broke."

Jake exhaled. "That man never stopped loving her. Not once."

Zena placed her mug on the porch rail and looked at Jake. "And you... you held me through every bit of it."

Jake chuckled. "Some nights I was just trying to hold myself. But we made it, Z."

She squeezed his hand. "We sure did."

They rocked in silence a moment longer, listening to the sounds of a house reborn.

Jake broke the quiet. "Think they'll be okay now?"

Zena tilted her head. "If love's the foundation? They'll do more than okay."

Jake nodded. "Then I think it's time we rest."

Zena leaned over and kissed his cheek. "Not too long though. You know this family—we get one quiet night, and chaos tries to RSVP again."

They both laughed, holding onto that porch moment like a bookmark in a well-worn story. Because the next chapter would come. But for tonight, the house was whole. And that was enough. The house was quieter now—just the low hum of fan on a stand in the living room the soft sway of sheer curtains against a breeze that smelled faintly of gardenia. Carolyn sat upright in bed, her hair freshly brushed thanks to Zena, who insisted on helping her look like herself again. Jesse sat beside her, stretching one leg over hers, tapping a rhythm on his knee like his thoughts had music behind them.

"I've been thinking," Jesse said.

Carolyn raised an eyebrow. "Dangerous."

Jesse smirked. "We've never done things the easy way. Maybe it's time we tried."

Carolyn smiled faintly. "Like getting married without chaos chasing us through the church parking lot?"

"Exactly," he said. "Simple. Small. Family in one room. No secrets. Just truth. Just us."

Carolyn blinked slowly, trying to absorb what it would mean to stand before her daughters, her parents, her brother, and tell them all: I choose him again. This time, we are going to make it all the way to the altar with no prison detours.

"I said yes," she whispered. "I meant it."

Jesse leaned forward, taking her hand gently. "This time, I want to build it right. No lies. No hustle. No running off in the middle of the night." Carolyn's voice cracked. "No pretending we're fine when we're not."

He nodded. "No pretending, period."

There was a knock at the door. Zena peeked her head in with a bag of grapes and her usual no-nonsense tenderness.

"You two decent?" she asked, eyes twinkling. Jesse grinned. "We're decent. Sentimental. Maybe plotting."

Zena stepped inside, setting the grapes down. "Well, I figured you might need help planning your wedding."

Carolyn blinked, then laughed softly. "Mama, I haven't even picked a date."

Zena shrugged. "So, pick one. You've got everyone you need. Jake and I already offered the backyard. We can string lights in the trees, put Miles and Ronnie on grill duty."

Jesse chuckled. "Only if Ronnie's allowed to wear a tux apron."

Zena pointed a grape at him. "That can be negotiated."

Just then Jordan walked in with a notebook. "If y'all are serious, I've already got a list started—dates, guests, venues, food options. Ronnie said he can borrow speakers from church and—"

Carolyn shook her head, eyes tearing up. "Y'all just knew?"

Jordan set the notebook on the side table and sat beside her. "We didn't wait for you to come back to start loving you. We never stopped."

Jesse reached for Carolyn's other hand and kissed her knuckles. "We're rebuilding a whole life, sweetheart. One vow at a time."

Carolyn looked at her daughter, her mother, and the man she had spent decades learning to love properly. She closed her eyes and exhaled a breath that had been held too long.

"Alright," she said softly. "Let's get married. Let's heal. Let's become a family again."

The next day, the ladies went to a bridal boutique in Charlotte. The sunlight filtered through the boutique windows, casting golden lines across the row of dresses as if heaven was laying out paths to new beginnings.

In Dressing Room 3, the air was thick with giggles, gasps, and the rustle of satin and tulle. Carolyn sat propped on a small velvet bench, her posture strong though her healing ribs protested. She wore a soft champagne colored dress and clutched Zena's hand tightly.

Zena—her steady anchor—had insisted on being there not just as her mother, but as the blueprint for resilience.

Jessica stood in front of the mirror, her yellow dress flowing like memory down her frame.

"Okay," she said, turning slightly. "Does it make me look like a daughter finally free of drama?"

Carolyn smiled, mist in her eyes. "It makes you look like someone who fought to come back. And won."

Jordan stepped up beside her sister. "It's perfect. Not because of the shape, or the stitching… because you feel right in it."

Amina leaned on the doorway, arms folded, watching. "I still say y'all need matching heels for this ceremony. Preferably something that could be used to kick bad decisions if needed."

Carolyn burst into a laugh so full it made Zena snort.

"Mama," Carolyn whispered, catching her breath. "Can you believe this moment?"

Zena looked at her daughter—fragile and fierce all at once. "Baby, I prayed for this moment through so many nights you weren't here, and through the ones where your name felt like a question."

Carolyn reached out and squeezed her mother's hand. "I know."

Amina moved beside Carolyn and knelt carefully. "You're about to start a new chapter with Jesse. And we're going to make sure this wedding is a celebration—not just of love, but survival."
Jordan nodded. "And healing."

Jessica turned from the mirror, eyes searching hers. "Can we all really be okay now?"

Carolyn reached for both her girls' hands. "We will be. Because we've got each other. And God saw fit to give me a second chance. I'm not wasting it."

Zena blinked back tears. "You've got people who love you. So fiercely. You just keep choosing us. That's all."

Carolyn leaned forward. "I want you all beside me. When I marry Jesse—when I become a mother again not with guilt, but grace—I want every woman who held me up to stand beside me."

Jessica whispered, "Then let's plan the hell out of this wedding."

Amina grinned. "With matching heels."

Jordan raised her ginger ale. "To dresses and forgiveness."

They clinked cups.

And for that quiet moment in a small boutique dressing room—they were more than survivors. They were builders of the life they never thought they'd get to wear.

Meanwhile, Jesse gathers with Jake, Ronnie, Bryce, and Miles to plan the wedding. The sun was steady overhead, filtered through a patchwork of oak leaves and clothesline shadows as Jesse leaned over the picnic table in Jake and Zena's backyard. A half-filled legal pad sat before him, annotated with scribbles, arrows, and notes in multiple styles of handwriting. A crumpled blueprint of the backyard layout was held down by a bag of nails and a can of grape soda.

Jake stood beside him, arms folded, surveying the yard like a battlefield he'd prepared to conquer again.

Ronnie kicked back in a folding chair, sunglasses on, chewing a toothpick. "So, we decided—no plastic chairs, right? Because if I see one grown man topple over mid-toast, I'm leaving." Jesse grinned. "Yeah, no cheap chairs. Mama Z's got a cousin who runs event rentals. Real wood. Real weight. No collapsing uncles."

Bryce stepped out from the shed, a coil of extension cords looped over one arm. "Sound system's good. Ronnie picked up the speakers from the church, and we tested them yesterday. No static."

Miles jogged up from the side gate, clipboard in hand. "We also got clearance to hang lights in the cedar trees—battery-powered, soft white. Whole thing will glow like a garden party with a purpose." Jake nodded, impressed. "Y'all boys might actually pull this off."

Ronnie smirked. "Please. I've done five block parties, two family reunions, and one emergency engagement celebration—ask me about it later. Point is, we got this daddy."

Jesse leaned forward, tapping a box labeled *ceremony arch*. "You think we go rustic? Or something classic?"

Miles looked thoughtful. "Rustic feels right. Y'all been through enough storms. Something rooted. Wood beams, wildflowers, light fabric draped over the top."

Jake smiled. "My girl deserves to walk beneath something that looks like it grew from love itself."
Bryce pulled up a crate and sat down. "Has she picked a dress?"

"She has," Jesse said quietly. "Champagne. Soft. She cried when she saw herself. Told me it felt like starting over."

Ronnie popped his toothpick out and leaned in. "Y'all got vows ready?"

Jesse paused. "I've got them in my head. Just waiting on the right words."

Miles flipped to an empty page. "We'll help with the setup. Day of, we're here from sunrise to finish. No excuses. No hold-ups. Just family."

Jake raised a brow. "We'll need a crew to prep the food too."

"Already planned," Ronnie said. "I recruited half the cousins. One even offered to smoke ribs overnight."

"Ooo wee. I bet I know which cousin that was. Only one man love cooking ribs more than I do and that's your uncle Charles. I consider myself to be a barbeque master, but that man there is a barbeque king! Jake said slapping his leg.

They all laughed. It felt good to be gathered in laughter and love, instead of tragedy and pain. Thid family had been through more than their share of storms, and now that God had seen fit to bring out the sunshine, they were more than ready to bask in the rays.

Jesse shook his head, smiling deeply. "This ain't just a wedding. This is a resurrection."

Bryce added quietly, "It's healing, and Lord knows we could all use something to celebrate. And nothing is more worth celebrating than love."

Miles leaned back, looking at the house where Carolyn sat inside with her daughters. "It's a love story with chapters no one expected."

Jesse looked at all of them—men who had carried him and his family through every trial—and nodded.

"It's ours now. And come Saturday night, we show her that this family doesn't just stand. It dances."

# Chapter Forty

(Jessica)
Grace in the Mirror

Jordan, Zena, and Amina prepared Carolyn for her walk down the aisle. The air in Zena's bedroom glowed with late-morning sunlight, bouncing off ivory lace and yellow satin. The scent of lavender oil and fresh magnolias filled the room. Soft gospel music played from a speaker on the windowsill— the kind Carolyn used to hum when no one else was listening. Today, every note felt like a prayer answered.

Carolyn sat at the vanity, her fingers resting lightly on her lap as Jordan worked her magic on her mother's makeup, dabbing concealer with precision and care. Amina fluffed layers of Carolyn's gown—the elegant champagne colored dress with subtle shimmer and flow that moved like mercy itself. Zena stood behind Carolyn, hands gently pressing her shoulders, as if grounding her in this moment.

"You nervous?" Jordan asked, tilting Carolyn's chin for eyeliner.

Carolyn gave a small laugh. "I've been married and divorced, had two daughters, spent time in ICUs and interrogation rooms... but yes. I am absolutely nervous."

Amina grinned, adjusting Carolyn's veil. "This ain't nerves. This is anticipation. You're walking toward the man who never stopped choosing you."

Zena leaned in, voice soft. "And you're walking toward the life you finally chose back."

Carolyn turned to her mother and took her hands. "I didn't deserve the way you held me through all my mistakes."

Zena smiled. "Maybe not. But I never loved you because you earned it. I loved you because you're mine."

Jordan paused, holding a lipstick tube mid-air, eyes misting. "You look beautiful, Mama."

Carolyn looked up. "You sound like someone who's forgiven me."

Jordan nodded, voice tight. "I did. A while ago. I just didn't know how to tell you until I saw you fight to be better."

Carolyn reached for her daughter's hand and held it to her cheek. "I'm still fighting. For you. For Jessica. For all of us."

Amina took the mirror from the dresser and turned it toward her. "Take a look, woman. This is who you are now."

Carolyn stared at her reflection. She didn't see the mistakes anymore. She saw the recovery. The strength. The love woven into every layer of her dress, every curl Zena pinned into place, every brushstroke Jordan laid against her skin.

"I never thought I'd get a moment like this," she whispered.

Jordan kissed her temple. "Then let's make it count."

Zena opened the door, the music growing louder from outside. "Time to walk," she said. "He's waiting."

Carolyn stood slowly, gathering her dress, her daughters, her sister-friend, and the version of herself she never thought she'd meet again. Jake and Zena both hugged their daughter, and as they prepared to walk out together, arm-in-arm toward the backyard, they carried more than fabric and flowers. They carried forgiveness. And the future.

The backyard had been transformed. Light strands draped from cedar branches like constellations brought low. Wildflowers lined the aisle in mason jars, and Zena's quilted pillows dotted the benches like welcome mats for the soul. Music hummed—soft, steady, a melody stitched together from gospel, memory, and grace.

Jesse stood beneath the arch Miles had built by hand and Ronnie reinforced twice, just in case. The arch glowed with candles tucked into lanterns, wrapped in fabric and forgiveness. Jesse wore a tailored gray suit, his posture proud but heart open. This wasn't about performance. This was about promise.

The crowd stood as Jordan, Jessica, Amina, and Zena emerged from the house—leading Carolyn, who walked with her father and a steadiness forged from every hardship she'd survived. She wore a soft champagne colored gown. Her hair framed her face in soft waves, and her eyes held a light that hadn't been there in years.

Carolyn clutched Jake's arm as she stepped into the aisle. The music swelled. Jesse swallowed hard. His lips parted, just enough to whisper, "Damn."

Carolyn's gaze met his and locked. And every step she took felt like a redemption arc set to a love song. Behind her, was her mother, Amina, and then Jordan and Jessica walked together—sisters in rhythm again.

Jessica's hand trembled. Jordan squeezed it.

"She's okay," Jordan whispered.

Jessica watched her mother step past decades of mistakes and land in the arms of the man who never stopped loving her. It almost undid her.

Carolyn reached Jesse, and Jake gently placed his daughter's hand into Jesse's. "You earned this," Jake said to both of them.

Jesse nodded. "We'll never forget it."

Carolyn gazed up at Jesse as tears welled in her eyes. "You waited."

"I wasn't letting go," Jesse replied. "Even when you thought I had."

They turned to face their family—Jessica, Jordan, Ronnie, Bryce, Amina, Miles, Zena, Jake, and BJ, who sat with a juice box, grinning at the flowers like they were made just for him.

The officiant stepped forward—an old friend of Jake's with a smile like sunrise. "We are gathered here today," he began, "to witness something extraordinary: a love that refused to quit."

Jessica felt her knees weaken. She watched her father take her mother's hand, watched her mother look at Jesse like he was the home she'd been running from and back to all her life.

"I left you," Carolyn said aloud, her voice firm.

"And I stayed," Jesse replied.

"I hurt you." She said

"And I never stopped loving you." He responded.

"I wasted years." Carolyn said tearfully

"And I'll make the rest of them count." Jesse replied confidently.

Tears flowed freely now. The officiant nodded, letting the words speak for themselves. "Do you, Jesse Braxton, take this woman—Carolyn Alexander—to be your wife, finally?"

"I do," he said.

"Do you, Carolyn Alexander, take this man—Jesse Braxton—to be your husband?"

"I do," she whispered. "Finally."

When they kissed, it wasn't dramatic. It was tender. Slow. Holy.

Jessica wept. Jordan held her. BJ clapped. And Zena closed her eyes, whispering thanks under her breath. They had made it. Not just to the altar. But through everything.

After the ceremony, it was time for a long-awaited celebration, At the reception, the happy couple sliced into the layered buttercream cake while Bryce tried to keep BJ from grabbing frosting with both fists.

"Wait 'til your grandma and grandpa dance," Bryce laughed, pulling BJ onto his shoulders.

Jesse turned to Carolyn, offering his hand once more. "Care for our long awaited first dance?"

Carolyn placed her hand in his, her voice warm. "Only if you remember how not to step on my foot."

They moved gently across the dance floor—no choreography, just knowing. Jesse hummed the tune under his breath. Carolyn leaned into him, tears on her cheeks and laughter in her chest.

Zena wiped her eyes. "This right here," she whispered to Jake, "is why you never stop praying." Jake grinned. "And why you never throw out a good man."

"Amen!" Zena agreed, hugging Jake and moving to the music.

Jordan pulled Jessica to the floor. "Come on, sis. You survived Miami, you can survive my two-step."

Jessica laughed, barefoot and glowing. "If I trip, I'm blaming trauma."

Amina joined with a dramatic twirl. "Let the women of recovery show off their rhythm!"

Miles and Bryce high-fived as Ronnie started a soul train line—complete with Zena sliding in for one gloriously off-beat shimmy that had everyone shouting. Even BJ danced, turning circles until he fell into a pile of giggles and frosting-smudged napkins.

Platters of ribs, sweet potatoes, collard greens, cornbread, and peach cobbler disappeared fast. Toasts were raised—Jake gave one that included two Bible verses and a joke about Jesse finally learning punctuality.

Jordan toasted her parents: "To the ones who proved that love doesn't expire—it just waits for you to grow up enough to appreciate it."
Jessica lifted her glass next. "To being home. And knowing what that means now."

As the moon rose, the music slowed. Couples leaned together, memories warm on their shoulders. Laughter quieted to murmurs of joy. Carolyn rested against Jesse's chest on a porch swing, eyes half-closed, her hand pressed to the new ring shining on her finger.

Jessica sat beside Jordan under a tree wrapped in fairy lights. "Do you think we get to keep this?" Jessica asked softly.

Jordan smiled. "We built it. We get to choose it every day." And they would.

Carolyn sat alone after the ceremony, writing to Jessica and Jordan. The house had gone quiet—still humming with warmth, but quieter now. Plates had been cleared, candles snuffed, BJ tucked in tight between Jessica and Bryce. The fairy lights strung across the backyard still flickered faintly, a soft reminder of the vows that had been spoken beneath them hours ago.

Carolyn sat in Zena's old reading nook near the window, wrapped in one of her mother's quilts, pen in hand, eyes misty but clear. A blank sheet of paper sat before her. She exhaled, grounded herself, and began to write.

*To My Girls—Jordan and Jessica, Tonight, I stood beside the man who has always seen the best in me, even when I couldn't find it for myself. I spoke promises with a voice I once thought I'd never use again. And I wore a dress that was stitched not just with thread—but with grace.*

*But before I move forward into this new life, I need to speak to you. I need you to hear me with no distractions. No interruptions. Just truth. I'm sorry. I'm sorry for the moments I wasn't your anchor, for the nights I chased what I thought was love while you both held each other like driftwood.*

*I'm sorry that your childhood had to feel like survival. I traded steadiness for spark. I put men before you. I put my ego before my motherhood. And still... you stayed. You loved me through bruises, absences, secrets. You loved me when I couldn't love myself.*

*Jordan—my first. My fierce. You became mother and sister and protector in one breath. You dried tears I never saw fall. You taught yourself how to raise a child before you were done being one. You deserved so much more—and yet you gave even more than that. You are the spine of this family, and when the world bent you... you didn't break. You stood taller.*

*Jessica—my heart's echo. My firefly. You chased light in places that tried to snuff you out, and I wasn't there to guide you. Because I wasn't looking. Because I wasn't listening. And yet— somehow—you returned. You carried pain, shame, weight no daughter should ever bear. But you walked back into our arms, trembling but brave. And in that moment, I saw God's grace in your eyes.*

*You both deserve a mother who chooses healing. A mother who protects. A mother who stays. And starting tonight, you have her. I don't expect forgiveness. I just hope you see me trying. Every day. In the way I speak. In the way I love. In the way I choose you—without hesitation. You are my redemption. You are my beginning again. All my love,*

*Mama*

Carolyn sat back in the chair and paused to soak up how blessed she was. She had made a lifetime of bad decisions that not only caused her to lose time with her family, but it had almost caused her to lose her life as well. She was so thankful God spared her life and gave her another chance to make it up to those she had loved the most and also hurt the most.

Her parents, Jesse, and most of all her daughters. It was how she hurt them that haunted her dreams the most when she was in the hospital. She never thought Jessica and Jordan would forgive her, let alone stand beside her as she married the love of her life.

Carolyn felt incredibly blessed. She folded the letter carefully and pressed it against her heart, then slipped it into a small box marked *For My Girls*. It would wait for morning—just like healing had waited for them.

# Chapter Forty-One

## (Jesse and Carolyn)
## What Morning Feels Like

Jesse and Carolyn talked quietly as the sun rose. The early light crept through the thin linen curtains of Zena and Jake's guest room, casting soft streaks across the quilt that covered Jesse and Carolyn. The world outside was still hushed—no car doors, no music, no BJ yelling for cereal. Just the rustle of leaves, and the familiar sigh, of a house finally resting.

Carolyn lay curled against Jesse's chest, her fingers tracing lines on his chest like a pattern she'd learned years ago but was only now remembering. "I didn't think I'd ever get back to this," she whispered.

Jesse tilted his head, brushing her hair back slowly. "To what?"

"Waking up next to you. No walls between us. No shame in the silence."

He smiled softly. "It's been a long time coming."

Carolyn shifted, lying flat now and staring up at the ceiling. "I used to think morning was just a start-over button. A way to forget the mess from the day before. But this—" she turned to him, eyes full— "this feels like the beginning of something we've never had."

Jesse leaned on one elbow, watching her. "Because now we're building it on truth."

"And grace," Carolyn added. "I didn't know how to accept that before."

Jesse ran his thumb across the top of her hand. "You were always reaching for love, Carolyn. You just didn't know it could be quiet. Gentle. Steady."

"I've always loved the storm," she said softly. "But maybe I was the storm."

"You were," he said with no judgment in his voice. "And I loved you through it."

Carolyn smiled, then turned serious. "What does it look like for us now? Beyond the wedding? Beyond the healing?"

Jesse thought for a moment. "It looks like breakfast on the porch. It looks like you writing again. Me teaching BJ how to fix bikes. You and Jordan holding space for each other. Jessica telling her story when she's ready. Zena baking when she's bored. Ronnie showing up uninvited with ribs."

She laughed quietly. "It sounds like a whole life."

"That's what I want for you," Jesse said. "Not survival. A life."

Carolyn blinked tears from her eyes, not from sadness but from the kind of relief that rewires a person. "I want that too," she whispered. "And this time... I'm not letting fear drive the car."

Jesse leaned in and kissed her temple. "It's parked in the driveway now."

They lay back, side by side, no urgency, no armor. Just skin and memory and the sacred quiet of morning after everything has changed. And for the first time, neither of them was bracing for impact. They were building.

Meanwhile, Jordan and Miles, were talking about love in the aftermath of healing. The backyard had returned to stillness. Fairy lights blinked above like distant stars, half the chairs were stacked, and the sound system had been powered down. A few fireflies meandered around the tall grass, and the scent of smoked ribs lingered like an echo of joy.

Jordan sat on the edge of the porch steps, barefoot, her bridesmaid dress bunched slightly beneath her. Miles joined her, two cups of iced tea in hand.

"I figured you earned one without someone asking you to make a toast," he said, handing her a cup.

Jordan took it with a quiet smile. "You're finally learning how to read the room."

Miles lowered himself beside her, elbows resting on knees. "That was beautiful today."

Jordan nodded. "I still can't believe it happened. My parents. That vow. That kiss."

"They rewrote the ending," Miles said. "You helped them get there."

Jordan stared out into the yard. "I used to think love was about proving something. That if it didn't fix the broken parts, it wasn't strong enough."

Miles turned toward her, voice soft. "And now?"

Jordan exhaled. "Now I think love just... stays. Not to fix, but to witness. To say, 'I see it all, and I'm not leaving.'"

Miles smiled. "You've lived that kind of love."

Jordan looked over at him. "You've given it."

Miles shook his head gently. "You earned it."

They sat in silence for a moment. Then she whispered, "I spent so many years bracing for impact. Protecting Jessica. Raising myself. Filling in the gaps Mama left behind."

"You did more than fill them," Miles said. "You built new space. Safe space."

Jordan bit her lip. "And what about us? You and me?"

Miles leaned in slightly. "That's the thing. We're not built on survival anymore. Now we get to build on peace. We don't have to rescue each other. We just have to love each other."

Jordan blinked, fighting tears. "I don't know how to do that yet."

Miles reached for her hand, threading their fingers together. "Then let's learn it slowly. Together."

She smiled, her voice barely above a whisper. "Okay."

And they sat there, iced tea in hand, healing in heart, watching tomorrow rise softly above the cedar trees.

The morning after the wedding greeted the Alexander family like a soft hymn. Sunlight streamed through the slats of Zena and Jake's porch, warming the remnants of a night filled with dancing, laughter, and vows stitched together with second chances.

Inside, the house exhaled slowly. Quiet conversations stirred in corners, the scent of biscuits wafted from the kitchen, and BJ babbled in his sleep, clutching a glittery ribbon like a treasure he refused to surrender.

Carolyn lay curled beside Jesse, her head resting against his chest. "I never thought we'd be here," she murmured.

Jesse kissed the top of her hair. "Here—and still becoming."

Downstairs, Zena stood over a skillet, flipping sausage links with a rhythm only she had mastered. Jake sipped coffee beside her, humming as he read the local paper. Jordan moved between cabinets, gathering plates, while Jessica poured orange juice beside Bryce, who held BJ against his hip.

"Alright, listen up!" Jordan said, placing a map in the center of the table. "We've got decisions to make. I for one want to be around all this love and support permanently, so I think, Miles and I are looking to relocate after we finish our respective internships."

Bryce leaned in. "Charlotte?"
Jake pointed to a circle drawn around *Jordan Springs*. "We are only ten minutes outside the city. Quiet but close. Charlotte has good schools and plenty of good jobs. I know a realtor who'll work with you when you are ready."

Jessica smiled. "Once Bryce and I finish at Clark next year, we're planning to move there too."

Zena raised an eyebrow. "Y'all finishing school first, right?"

Bryce nodded. "Absolutely. We promised ourselves and we promised you."

Carolyn wiped her hands on a dish towel. "I want a little garden. And a porch swing. A place where BJ can run without fear. A place where you girls can come and sit without needing a reason."

Jordan looked at her mother. "You deserve that peace."

Amina entered from the hallway, brushing sleep from her eyes. Ronnie followed close behind, coffee in hand, offering her his seat.

Zena watched the quiet exchange, then asked with a smirk, "Y'all just friends or is there something growing in this garden too?"

Ronnie chuckled. "Working on it. Slowly."

Amina winked at Zena. "You know I don't do fast."

Jake clapped his hands. "Then it's settled. We build roots. We stop surviving—we start planting."

# *Chapter Forty-Two*

## (Family)
## Porch Proposal

Later that morning, as the sun climbed higher and the family shifted into packing and planning modes, Miles walked up behind Jordan on the porch. She was sketching house designs in her notebook, BJ now napping in a nearby lounge chair with glitter stuck in his curls.

"I got something for you," Miles said, slipping a velvet box into her hand.

Jordan blinked. "You serious?"

Miles nodded, taking a breath. "I don't know what forever looks like, but I know I want to build it with you. Marry me—not just for today—but for every quiet morning and every loud family dinner."

Jordan opened the box slowly, her heart thumping wildly. Inside sat a simple rose gold ring—elegant, strong, her style. She looked up, eyes glistening. "You asking me to build with you?"

Miles smiled. "I'm asking you to design the blueprint of my life."

Jordan laughed through her tears. "Then yes. Absolutely yes."

As midday arrived, the family gathered on the lawn, lemonade and peach cobbler in hand. Ronnie raised his glass.

"To new beginnings—every last one of them. To engagements and graduations. To gardens and glitter. To family showing up even when it hurts."

Carolyn stood next, Jesse beside her. "And to choosing love, again and again."

Jessica stepped forward. "To building a life no one thought we'd get to live. And to fighting for the joy that follows us home."

Zena smiled at her daughter, her son, and all the ones they'd gathered into their hearts. "And to the ones we've lost, the ones we've found, and the ones who still need rescuing."

### Final Moments: Questions on the Horizon

As the camera pans out, so to speak, and the family begins packing, planning, and dreaming together, a few question linger.

Where is Joe? He vanished from Miami under the threat of Arturo Delgado. But men like him don't disappear quietly. Will he return, searching for revenge or closure?

Can this family hold onto joy with shadows still lingering? Will Jessica and Bryce build the family they once only dreamed of? Will Ronnie and Amina plant something sturdy enough to grow? Will Jordan and Miles make it down the aisle? Or will a person from their past interrupt their plans? And is healing ever truly finished?

One thing's certain: love has returned to the Alexander family. But the story isn't done.

### End of Book Two

*Next: "A Beautiful Ending" – the final chapter in the trilogy.*

www.ingramcontent.com/pod-product-compliance
Lightning Source LLC
Chambersburg PA
CBHW060406260626
47160CB00006B/2451